Betrayal

Also By Christopher C. Tubbs

LADY BETHANY
Graduation
Betrayal

SCARLETT FOX
Scarlett
Freedom
Legacy

CHARLEMAGNE GRIFFON
Buddha's Fist
The Pharaoh's Mask
Treasure Of The Serpent God
The Knights Templar

DECOY SHIPS
Kingfisher
The Warley

BETRAYAL

A LADY BETHANY ADVENTURE

CHRISTOPHER C. TUBBS

LUME BOOKS
A JOFFE BOOKS COMPANY

Lume Books, London
A Joffe Books Company
www.lumebooks.co.uk

First published in Great Britain in 2025 by Lume Books

Copyright © Christopher C. Tubbs 2025

The right of Christopher C. Tubbs to be identified as author of this work has been asserted in accordance with the Copyright, Designs and Patents Act 1988.

This book is a work of fiction. Names, characters, businesses, organisations, places and events are either the product of the author's imagination or are used fictitiously. Any resemblance to actual persons, living or dead, events or locales is entirely coincidental. The spelling used is British English except where fidelity to the author's rendering of accent or dialect supersedes this.

No part of this book may be used or reproduced in any manner for the purpose of training artificial intelligence technologies or systems. In accordance with Article 4(3) of the Digital Single Market Directive 2019/790, Joffe Books expressly reserves this work from the text and data mining exception.

Cover design by Imogen Buchanan

ISBN: 978-1-83901-597-7

Clean Up

The Honourable Bethany Stockley — tall, elegant, beautiful and educated, codenamed Chaton by the British Secret Service and currently known in these parts as Rosa Collins for the purposes of her mission — crouched in the filth at the back of a cantina in Veracruz dressed as a beggarwoman, with filthy hair and ragged dirty clothes. Her latest mission was to assist the Americans in their bid to eliminate the Colombian privateers who increasingly threatened their shipping. Beth's boss, Admiral Turner, head of Military Intelligence Overseas, had given her a free hand and told her to do whatever she had to.

The two men in the back room of the cantina were of interest to her; she wanted to know what they were talking about. To all the world it looked as if she was a vagrant, searching the rubbish for something to eat; in fact, she was listening intently to their conversation through the open window between them.

One of the men, a Colombian, was forcefully making a point.

"I want the names and cargoes of the ships. Your agent has the list of sailings, and you will copy it for me."

"But, Señor López ... he keeps it in the safe now, and has done so since Señor Luna was killed."

Beth knew all about *that*; she had killed Señor Luna herself, and left the warning note pinned to his body. Luna had been selling the sailing lists to Colombian privateers and Beth had caught him red-handed when he tried to sell the list to her. The outraged local authorities, who were as corrupt as Luna was, were now looking for his murderer. They had already interviewed Beth because, given the undercover nature of her work, she was posing as an American trader and the current sailing list had American ships on it. But they had no evidence, and so had to let her go.

López didn't care about security measures, or Luna's death.

"You will get me the list, or your family will suffer. That's a very pretty daughter you have — she would fetch a good price on the block."

Rivera caved in. "I will get the list, please do not hurt my family."

"I want it by Friday."

Beth had heard enough and shuffled away, dragging a foot as if disabled. Once she was clear of the cantina, she resumed walking normally and headed back towards the safe house, which the Secret Service used as a base in Veracruz.

Manuela, the resident agent, opened the door to Beth's knock and grinned at the sight of her. Beth looked at her enquiringly, because something was obviously up, but the urge to make her grubby body clean overcame her curiosity, and she stepped past Manuela into the dim interior.

Almost immediately, Beth sensed another presence, and her hand went to the karambit dagger hidden in her sash. Then she caught the scent of tar — and man. She let her eyes adjust … it was Richard Brazier, the captain of her schooner, the *Fox*. He wrinkled his nose as she stepped closer.

"Pee-ew, you stink."

"I know; it's part of my charm." Beth smiled sweetly at him.

Richard laughed. "We have a communication from London. Came in on a merchant ship."

"What does it say?"

"No idea, it's in code. But there is a second envelope, from Seb."

Seb was her fiancé, Sebastian Ashley-Cooper, son of the Earl of Shaftesbury and also a British agent with the codename Lancelot.

Beth rolled her eyes. "I will look at it after I am clean."

"Good, because the smell is making me gag."

"Give me the letter." Beth poked her tongue out at him as she left and went into the back room, where a tub of hot water was waiting. She stripped and sank into it.

The letter from Sebastian, her betrothed, relayed some of the goings-on concerning her family in Burma, where her father was the British ambassador. Most of the news was mundane, but an encoded section gave her details of various undercover operations. Tears filled her eyes; it could be months before they saw each other again.

Freshly bathed and dressed in a typical Mexican skirt and blouse, Beth sat down at the kitchen table to decode the message that accompanied Seb's letter. It was from Admiral Turner, the head of Military Intelligence Overseas.

Americans happy with progress so far. They have identified a Colombian who calls himself El Dragon. He is targeting their ships. Stop him.

M is still in Asia, do not expect your mother and father home soon. Lancelot sends his love.

Contact in Colombia is Lucifer, you can find him in Cartagena at a cantina called La Orquídea Morada.

The message went on to provide the usual recognition phrases and further details.

Beth wondered about El Dragón. Was he López? Then she thought that López might call himself the Wolf, as his name was derived from that, but, she told herself, surely it wouldn't be that easy.

When she had finished reading the message she found that Richard was still waiting, so she told him the news.

"So, they have a name and that's it?" He sniffed, clearly unimpressed.

"That's about it. Why don't you and the crew keep an ear out for any mention of him? If he has gained the Americans' attention, he must be quite active."

Richard rose to leave. "Will do, boss."

As Richard departed, Manuela sat down opposite Beth and rested her hands on the table. "I have not heard of this Dragon. He is not based here."

Beth sighed. "It would be too easy if he was."

Beth's first priority was to deal with López and his blackmailing of the shipping clerk. She wanted — no, she *needed* — to eliminate that particular privateer at sea, out of sight of the authorities. In Mexico, letters of marque were being issued to anyone who could pay the bribes. Officially, those letters only permitted the privateers holding them to attack Spanish and Portuguese ships, but many were tempted by the rich cargoes carried by British and American vessels. Beth had been sent to Mexico on a mission to stop that, and so far she had enjoyed quite some success. Increasingly, privateers tended to avoid British and American ships — on the grounds that most of their colleagues who had attacked them had subsequently disappeared.

Beth's entire operation was being funded by the British Secret Service, and consequently, any profits she made from selling captured hulls and cargoes, indeed any loot she secured at all, became the property of the Service. So far on this mission she had sold the goods and hulls in Havana, Tortuga and, occasionally, Jamaica, where her family held a pair of plantations.

As Beth considered these matters, Garai — her mentor, fellow agent and member of her father's Special Operations team, the Shadows — walked in from the courtyard at the back of the house, where he had been exercising. His tanned body glistened with sweat, which emphasised his muscles. At fifty, he was still fit and very attractive; Beth noticed that Manuela looked at him and sighed even though she knew as well as Beth did that Garai preferred the company of men and was, in any case, celibate.

"Turner?" Garai said, looking at the letter.

"Yes, giving us a target with no information other than that he calls himself El Dragon."

"Compensating for something?" Garai snorted.

"Probably," Beth said, and laughed. "We need to visit Mr Rivera."

"I'll get ready."

Beth already had a list of shipping that covered the next few weeks, but it was intended to help agents find suitable berths for travellers or cargoes, so it only listed the larger ships that tended to run regularly and took passengers. She read it carefully then took another paper and studied that; then she took out her forgery tools and selected a sheet of paper from her stock. She copied the list — replicating the handwriting on the second paper and replacing the name of one of the American ships with that of the *Brunswick*, which was the name currently used by her own ship, the *Fox*. She listed it as carrying a cargo of silver bullion.

Satisfied, she rolled the paper up and put it into a woven straw bag which she carried over her shoulder. At that moment, Garai came down the stairs in fine attire, looking every inch the Mexican gentleman.

"Very handsome," Beth said.

"Thank you. I try," he replied, then grinned and held out his arm for her to take. "Shall we?"

The pair left the house and walked to the offices of Rivera's boss, the shipping agent. One building on the same street was boarded up; somebody had pasted a poster on the door, advertising a reward for information leading to the arrest of Señor Luna's killer.

The shipping agent's office was three doors further down, and on the first floor of the building. Having climbed the outside staircase, they knocked and entered. Rivera was in the outer office.

"Can I help you?"

"Is your boss in?" Garai asked. He needed to be sure the answer was "no", although they knew that the man rarely got to the office before ten in the morning and took a three-hour siesta from twelve.

"No, he is not here at the moment. He will be back at three."

"Good, then we can talk to you in private," Beth said.

Rivera looked alarmed and Beth treated him to her best smile. "We know that López is blackmailing you to give him the shipping list."

"How … ?"

"Never mind how, we are here to help you." Beth took the rolled-up list from her bag. "You will give him this."

Rivera took the paper and unrolled it. "That is my handwriting!"

"It is. You will give this list to López."

He scanned the names. It *looked* genuine. "But …"

"Just do as I ask and López will not be a problem for you anymore." She touched his arm. "And your daughter will be quite safe."

As Garai and Beth left, Rivera shook his head. How on earth had they got hold of the current list? And how did it come to be in *his* writing?

It was a waiting game now. Beth had discovered that the espionage business, and the role of an agent, involved lots of tedious waiting, watching and following. The exciting bits were few and far between.

Manuela had a team watching the docks and kept Rivera's house under observation. López stayed on board his ship at night and frequented taverns during the day, meeting other captains and talking to agents. At Beth's suggestion, Manuela had got a job as a serving girl at one of those taverns, and reported that he was a boastful type who liked his rum.

The docks were always being watched by López's snitches and independent informants, which was nothing unusual, but there were two men specifically watching the *Brunswick*, which was. The day before the *Brunswick* was due to sail, a nondescript closed cart turned up, escorted by eight tough-looking outriders armed with rifles who loaded four large, heavy chests onto the ship. Then, free of their burden, the riders dispersed into town to drink their pay. When asked, they said that they were guards employed by a silver mining company. The delivery sparked a mass exodus of watchers, who rushed off to sell their information.

The crew of the *Brunswick* also welcomed aboard a fancily dressed female passenger, who was accompanied by a manservant. She had auburn hair, which was unusual in the area. They sailed on the next ebb tide, destination New Orleans.

From the northern end of the docks another ship left as the *Brunswick* rounded the headland. A schooner with a large crew — and black sails.

Beth changed into her fighting leathers as soon as they were sufficiently far away from the dock not to be seen. She complemented the leathers with a wide-brimmed hat that had an ostrich plume in the band. On her belt she wore a rapier and main gauche, while a pair of pistols holstered in leather sleeves adorned her bodice. Her cat, Fernando, stalked the feather from the top of her dresser. He had joined Beth from the street, turning up at the house and adopting her. He was a big tabby — of around a year old, she guessed — and happy to follow her onto the ship.

On deck, she relished the fresh air. Without the overpowering stench of humanity that dominated Veracruz, she could smell the earthy tones of the land and the ozone freshness of the sea. Richard approached from the weather side of the quarterdeck.

"Good morning."

"Are we being followed?" Beth asked.

"Oh yes, black sails on the horizon. I expect they will move up overnight and attack at dawn."

"That tends to be their standard modus operandi." Beth frowned. "We will let them, which is ours. Then the men can have some live fire practice."

"The boys are looking forward to a bit of exercise," Richard said, with typical deadpan humour.

Beth wasn't fooled; she knew her captain had a mischievous streak a mile wide. "What's the betting?"

Richard grinned. "Two to one that we take the ship and keep it, four to three that we sink it, evens we take it and sell it."

Beth laughed; the crew were notorious gamblers, and the book was kept by the purser. All bets were limited to a guinea maximum, on Richard's orders. Beth didn't bet, as that was unfair. She was the one making the decisions, after all.

Fernando appeared from below decks with a rat in his mouth and proudly showed her his prize. She knelt and ruffled his head as he rubbed up against her. Then, the rat twitched. Fernando quickly tired of the fuss and returned to playing pat and chase with his prey.

They kept lights burning all night, and two hours before dawn the ship's longboat was launched with a mast stepped and crewed. It had covered lights mounted in the same pattern as those seen from astern on the *Fox*. One by one the *Fox*'s lights were doused, and the corresponding light uncovered on the longboat. The *Fox* beat to windward and went to quarters an hour before dawn. The carronades were loaded with chain but not run out.

"Have they moved up?" Beth asked Richard, who was peering through a night glass.

"They are a half-mile behind the longboat. When the sun comes up, they will accelerate."

"Will they see us?"

"Not immediately, we will still be in shadow for a moment."

Then the sun peeked over the horizon, illuminating the schooner and longboat. Beth imagined their followers' surprise as they realised they had been duped, and their shock when they saw that the *Fox* was abeam of them.

Richard gave the order: "FIRE!"

The guns roared and chain howled across the water, leaving a shimmer in the air as it passed. It was well aimed, and the schooner's rigging suffered.

They closed; the privateers responded. Chain dealt blows to the *Fox*'s rigging, but no one was hurt. Beth stood on the quarterdeck and urged her gunners to reload as fast as possible. Their second broadside brought down the top half of the schooner's foremast.

"Prepare to board!" Richard bellowed, as the gap closed to a mere fifty feet. The men knew the drill. Swivels, loaded with grapnels attached to ropes, were fired into the other ship's rigging. Then the swivels were swapped for new guns, loaded with canister shot. The crew hauled on the ropes to pull the ships together, and as they touched, gunners fired the swivels and carronades, sending canister shot blasting across the privateer's crowded deck, leaving it strewn with dead and wounded men.

Beth leapt up onto the rail, gave a rallying war cry and jumped the gap, followed by her men. Pistols in hand, she shot the first man, and pistol-whipped then shot the second. Then, to the surprise of those enemy sailors who hoped she was out of bullets, she re-cocked both guns. They were six-shot pinfire revolvers, a present from her betrothed.

Clearing a path, Beth made her way to the quarterdeck, where she expected to find the captain. She shot one more man — and there he was.

"López!" she cried, and he spun to face her.

"*Who* in God's name are *you*?"

"Rosa of the *Fox*."

"Rosa the Fox?"

"Whatever. On guard!"

She swapped her pistols for her sword and main gauche. He was armed similarly and moved smoothly to engage. His footwork was good, he had good balance and a supple wrist. A worthy opponent.

Beth was cautious against this unknown quantity. She parried his first probes and tried a simple attack of her own, which he parried with a flick of the wrist and a sneer. Stepping to the left, she moved towards his sword arm. As she expected, he stepped to keep things square — to where he thought he had an advantage.

He parried her next attack with his main gauche and flicked his sword in a lightning-fast attack to her throat. She caught his sword with her main gauche and let it slide down her blade, catching it in the quillons. A sharp twist of her wrist and his blade snapped off, halfway along its length.

"Oops," she said, as he looked at it in surprise.

"Bitch!" he said and attacked with the sword-stump in his hand.

"Absolutely," she said, as she pirouetted out of the path of his charge and ran him through the kidney via his back.

López staggered a couple of steps, then collapsed to his knees as the shock hit him. Beth watched as he slumped to the deck, face down.

She turned and swept her sword across the lanyard that carried the defeated crew's flag, and it floated to the deck.

Havana and Tortuga

The prize was taken to Havana and put into the hands of their regular broker.

"*Buen día*, Señorita Rosa!" Ernesto greeted Beth as she walked into his yard accompanied by her cox, Carlos. Ernesto's dog, a massive white animal, followed him — and she was followed in turn by half a dozen bundles of white fur. As Havana was a regular haven for privateers and pirates alike, Beth maintained her cover identity at all times when she was there.

"Ernesto, good day. I see that Maggy has had puppies!" Beth knelt down and called the fur-bundles over to her. A couple held back, four came forwards eagerly, and one climbed on her lap while the others circled Beth, sniffing her leathers. She picked up the pup in her lap and gave it a cuddle; in return, it washed her face with an eager soft tongue.

Beth was in love.

She held it out so she could see if it was a boy or girl. It was most definitely a boy.

"He likes you; you should take him," Ernesto said, and grinned.

Maggy walked over and sniffed the pup, then headbutted Beth

for some fuss. Beth ruffled Maggy's head then put the puppy on the ground; he promptly sat down in front of her.

"Should I take him, Maggy?" Beth asked, looking into the animal's eyes.

Maggy pushed her head into Beth's chest in reply.

"He is seven weeks, old enough to leave the nest," Ernesto said.

"Will he be as big as Maggy?"

"Bigger! His father was a big dog, even for this breed."

Beth had a sudden thought. "You've never said what breed it is."

"She is from the Pyrenees, we call them *Grande Perro Pirano*. They are used to protect the flocks."

"So, a big shepherd dog, then. Can I buy him from you?"

"No, he is a gift."

Beth stood up and hugged him, then picked up the pup and held him at arm's length. "I will call you Fede, short for Federico. The peaceful warrior."

Fede wagged his tail, making his whole body wiggle. Beth hugged him. Then she turned her thoughts back to business.

"We have a ship to sell, another schooner."

"I saw you come into the harbour; she is the *Dolphin*. Did you kill her captain?"

"They attacked us, and he and I fought."

Ernesto knew what *that* meant; she had a reputation for not taking prisoners.

"Good. He was a pig."

Beth smiled. "Will you send a crew over to move her into the yard? Her rigging needs some work."

"Yes, Pedro will take care of her."

They closed the deal with a glass of wine and as they drank, Beth noticed that none of the pups or Maggy approached Carlos. On the contrary, Maggy sat near Ernesto and looked at Carlos with an expression that suggested she did not trust him.

Beth put Fede on a lead that Ernesto supplied, and he happily trotted next to her as they went back to the *Fox*. The puppy was quite content: he liked Beth and had felt a bond with her from the moment she picked him up. This would develop as he grew, and his protective instincts would in time encompass Beth and her crew.

But he didn't like Carlos. Carlos smelled wrong.

Keen to find out more about El Dragon, Beth started asking at the dockside bars to see if anyone had heard of him. The first few bars turned up nothing. No one had heard of El Dragon. In fact, Beth was beginning to think that he had never existed … until she walked into a cantina set slightly back from the docks and heard three old men reminiscing. One in particular was well into his cups.

"It was '92, and I was sailing with that devil Dragon. He was a beast, had no mercy for anyone. We caught this ship with settlers aboard. They only had tools and stuff for their houses — but he was sure they had money hidden away. He tortured the children in front of the parents, then the women in front of the men, and finally he killed the men by gutting them and throwing them to the sharks. He killed everyone, then burned the ship." His eyes welled with tears. "Those poor little ones."

Beth went to the bar and bought four beers. She placed them on the table and pulled up a chair.

"Mind if I join you?"

One old man smacked his lips and took a tankard while leering at Beth. "Don't mind if you do. Pretty girls are always welcome."

She gave him a smile, then tipped her head towards the drunk, who was alternately sobbing and hiccupping. "Your friend there mentioned the Dragon."

"Oh, he's been gone many a year."

"What happened to him?"

"He got caught and hanged, that's what."

The drunk had by now found the full tankard and looked up from taking a long pull on it. "No, he wasn't hanged. They put him in a gibbet over Port Royal. Took him days to die."

"They killed only him?" Beth asked.

"No — the British hanged the officers but they sold us crew into slavery." The old man pulled up the sleeve of his shirt to show a slave's brand, which had been struck through with an over-brand. "I was freed when the plantation was sold. The new owners didn't want to keep white slaves."

"El Dragon hasn't been seen since?"

One of the other men leant forward and said, in a soft but sinister voice, "His ghost is said to roam the main, dragging sailors to Davy Jones's locker, never to be seen again!"

The old men peered at her. She played along and looked shocked, as the old men cackled at their own joke.

Having tried and failed to find out more about El Dragon, Beth asked Richard to prepare to sail. Carlos hadn't returned from wherever he had wandered off to and Beth wasn't about to wait for him. However, he arrived in the nick of time and jumped onto the deck as the crew started warping the ship from the dock.

"You should have been back an hour ago. I was about to mark you as run," Beth scolded him.

For a second, anger flared in his eyes — but he got it under control and apologised. "I'm sorry, skipper; I was with a woman and forgot the time."

Beth shook her head. "Men!" But as she said this she thought, *He looks as though he wants to lash out.*

Fede wandered over and pointedly sat in front of her, looking up at Carlos's face. Beth looked down at him, her head cocked to one side in thought. *You know what? I don't think he likes you.*

They raised sail as soon as they had sea room. "Where to, boss?" Richard asked.

"Jamaica — I need to look into the prison records," Beth replied.

"Your wish is my command."

They sped out of the bay under full sail, inviting curses and shouts from ships they shaved past. Richard was having fun and the crew loved it. Beth grinned; it was just the behaviour one would expect from a cocky privateer. The *Fox* swung around, to run down the north coast of Cuba. Far enough north to avoid the Cays, but not so far out as to make navigation difficult. They were out of the hurricane season and enjoyed the steady northeasterly trade wind.

"Skipper, there's a sail that keeps popping up on the horizon, off the port quarter," the lookout reported.

"Following us?" Beth asked.

"Probably," Richard said. "Do you want me to lose them?"

Beth considered this for a moment. "No, we will worry about them later."

Richard gave her a look. He preferred to deal with situations like this head on.

"You don't agree?" She smiled.

Richard frowned, looking aft. "I don't like being followed."

"Well, in this case, we need to give them some rope."

"Why?"

"I will tell you when I know."

As Beth walked away, Richard watched her go. *She can be annoying at times*, he thought.

The sail dogged them along the north coast until they got to the passage between Haiti and Cuba. Beth, who had been conscious of *something* nagging in the back of her mind for the last few days, suddenly issued an order.

"Set a course for Tortuga."

"Tortuga?" Richard said, surprised.

"You know, the island just north of Haiti." Beth seemed to be distracted.

"Why? I thought the clues were leading you to Jamaica."

"Exactly, which is why we are going to Tortuga."

Richard shook his head. He had no idea what she meant, but he complied — and they soon entered the strait between Haiti and Tortuga, approaching Port Vincent, where they anchored in the harbour.

Beth stood with Garai as they watched the sailors drop anchor then reverse the foresails to drive them backwards.

"Father told me he had quite an adventure here," she said.

"It *was* a little entertaining," Garai commented.

"Pfft, so getting shot at, running from a mob, burning all the ships in the harbour and capturing the *Silverthorn* — is that what you call 'a little entertaining'?"

"Well, technically we didn't capture the *Silverthorn* here," Garai said, deadpan.

Beth gave him a sideways look but decided that the veteran wouldn't give an inch and changed the subject. "Come ashore with me."

"Of course. Do we need tools?"

She knew he meant weapons.

"Only the usual."

"I will meet you at the port."

They stepped ashore and were ignored by the locals, who were used to strange ships turning up. Beth found this lack of attention rather refreshing. A local bar beckoned. It was called the Jolly Roger.

"Did pirates really come here?" Beth asked the landlord, wide-eyed. She was dressed as a wealthy tourist, who had come to see the notorious den of iniquity that was Tortuga.

"They did indeed. The Scarlett Fox, Morgan, Blackbeard, Collins, Anne Bonny. They all came to Tortuga at one time or another."

"Oh my!" she said, feigning awe. "What about El Dragon?"

"Who?"

"El Dragon, in Jamaica they said he was a great pirate."

"Then someone has been pulling yer leg, missy. El Dragon weren't nothing but a poor imitation of Edward Teach — you know, Blackbeard."

"He wasn't?"

"Nah; he tried to be like him, but was just a murdering git with no style."

Interesting.

Just then, a drinker who had been listening looked up. "You got a lot of interest in the brotherhood."

"Pirates are exciting!" Beth simpered.

"Well, you better be careful. There are still some who hold to the old ways."

"Are there? Oh my!"

"Jack Cunningham, for one. He will pluck out your eyes if you cross him."

"Now, Abel, don't go frightening the young lady," Paola, the barmaid, said.

Abel wasn't to be deterred and stood up, looming over Beth threateningly.

"You ask too many questions, missy." He took a step forward; Garai moved in and the man landed flat on his back on the floor.

"Woah, now! No need for that!" the landlord cried.

Beth made a placatory gesture. "Forgive my man, he is sometimes ... overprotective."

Abel grunted something, a dazed look on his face.

"But then—" her face hardened — "he probably just saved his life."

The landlord sensed the change in atmosphere and reappraised the girl before him; a girl who, just a moment before, had been an empty-headed tourist. Beth put her tiger's-claw knife on the counter. "Now tell me, who are the currently active pirates?"

Paola looked at the knife. "You been holding that all the time?" she said, wide-eyed.

Beth glanced at her. "Never go anywhere without it." She turned her attention back to the landlord. "Now speak."

He looked at the knife, then at Beth, and gulped. "There are a few skippers who will take an opportunity if one presents itself like. It's a big ocean and nobody asks where cargoes come from."

"That's fair if you have a letter of marque, but it will get you hanged if you don't," Beth said.

The landlord looked at her suspiciously. "Are you the law?"

"Me?" Beth laughed. "I'm Rosa of the *Fox*."

They looked at her blankly.

"You haven't heard of me?"

The landlord and Paola looked at each other, then back at Beth, and then shook their heads in unison, their faces blank. Garai gave a chuckle — which grew into a full-throated laugh.

"So, what did you learn?" Richard asked, as they shared a glass later that evening.

Garai started to chuckle. Beth glared at him, and he got himself under control.

"Am I missing something?" Richard said.

"No," Beth snapped. "We were told that El Dragon was a poor imitation of Blackbeard and wasn't a very good pirate."

"Blackbeard! That explains the Dragon's excesses," Richard said.

Beth replied, "Blackbeard wasn't the worst of them, Ned Low was a real sadist. Blackbeard worked hard on his reputation, to make it easier to take ships." Then she paused, as if contemplating something. "We will sail for Jamaica in the morning and see if that ship continues to follow us."

Record Rummaging and a Visit Home

Two days later, Beth and Garai walked into the courthouse in Kingston, Jamaica, which had a dusty old records room cared for by an ancient archivist by the name of Miss Agatha. She had, apparently, been there for years — but nobody knew exactly how old she was, or when she had first started the job.

Agatha had a pronounced accent from the English West Country.

"How can I help you, my lover?" she said with rounded vowels and not an "h" to be heard. Beth would have bet a guinea that she wouldn't hear the letter "t" at any point in the ensuing conversation, either.

Beth smiled. "Sometime in '92, a man who went by the name of El Dragon was sentenced to death by gibbet. I was wondering if there were any records of the trial or his background."

Agatha went to a cabinet of small drawers and pulled one out. It was long and full of cards. She rifled through them until she found what she wanted. Then she frowned and went to another drawer and repeated the process. Now armed with two cards, she beckoned Beth to follow her.

They walked along long shelves filled with everything from scrolls to parchments to leather-bound books. Now and then, Agatha stopped, and Beth noticed that she was checking numbers — which had been burned into the edge of the shelves — against the card. She pulled out a book, then went to another row and found another shelf with a number that corresponded to that on the second card. This time, she pulled out a much bigger file that had a thin wooden cover at the front and back. She took the book and the file to a table and sent up a cloud of dust when she put them down.

"Not been down yer for many a day. Now, let us see."

Beth congratulated herself on an accurate prediction — Miss Agatha swallowed the letter "t" every time.

"This yer is the court records." She opened the book and flicked through to the beginning of 1792. "Here we are, June 1792. The Crown versus Miguel Ortega, otherwise known as El Dragon. Charged with piracy, rape, buggery, theft, murder and torture. The records cite three incidents where he took ships." She pushed the book across the table to Beth, who pulled up a rickety chair and read. She remembered the old drunk.

"Some of his crew gave evidence against him. I think I probably met one of them."

"It were thirty odd years ago, so he must be old," Agatha said, sounding surprised.

"He was, and still haunted by it. Aah — here it says that the ones who gave evidence had their death sentences commuted to slavery. The man I met had a brand."

The court record didn't tell her much about Miguel's background, only that he was Colombian. As Beth read, Agatha was rifling through the file, which turned out to contain back copies of the *Royal Gazette* newspaper.

"Here is the broadsheet from the day of the execution."

She produced a single large sheet of paper, printed on both sides. One section was titled "Criminal Court Proceedings", and about halfway down the column was a paragraph covering "The Trial of Miguel Ortega".

The pirate Miguel Ortega, also known as El Dragon, was captured by HMS Warsprite on the 19th day of May in the year of our Lord 1792 and brought to trial on the 17th June in Kingston. Sir Adam Williamson, governor, presided. The court heard the charges of piracy, rape, murder, molestation, buggery, theft and torture read out by the prosecution, who went on to provide witnesses from Ortega's own crew who testified to his guilt. In his defence, Ortega said he was born and grew up in Barranquilla in Colombia, where he was daily abused by his father and uncles and forced to work on fishing boats from the age of six.

Sir Adam was not moved to pity by this plea of mitigation and sentenced the rogue to be hanged in a gibbet from the walls of Fort Charles until he was dead, his body to be left there three months thereafter to act as a warning to others. The officers and crew were sentenced to death by hanging. The defendants who gave testimony against Ortega had their sentences commuted to slavery on Antigua.

"Well, there we have it. I suppose our next stop is Barranquilla, to find out more and see if it is someone from there who is trying to resurrect El Dragon," Beth told Richard and Garai when she returned to the *Fox*. "But first I want to visit the plantations."

"How long will you be?" Richard asked.

"A few days at least. Why?"

"The *Fox* needs her bottom cleaned, and coppering. That will take at least a week, probably closer to two."

"Then we will be back in two weeks," Beth told him.

Garai knew that her use of "we" meant he would be going to the plantations with Beth, and so he prepared accordingly.

He extracted riding breeches, silk shirts, high riding boots to protect against thorns, a tailcoat and a wide-brimmed hat from his baggage.

Then he meticulously cleaned, sharpened and oiled a pair of wicked-looking curved daggers that were similar to, but larger than, Beth's. Garai preferred a sabre to a rapier and his was a fine example of the swordsmith's craft. It was a 1796-pattern officers' light cavalry sabre, with a thirty-three-inch curved blade that was wider at the point than the hilt. Fullers ran almost the entire length and on both sides of the blade, which was sharpened on one edge except for the last six inches; *that* section was sharpened on both sides, making it perfect for stabbing. It was a brutal weapon even when wielded by a novice, but in Garai's hands it was truly deadly. He wore the sabre on his belt with a machete on the opposite side to balance it. His revolver was holstered under his arm, while on his saddle he would carry a rifle and a pair of double-barrelled pistols.

When Garai was ready, he went on deck to see if Beth was. He smiled wryly when she told him she would be at least another half-hour.

"I will go and find a carriage and horses, then," he told her.

"Riding horses would be better. Get four, so two can carry our packs."

We must be in a hurry, thought Garai, as he went to visit the local livery stable.

He was met by the proprietor, Silas Grimes. "I have horses to suit most riders, what do you need?"

"Horses with pace and stamina, four of them," replied Garai.

Grimes looked Garai over. "I can see you are experienced — what about the others in your party?"

"There is only one other. She is an excellent rider."

"She? So you will need a side saddle?"

Garai laughed. "I wouldn't suggest that within her hearing! No, normal saddles will be fine — and pack harnesses for the other two."

Grimes led Garai around the yard to a paddock, where horses stood around eating hay from a basket and snoozing. Garai climbed over the rail and walked among them. Having checked them over, he chose two sturdy animals that looked strong enough to carry loads all day: these would take the packs. In a separate corral were three black horses with flowing manes and tails.

"Friesians?"

"Yes," Grimes said, impressed that Garai recognised them. "Two geldings and a stallion."

The stallion snorted and stepped forward with high steps. He had bright, intelligent eyes and held his head high on an arched neck. Garai stepped through the rail and held out his hand, upon which he had an apple.

"Hello, my beauty; you're a fine lad now, aren't you?" he said softly. The stallion stepped towards him and reached out for the apple. Garai stroked his neck as he crunched it.

"What's his name?"

"Emperor," Grimes replied.

"I'll take him." He moved onto the geldings and liked what he saw. Both were around sixteen hands and very well kept, but one appealed just a little more than the other. "And this one?"

"That's Gregory."

Garai looked them over again; they were both excellent specimens of the breed. He turned to Grimes and spat on his hand in the traditional manner of horse dealers beginning negotiation of the price.

Beth stepped down the gangplank just after dawn to find Garai strapping her bags into the pack horses' panniers. There were no riding horses in sight. The air was cool and the docks quiet.

"Are we walking? I will need to change my boots."

She was wearing a riding habit over her leather trousers, and a cloak over her shoulders to conceal her leather bodice. Her hair was tied in a ponytail. Beth wore her rapier at her left with a main gauche on her right, and pistols were holstered in the sleeves that had been stitched to her bodice. Her boots were high and laced up at the front, with Cuban heels and slender, blunt, silver spurs. Slim throwing knives were set in hidden sheaths in the uppers of her boots, their pommels looking like silver decorations.

Garai grinned and put his fingers to his lips, emitting a shrill whistle. At once the sound of hooves echoed, and two horses appeared from between the warehouses, led by a single man.

"Oh. My. Lord," she said as they came into view.

For a moment, Beth seemed to regress to her six-year-old self, seeing her pony for the first time. She stepped forward and stopped, as if uncertain the animals were real.

Garai grinned and tossed her an apple. "The one on the left is yours, his name is Gregory." Garai stepped over to the other horse and took his bridle.

Beth advanced slowly, keeping eye contact with Gregory, her hand held out with the apple. He whickered and stretched his neck to take it, his lips soft against her hand, his breath warm. She stepped in close, and he nuzzled her shoulder. She whispered in his ear and stroked his nose, then ran her hand down his powerful, arched neck. His long, flowing mane was beautiful. It had been meticulously brushed out and covered one side of his neck entirely. His coat glowed in the morning sun.

Beth noticed that her rifle was already in a saddle holster and that a pair of saddle pistols were also in place. The saddle was of the Spanish/Mexican Californian style, with a high-peaked pommel, high cantle and long stirrups. It was decorated with fancy stamping in the leather and was a work of art.

"Like him?" asked Garai.

"Did you buy them?"

"Why? Do you want to keep them?"

"God, yes." Beth seized the pommel and lithely swung herself up into the saddle. The stirrups were too long for her liking, so she shortened them a little. "Well?" she said, looking impatiently at Garai.

"Well, what?" he replied, teasing her.

"Are you going to mount up so we can get going? And did you buy them?"

He laughed as he hopped to get his foot into the stirrup and then swung himself up into the saddle. "Yes, I did."

Beth kicked Gregory on, and Garai reined Emperor in alongside her. The pack horses' reins were connected to a ring on his saddle's cantle and they followed along behind him. They walked their horses across the cobbled surface of the dock, getting the feel of their saddles, reins and the horses themselves. Emperor was impatient to get going, but Garai was more than a match for him.

Beth discovered that, like her steppe horse, Polina, back in England, Gregory had been trained to respond to neck-reining, so she held them loosely in her right hand, her left hung relaxed at her side. The cobbles gave way to a dirt road, and she nudged him into a trot. His action was smooth and even, and with the Spanish-style saddle she didn't have to post.

As soon as they cleared the town, Beth tried a canter and Gregory accelerated. Garai struggled to keep Emperor from galloping after him, which wouldn't be good for the pack horses.

"We can race later, when we get to the plantation," he called as he sensed Beth's desire to let her horse have its head.

Beth reined Gregory back into a slow canter. She had the feeling he could keep that pace up all day.

"We will need a few mares."

Garai immediately understood the statement, having known Beth since her childhood. "I thought you might think that. I suppose you want to breed them?"

"How could I not? They are magnificent!"

At the end of the day they reached the Blue Mountain plantation, and as soon as they were recognised a hue and cry went up, spreading the word that Princess Bethany was home. As they rode along the long drive to the main buildings, children came out and ran beside the horses, and soon dogs barked and joined with the children. Emperor showed off, prancing along with a high step, his neck arched elegantly. Gregory mimicked him, not wishing to be outdone.

Phineas Calthorpe, the estate manager, met them in front of the house.

"Miss Beth, this is an unexpected pleasure!"

"Hello, Fin. How are you?" she said as she slid from Gregory's back.

"Very well, thank you." Phineas hugged her and shook Garai's hand. A pretty woman came out from the house; she wore bright clothes that complemented her skin, which was the colour of milky coffee.

"This is Jasmine, my wife."

"You got married? Congratulations!" Beth gave the woman a warm hug and kissed her on the cheek.

Jasmine looked at Beth's fighting gear and chuckled, amused. Beth was living up to her reputation. "We need to get you dressed properly. The people will want to see you."

As a couple of men carried their bags into the house, Jasmine joined Beth in her room and helped her to unpack.

"So, where did you meet Fin?" Beth asked as she hung a dress in the wardrobe.

"We met at a party on the beach at Annotto Bay. The workers from both plantations were celebrating the new year there." Jasmine's voice, rich and accented, conveyed her joy at the memory. "He was talking to Arny Strong, the under estate manager for the Den. When our eyes met ... everybody else just faded away."

Beth sighed; it was all very romantic. Meanwhile, Jasmine shook herself back to reality. "Now, what are we going to dress you in?"

Beth held up a skirt that she had last worn in Havana a scant few weeks ago. "How about this?"

"Hmm, what about a blouse?"

"I only have a white one."

"I can lend you a nice green one that will show off your hair, if you like."

And so, shortly afterwards, Beth emerged from her room, dressed in a traditional bandana skirt of emerald-green cotton that hung to her calves, with a matching top that featured ruching on the bust line and shoulder seams. She went barefoot and the only weapon she carried was a silver dagger, which was sheathed in a garter on her thigh.

Beth's skin, tanned from sailing, glowed in the setting sun as she walked out of the house and down the steps of the front porch to be greeted by the workers.

Clearly, a party was called for. Rum punch was served from a large cauldron and food was laid out on trestle tables. Music was provided by a group of men who played guitars, pipes and drums. Everybody danced. Beth, who remembered her last foray into drinking rum, drank in moderation. That evening, she was able to forget her duties and her mission and just enjoyed herself.

The party wound down at midnight; most people there had to be up for work at six the next morning. Beth, however, slept in and eventually awoke with a feeling of contentment.

It didn't last. As soon as she had finished breakfast, she became aware of a commotion outside. She went out to see what it was all about.

Manhunt

Within the hour, Beth, Garai and two of the plantation overseers had mounted their horses. A pair of bloodhounds were barking and howling; their handlers, on foot, held them on long ropes. The riders were all dressed for a journey across country, with high leather boots and leather chaps to protect them from thorns in the brush.

A woman's body lay under a bloodstained sheet on a trestle table outside a worker's house, her family weeping and wailing around her. Lilibeth had been discovered when she failed to appear for work, at which point her sister had gone to check on her. Lilibeth had been stabbed many times in the stomach and chest in a frenzied and brutal attack. The perpetrator was nowhere to be found.

Garai, who was no stranger to violent death having been a fighter and agent for many years, examined the body. A head wound suggested she had been knocked out, or at least stunned. She had been gagged, and the blood on her thighs indicated she had been raped before she was killed — she probably hadn't been able to scream for help. Garai thought she had been dead for several hours, maybe since midnight.

A headcount found one other person missing: a man called Stanley, who had been unsuccessfully wooing Lilibeth for the last year. If he had killed her at the end of the party, he had a ten-hour head start on them. The dogs were taken to Stanley's hut to get his scent, then out to a relatively empty area of the plantation. They scanned back and forth until one dog howled and started off, heading out towards the perimeter with his handler trailing along behind him on a long line.

The search party soon came to the cactus fence enclosing the property. Such barriers were an effective way of keeping goats and other livestock from entering the plantation, but one had a hole in it.

"The cuts are still weeping, he cannot have passed through here more than a few hours ago," Garai said.

"We will have to go out the gate and circle back around," Beth declared.

The dogs picked up the scent again and set off through the wilderness, towing their handlers behind them. The searchers followed in a line, their horses keeping them out of the reach of the low scrub's thorns.

Beth examined a bush as they passed and shuddered, thankful she wore her fighting leathers. The thorns were more than an inch long and razor-sharp, but regardless, Beth spotted an iguana perched on a branch and chomping on some tender new leaves. *Damn, but you are tough,* she thought.

In time they reached a clearing with a stream. The dogs milled around the bank.

"He has taken to the water to hide his scent," a handler told them.

"Did he go upstream or down?" Beth asked.

At this, Garai dismounted and stepped into the stream. First he followed it upstream until it entered the brush, then turned and followed it downstream. He stopped and bent to look at something.

"A rock has been turned here."

He moved on and stopped at the edge of the clearing.

"There's another here. He went downstream."

As the stream provided a path through the brush, which was thicker on the banks due to the readily available water, they followed it. After a mile or so, they came to a track. The dogs set up a din of howling and followed it downhill towards the coast. Now was the time for speed: the dog handlers were hoisted up behind the riders and the dogs let loose.

As they cantered down the track following the dogs, Beth could see a row of footprints in the dust. At first they were close together, but became further apart — presumably the man had broken into a run.

Suddenly, the dogs veered into a side track leading back up into the hills. Beth got a shiver of warning: something wasn't right.

"STOP!" she shouted, and pulled Gregory to a halt.

"What's up, boss?" Garai asked.

"Why would Stanley head back into the hills?"

One of the dog handlers pointed ahead to a ridge with a slot in it. "He's heading for the Maroons' community near Buff Bay; this track goes down there once it gets past that ridge."

"Are there any people up here?" Beth asked.

"Some. Those that don't want to be found by the authorities, mainly."

"He could be hoping to find a ship," Garai said. "They stop in Buff Bay to collect cargo from Charles Town."

"You—" Beth pointed to one of the overseers — "go to Kingston and find the skipper of my ship, the *Fox*. Tell him that I want him to take her to Buff Bay and stop any ships from leaving." Beth pulled a ring from her finger and gave it to the man. "Give him this, so he knows the order comes from me."

Then, Beth pulled her rifle from its scabbard on her saddle and fired a shot into the air. As she reloaded, she shouted towards the brush where her instincts told her someone was hiding. "If you attack, I will kill every one of you, with no exceptions. Show yourselves and we will leave you alone. The only man we want is the one who passed through here this morning."

A man stepped out onto the track, followed by half a dozen more. All were armed with spears and machetes. Beth heard gasps from the men behind her and a chuckle from Garai.

"How did she know?" someone muttered.

Beth pointed her rifle casually at one of the emerging men, a filthy individual dressed in rags.

"You. Are you the leader?"

"Sort of," he replied, shuffling his feet. He had a Yorkshire accent.

"Have you seen a stranger pass through here? When did he pass?"

"About three hours ago, I reckon."

"Why didn't you stop him?"

"He were covered in blood and didn't even have a knife on him. He weren't going to bother us, so we let him go."

It was clear she could learn nothing more from this man, so Beth kicked Gregory forward, pushing the men to the side of the road. She reached into her saddlebag as she passed and tossed them a loaf of bread, before kicking the horse into a canter.

They ate lunch in the saddle as they crossed the ridge. Beth thought they were probably only an hour or so behind Stanley now. However, as they rode into the next valley the trail led them to another river.

"Damn it! He's taken to the water again," Beth cried.

Garai looked the river over and walked the bank.

"It's too deep to wade and too fast anyway. He went in here," he said, kneeling by a mark in the bank. "He was dragging something. Looks like it was probably a log."

One of the dog handlers stepped up and looked at the drag mark.

"No, boss, that was a dugout boat. See, the bottom of the scrape has a line from the carved front."

"If there was a boat here, then either he pre-planned this or someone else brought it upriver," Garai said.

"Search the area," Beth said.

It did not take long for the dogs to find the bodies of two teenage boys, thrown one atop the other in the brush. Beth examined them when they were laid out in the open.

"Bashed in the head of one and stabbed the other. They are still warm. Anyone have any idea where they came from?"

One of the trackers shook his head but the other stepped forward. Tears ran down his face.

"One of them is my cousin's boy. They live in Tranquility."

"Wrap them in blankets and make a travois to carry them," Beth ordered. While she knew that this would delay them, she was prepared to take the time required to honour the dead boys. They had been innocents, in the wrong place at the wrong time. Their families needed to know what had happened, and to bury them.

The men took little time to make a travois. They cut poles from a stand of trees, and used reeds to bind them together. The bodies were carefully laid side by side and secured before they set off downstream to Tranquility.

They entered the village as dusk was falling, and found the boys' parents. Beth let the plantation men tell them of the fate of their children, and as they did so a great wailing rose up from the women of the village. The men were understandably angry, and one, who appeared to be the head man, sat with Beth to discuss the matter.

"You say the man who did this killed a woman on your plantation?"

"Yes, sometime around midnight last night. We started looking for him this morning."

"And you followed him to where you found our boys." It was a statement, not a question, and Beth nodded. "You still think you can catch him?"

"We think he is either heading for the Maroon community at Charles Town or will look for passage out of Buff Bay. If he is looking for a ship, he will be disappointed; mine is blockading it."

The head man nodded. "I will come with you, with two of our men. I want to see justice done." The look on his face told her he would brook no argument.

"We leave at dawn," Beth said.

There was a church in the village and the boys' bodies were placed there overnight. They would be buried the next day, before they started to stink. Beth and her men were given a house to sleep in, but none of the men really slept much. They were up and ready to go at first light.

The road down to Charles Town was good and they made fast progress even with the three villagers running beside the horses. The men were all hunters and could maintain the pace for hours if need be.

"The Maroon community is before the main town in a valley that runs south-east," the head man said as he loped along holding Beth's stirrup.

"Are they friendly?"

"They keep themselves to themselves. There is a lot of history between them and the freed slaves."

They turned into the valley where the Maroons lived and stopped before a brush fence that ran across the route, cutting off access. It had a gate in the middle which was manned by two men.

"What do you want?" one demanded.

"We are looking for a man who would have got here late yesterday or early this morning," Beth said.

"Why?"

"He has murdered three people — a woman and two teenage boys."

The men looked at each other. "Wait here," the larger of the two said, as the smaller one ran off up the road. Beth dismounted and signalled for the others to do the same.

The head man, who was called James, stepped up and faced the guard. "He killed two of the sons of my village. If he is in there, you had better hand him over."

"Or you will do *what*?"

Beth stepped up to stand beside the head man. "I will burn your community to the ground."

"You may be dressed in fancy leathers but we are Maroons and we can fight."

"And I am Beth, of the Blue Mountain and Den plantations, and I have enough men with me to do what I say."

The big man looked down his nose at her, and she was about to knee him in the balls when one of her men spotted the other man returning.

"The one you want is in the town. Three of you can come and get him," the smaller guard told them.

Beth, Garai and James mounted up and followed him. Around a bend in the valley was a town — if a road with around twenty buildings lining it can be called a town. At the far end of the street stood a group of men. Beth pulled up and dismounted. James and Garai, who had shared Emperor, slid to the ground nearby. Garai handed a saddle pistol to James, who tucked it into his belt.

The two men came up to stand on either side of Beth, and the three walked in line down the street. Beth scanned the rooftops and the tower of the church. A movement caught her eye, and she cocked her head at Garai, who glanced and nodded.

A breeze kicked up a dust devil that ran across the street ahead of them. The sun rose in the sky, its heat evaporating any sweat that broke out on a brow. The men at the other end of the street spread out into a line. Another dust devil skittered past, and a window banged.

They stopped fifteen yards from the line. "Where is he?" Beth said.

"Inside," replied a man in the centre of the line.

"Are you going to hand him over?"

"How do I know you are telling the truth? How do I know he is the right man?"

"He will be tried according to the law in Kingston. If he is innocent, he can prove it in court."

"White man's justice?"

Beth sighed; she had feared this response. The Maroons were justifiably sceptical when it came to "justice".

"I am James, head man of the town of Tranquility. He killed two of our boys, this we know. They are burying them this morning. He bashed in the head of one with a rock and stabbed the other to death with his friend's knife, just so he could take their canoe. He must be handed over to me for justice."

"We have had good relations with Tranquility. Where did he kill the woman?"

Beth held out her hand, which bore an iguana tattoo. "She was a woman of my people, the people of the Blue Mountain and Den plantations. He stabbed her to death and left his knife in her belly."

The sight of the tattoo caused a ripple of tension to run down the line.

"We know of you; they say you are of the blood of the Scarlett Fox."

"She was my great-grandmother."

At this, the man turned and waved towards the building. A man was dragged out. He seemed reluctant to face Beth as he struggled and pleaded with his captors.

"We held him as soon as we heard what you said. He denies it."

"Does he have scratches on his body, from fingernails?" Garai asked.

A man leant towards the leader and muttered to him.

"Yes, he has scratches on his neck."

"I thought he would. I found skin under the dead woman's fingernails."

Stanley began to wail. "She is lying! They are all lying! I didn't do it."

Beth looked at him with utter contempt. "I have men at the gate who can identify you. Men who have known you all your life."

The two overseers from the plantation came and looked at the suspect with hard eyes. One spoke confidently. "He is Stanley, he was born at the Den plantation and moved with his mother to the Mountain when he was five years old. His mother, God bless her, is so ashamed of what he's done we're watching her in case she tries to kill herself. He has a scar on his ribs from when his donkey ran into the brush and a thorn ripped his side open, when he was ten."

The shirt was ripped open and there was the scar, just as the man had described.

"He had been mooning over Lilibeth for a year or more. We think he got drunk at the party to celebrate Miss Beth's homecoming, then followed her to her tent and killed her. The priestess has cursed him."

That was news to Beth. She knew nothing of a priestess, let alone a curse. What she did notice was that the Maroons suddenly looked worried. Meanwhile, the effect on Stanley was astonishing. As he fell to his knees praying and gabbling, the men holding him stepped back as if he was unclean.

"What was all that about a priestess? I assume she is not of the regular church," Beth asked one of the men as they rode back the way they had come. The prisoner was stumbling along behind them, his wrists tied to the saddle of a horse by a long line.

"She is the healer and witch woman. You know her — she was the one you met when you first came here."

Beth had visited the year before and discovered her ancestor Scarlett, the famous Scarlett Fox, had been treated as the queen of the people. Their ancestors had worked the plantations as free men and considered her to be their princess.

"The one who did my tattoo?"

The man nodded. "She put a curse on him."

Beth knew nothing about the strange religion that was part Christian and part Obeah and quite frankly didn't want to, but couldn't resist asking, "What kind of curse?"

"That his soul will be trapped forever in his dead body and never go to heaven or hell. She will complete it when he is in front of her."

Beth sent a message to Malakai, the company agent in Kingston, before they set out on their return journey, asking him to bring a judge to the plantation. As they passed through Tranquility, they had to stop the townsfolk from stoning their prisoner to death. They were joined by a delegation of Tranquility's townsfolk, including the boys' parents.

The next day, the judge arrived at the plantation. He was bad tempered, and Beth knew that Malakai practically had to drag him out of his house to be there.

"If you know he's guilty, why not just hang him?" snapped Mingus Fisher as he was introduced to Beth.

"Every man is entitled to a fair trial," Beth said, a hint of warning in her voice.

The judge opened his mouth to reply, but Malakai saved him by stepping on his foot.

A court was set up in the courtyard in front of the plantation house; the judge sat at a desk on the porch. He slapped his wig onto his otherwise bald pate and called the court to order.

"Who represents the prosecution?"

"I do. I am the Honourable Bethany Stockley."

"And who is acting for the defence?"

Malakai pushed a second individual forward.

"I am; Reginald Smythe, solicitor."

"They dragged you out here as well then, Reg." The judge smirked. "Have you spoken to the defendant?"

"I have."

"How does he plead?"

"Guilty on all counts, milord."

"Do you have a confession?"

"Yes, milord."

The assembled crowd of witnesses jeered and shouted.

"Any mitigating circumstances?"

"The killing of Lilibeth was a crime of passion, milord; he has no excuse for killing the two boys."

The judge turned to Beth. "What punishment do you seek?"

"The killing of two innocent boys deserves nothing less than execution by hanging. The bereaved families request that his body be buried in unconsecrated ground."

Stanley collapsed and was dragged to his feet by two men acting as court ushers.

"Is there anything you want to say before I pass sentence?"

Stanley shook his head.

"Then Stanley, I sentence you to be hanged at dusk today — might as well get it over with — and your body shall be buried in ground that has not been consecrated. Court dismissed." He turned to Beth. "Happy?"

She smiled sweetly. "Why yes, thank you."

"Then the least you can do is get me a drink. A good stiff one."

A rum punch had already been prepared and Beth ladled some into a glass with ice and mint. Looking back towards the judge and noting his grumpy face, she picked up a bottle of rum and topped the glass off with the neat spirit. She took it out to him just in time to see an old woman shaking something over Stanley — she took the substance from a bowl and dispersed it using a bunch of twigs.

"What's she doing?" Beth asked Fin.

"A curse ritual — that's chicken blood, and the twigs are from a manchineel tree. She is sealing his soul in his body."

"I heard she was going to do that. He seems to believe in it."

"He does; the priestess is seen as powerful and Obeah is probably followed as much as the regular church. It is very unusual for this priestess to carry out this kind of ritual — she normally restricts herself to healing."

The evening came, by which time a gallows had been erected. There was no trap; the condemned would stand on a barrel, which would be kicked away to drop him. A pair of workers brought him out. He had been held in Lilibeth's hut with the priestess the whole time. Her chanting had not stopped since the trial.

The condemned man was placed on the barrel and the noose put around his neck with the hard eye at the back. A hood went over his head. The old woman shouted something in a language Beth didn't understand and danced around the gallows to the sound of drums. She ended with a flourish as the drums reached a crescendo. The barrel was kicked away.

It took almost half an hour for Stanley to stop struggling. Beth was slightly sickened by the time it took, but in the end the deed was done. Stanley was cut down and buried outside the plantation's perimeter. A large rock was placed over his grave — it had symbols painted on it in chicken blood.

The Den

Beth and Garai moved on to the Den the next day; Beth had experienced enough excitement for the time being. The trip only took a few hours, and she entered through the Den's gates with the warm feeling of coming home. She did not understand that at all. Why did she feel such a connection to the place?

Word had reached the plantation that she was on her way, and a reception committee was waiting for them. Once the greetings had been made, she took a few moments to be alone on the porch outside her room and soak in the feeling of warm recognition that wrapped around her. She closed her eyes and must have dozed off, as she dreamt that Scarlett, her great-times-five grandmother, sat beside her.

"This was always home for us, even while we lived in England," Scarlett said. Beth looked at her and saw the family resemblance.

"You look like my mother."

"She is beautiful, but you are more like me. But I have a warning. Beware of him that is close to you."

"What? Who?" Beth asked — but she had woken, and the dream ended.

"What did you say, ma'am?" asked Delia, her maidservant. She had come to tell Beth that dinner was ready.

"Oh, nothing. I was having a dream."

"Dreams are important, ma'am. That's when the spirits come talk to us," Delia said, crossing herself.

Beth thought about that. Did her great-grandmother really visit her in a dream? Or was it her own subconscious, realising something that she should take note of? She had read John Norris's *An Essay Towards the Theory of the Ideal or Intelligible World* and had a limited understanding that the mind operated partially outside one's consciousness.

Beth went to dinner and later, when she was preparing for bed, Delia said, "You should talk to the witch woman about your dream. It could be important, ma'am."

"Please call me Beth. Is there a witch woman here at the Den?"

"Yes, Miss Beth, every plantation has one. But not every owner knows that."

Two nights later, the dream was repeated, and Beth awoke feeling alarmed. She got out of bed and pulled on a robe before stepping out onto the veranda. The night was still, with a slight breeze that was enough to cool her. She looked towards the village of houses where the workers lived. There was a solitary fire burning in the central yard around which the houses stood.

Barefoot, she walked across the yard towards the flames that seemed to form a beacon beckoning her towards it — and as she got closer, she could see a solitary figure sitting beside the blaze.

"I've been expecting you," the figure said.

"You are the witch woman?" Beth asked, knowing that she was.

The old woman sat back and smiled. "I am Mama Felice; I look after the people here and keep them free of evil spirits. Sit down, child."

Beth sat on a log and gazed into the flames, which seemed to dance and sway with a rhythm.

"You were dreaming."

"Yes." The flames were hypnotic, and the smoke smelled sweet.

"Tell me."

Beth told her about the visit of Scarlett, and the warning, and how she felt a presence whenever she was at the Den. There seemed to be drums being beaten far off in the background — then Beth smelled dry grassland.

"The ancestors protect us, and yours is warning you that someone close wants to harm you. She cares for you."

A voice in the back of Beth's mind said that much was obvious. The old woman produced some cowrie shells and scattered them on the ground in front of her. She studied them closely.

"I see a man with two masters. You are one; the other ... I cannot see him, but his soul is black. He is patient. There is a spirit beside him." Then the old woman sat back, a troubled look on her face. "He is using the spirits to hide himself. You need to take care."

Beth woke the next morning and remembered the visit to the old woman. She sat up, and something bumped on her chest. She took it in her hand; it was an amulet fashioned from a shell and woven stems of some kind of herb. It hung around her neck on a leather thong. She dimly remembered the old woman putting it on her and saying, "This is for protection. Do not take it off until you have killed the other master."

* * *

The rest of the visit went as planned; they met the workers and toured the plantation. Then Beth paid her respects to her five-times-great-grandmother's grave in the crypt below the house. She sat for a while and just chatted to her — and came away feeling more at peace. Then she sent a message to Richard to bring the *Fox* around to Annotto Bay, where she planned to treat the crew to a feast.

Richard had to work the *Fox* well out to the east to get enough sea room to bring her around Morant Point and head north-west up the northern coast of the island. The ship passed many fishing villages, set into bays with boats pulled up onto sandy beaches and backed by forest that climbed up the hills as one looked inland. Between the bays the coast was rocky and impossible to land on. Richard was wary of coral outcrops and resisted the temptation to get too close.

Occasionally, they would pass land that had been cleared of trees and put to use for agriculture. A road that seemed to follow the coast came and went.

"Annotto Bay should be coming up soon," the master said to Richard.

"Reduce sail. I want two men in the chains. We will go into the river," replied Richard, recalling that Beth had told him her grandmother used to take her ship in behind the bar and some way up the river.

The men on the chains started to call out the depth, as they reduced sail to just jibs, spanker and the fore topsail. They proceeded cautiously at walking speed.

"Three fathoms, sandy bottom and shelving!"

The *Fox* drew just under twelve feet of water.

"Heave to, back the foresail," Richard barked and the ship came to a rapid halt. "Bring a boat around and sound the entrance. I do not want us aground."

Midshipman Stephen Donaldson commanded the boat and found that there was a rig of silt across the entrance, which had a dip in the middle that was two and a half fathoms deep and only thirty feet wide. The rest of the ridge only had a fathom and a half of water over it. The boat crew marked the edges with buoys. When Stephen returned and reported, Richard looked thoughtful. "The tide is no help, it only changes by six inches or so here. We are twenty-four feet wide at the waterline, so there is no room for error," he said.

"Three feet of clearance all around, that's a tight squeeze. A slight shift in the wind and we will be aground," the master commented.

"Yes, so we will kedge her through. I want an anchor set dead centre a half-cable into the river, and another dead astern. The two are to be connected by a cable that runs down our centre line via the capstan."

Stephen understood; the cable would run through the fore and aft bulwarks with the capstan in between. As the capstan was turned, it would pull in on the foreword anchor and let out the aft, hopefully keeping the ship straight as she passed through the gap. It was a novel approach.

The ship's boat was soon busy, as the anchors had to be set as precisely as possible. Two hours later they were ready. It had taken time, but rushing would only have got them into trouble.

Richard called out the order to man the capstan. Then when the men were ready, he ordered, "Step slowly men, we need to see how she reacts."

The men heaved and stepped, the rope tightened, and the ship moved forwards. Richard stood in the bow watching as she did so.

So far, she was approximately central and moving forwards around twelve feet for every rotation of the capstan.

Richard was so intent on this observation that he didn't see the figures on large black horses watching them from a hilltop.

The bow passed between the buoys. The current pushed it slightly to port, but they were within limits. Just. He resisted the temptation to speed things up and kept the men at their steady pace. He walked down the port gangway as they passed the buoy, watching for any deviation.

The current's got more of the hull to press against, he realised as the cable tightened and stretched a little bit as the pressure increased. He ran back to the bow and peered at where the cable disappeared into the muddy water. It looked firm. His stomach tightened.

"We're through!" Stephen called from the quarterdeck.

"Avast hauling. Set the jibs, spanker and fore topsail."

As soon as he had sail pressure on the ship and could hold her against the current, Richard had the stern kedge brought in so they could release the cable. "Buoy the cable and tie it off against that tree over there. We will need it when we leave," he shouted.

Beth and Garai had watched the whole thing from their vantage point on the top of the hill.

"It must have silted up over the years," Garai said.

"I will ask them to dredge it, so next time we can use the river better. Let's go down to the dock," said Beth.

The dock was around a bend in the river where it was at its widest. They were waiting when the *Fox* came alongside. They sat on their horses and waved. Richard waved back, and once the *Fox* was securely tied off he came ashore. Beth dismounted to greet him.

"Nice horses," Richard said, when the greetings were over.

"We got them in Kingston. That was a tricky entrance!"

"Somewhat," Richard said, with his usual understatement.

Garai shook his hand. "What gave you the idea of using two anchors like that?"

"There is a chain ferry across the Thames at Harlow. Always follows the same path, every time it crosses. I thought the same principle would work here."

Beth laughed; there was nothing new under heaven. "Get the men ashore and we will lead you to the Den."

"Let me organise a harbour watch first," Richard said and went back aboard.

Beth wanted to tell Richard not to bother, but she knew he would never leave their ship unattended. He picked a responsible mate and several members of his crew who were in trouble after a sojourn ashore in Kingston. They would miss out on the feast as punishment for wrecking the Jolly Roger tavern in a fight with some regular navy men.

Beth offered Richard her hand and a stirrup. "You can ride behind me."

He politely declined. The thought of sitting close behind her was already making him uncomfortable; he dreaded to think what would happen when the horse started moving. "I need the exercise," he said, and began to walk.

The column of men snaked its way inland to the Den, where they were enthusiastically greeted by the workers. An ox had been slaughtered and then roasted over a pit for a day and a half. There was goat stew, jerk chicken, fresh bread, rice and peas, greens and fruit aplenty.

Casks of ale that had been brewed on the plantation were broached and tankards passed around. Soon the sound of singing and laughter filled the air.

Beth found Carlos, her coxswain, standing off to one side, eating a plate of food.

"I didn't know you had property," he said.

That made sense to Beth; she didn't talk about it on board the *Fox* and she hadn't let him ashore with her in Jamaica.

"It's been in our family for generations."

"Has it?" he muttered.

She didn't answer as she thought that a rhetorical question. Instead, she said, "Oh look, the girls are going to dance," and wandered off.

Carlos watched her go and his expression hardened. A little way off, an old lady watched him with narrowed eyes.

Barranquilla

The *Fox* negotiated the exit from the Wag Water river just as she had entered it and, once clear, set sail for Barranquilla. Which was easier said than done, as the port lay pretty much due south of the western tip of Haiti. That meant they had to beat against the wind and current to the east until they got south of Haiti, and then had to steer a course that allowed for the Caribbean current and prevailing easterly winds.

It took five days to make the easting and another three to cross the Caribbean Sea on a course that pointed more towards Aruba than Barranquilla. However, the leeway resulted in their making land just a couple of miles east of the bay of Santa Maria. There was a lagoon — more of a swamp, really — protected by a double bar behind it. The place was infested with mosquitoes.

"What a shithole, no wonder El Dragon wanted out of here," Richard said as he swatted a bug from his neck.

"Carlos, do you know this place?"

"I have only been here once. There is a dock inside the lagoon by the main town."

"How do we get in?"

"There is a gap in the first bar over there and another in the second bar slightly to the south-west."

Richard addressed Beth. "We can go into the lagoon, but that exposes the crew to the mosquitoes and fever from the swamp miasma."

"You're saying it's better just to risk me and Garai?"

Richard blushed. "Well, I wouldn't put it quite like that."

Beth grinned at him. "Father told me to bring citronella oil for occasions just like this."

And so Beth and Garai stepped down into the ship's boat, smelling sweetly of citronella. The boat's crew had also been given some and had great fun posing as if they were applying perfume, dabbing it behind their ears and rubbing it into their wrists.

The dock, which was only just worthy of the name, was a single plank running across the top of a line of piles driven into the mud. The place smelt of decaying vegetation and shit. The latter came from the local practice of dumping human waste onto the fields as fertiliser.

"My God, it will take days to wash this stink out of our clothes," Beth said.

"Don't trip, or it will take a month," Garai joked.

Even Fede, whom Beth had brought along for some exercise now that he was the size of a fully grown sheepdog, sniffed the ground disdainfully. They made their way to the village and were met before they got there by a delegation wielding rusty mattocks and machetes.

"Friendly bunch," Beth said, under her breath. Then she plastered on a smile and asked, "Is one of you the local mayor?"

One of the men, who carried a large cleaver, looked at Garai. "Your woman speaks for you?"

Garai laughed. "This is Rosa of the *Fox*, a privateer. Do not insult her or she may cut off your balls and feed them to you."

The men laughed. "In this town, our women know their place."

Beth cocked her head to one side and gave the man a direct look, which — if he had been paying any attention to her at all — would have warned him.

As it was, he jumped so hard when the bullet smacked into the dirt at his feet that he dropped his cleaver. "*Madre Mia!* You crazy bitch!"

Beth held the pistol loosely in her hand, a wisp of smoke rising from the barrel. "Your woman should have told you not to bring a knife to a gun fight," she said.

A commotion came up from the houses and a group of women stormed forwards, berating the men for their lack of hospitality. A rather plump matron came to the front and pushed the man aside. "Señora, forgive our husbands for their rudeness. They are simple farmers and fishermen," she said.

Beth treated her to a dazzling smile and put her pistol away. "I am Rosa," she said, and swept off her hat in a bow. "What is your name?"

"Manuela, my lady. Is that hair your natural colour?"

Beth held up a lock of her hair and looked at it. "Yes, it is."

"Please come to our village and have some refreshment."

Even with the citronella, Beth and her crew were bitten several times as they walked. They soon found that the ramshackle houses visible from the dock were mostly fishermen's huts and the main town lay behind them. Well-made houses lined the street and they stopped at a cantina, where the woman and her now-quite-docile husband asked them to sit down. They were served chocolate in earthenware mugs.

"Now, how can we help you, Doña Rosa?"

Beth briefly described her interest in the current wave of piracy and told her, "I want to know anything you know about the pirate El Dragon."

Manuela spat on the ground to the side of the table. "That ass. He disgraced this town."

Beth was surprised at her vehemence. "He is remembered, then?"

"He is — and some idiots want to build a memorial to him." She looked at her husband, who tried and failed to look as if he didn't know what she was talking about.

Beth looked to the husband, and asked him directly, "Why would you want to memorialise a man who was executed for terrible crimes?"

"He was famous, a real pirate," the man replied lamely.

"He was a murderer, rapist, torturer and thief. Apart from that — a real hero," Beth said, then shook her head and turned back to Manuela. "I know he came from here. Has anyone local wanted to follow in his footsteps?"

Manuela shook her head. "None of them have the guts to do that. They just talk about his so-called exploits in the cantina in the evenings. Making him out to be some kind of hero, and it all happened thirty years ago."

Beth gave the man a hard look. "Let me tell you about your hero's exploits." She went on to give a no-holds-barred account of his crimes, victims and ultimate fate in a gibbet.

"So, you see, if someone is trying to resurrect the name of El Dragon, we need to put a stop to them."

"You should ask at the town of San Salvador, which is on the river," Manuela suggested. "It is more concerned with trade, and they may have heard something."

* * *

To get to San Salvador, they sailed the *Fox* up the River Magdalena, where they found a busy port where goods from the interior were traded and shipped to locations far and wide. As is usual for such a port, there were plenty of saltwater sailors who would talk for the price of a beer.

To speed things up, Beth sent Carlos out to cover some of the bars, while she and Garai covered the rest. They came up with nothing and met up with Carlos at the end of the day.

"I hope you had better luck than we did," Beth said as they sat at a table in a bar close to where the *Fox* was docked.

"I found a group of sailors who were just about to depart. They told me that they had heard talk of a privateer who operates out of a secluded bay to the south of Cartagena, near the town of Pendales on the Baru peninsula. He has a ship called *El Dragon*."

"Hmm, that makes some kind of sense," Beth said, and pondered his words. "We should at least look into it."

They sailed on, covering the ninety miles to the peninsula and creeping along the coast, looking for the bay. The chart showed little detail, and Richard and the master made notes and sketches as they progressed. Cartagena Bay, with the sheltering Isla de Terra Bomba, ended with the Polonia peninsula which curved up to the north. South of that, the land was largely uninhabited, and they almost drifted down the coast on the prevailing current until a lookout called, "Deck there! There be an inlet coming up."

"Carlos, do you think this is it?" Beth asked.

"It could be, but there may be more."

"Take us in, we will have a look," Beth told Richard.

"Bring the ship to quarters, Stephen. Prepare to wear ship! Two men in the chains."

The crew operated with practised ease and the ship was ready for battle as she swung around to head a little south of east into the inlet. That inlet narrowed before opening out into a reasonably-sized bay that was about three-quarters of a mile deep.

They sailed down it, watching the shore for signs of a camp or anything that would constitute a base for a privateer. They found nothing.

"Looks like this isn't the one. But It looks like a good place to overnight," Beth said, and sighed. "Let's drop anchor here, it is relatively free of mosquitoes."

The ship came down from quarters and the men relaxed. It was a peaceful place and though it was sheltered, a light breeze blew constantly, keeping the temperature moderate.

In the morning, they breakfasted before getting the ship ready to sail. Beth inhaled the scent of trees coming from the land, then stiffened as the lookout shouted, "Deck! There are masts at the entrance!"

"What?" Richard said, and went to the ratlines to climb up and have a look for himself.

Beth watched him and was about to call up — but then, everything went dark.

When she awoke, Beth was laying on her side with her arms tied behind her back. She retched as nausea washed over her. She tried to move but found her legs were tied as well. Her head hurt. She closed her eyes until the pain lessened a little and the nausea passed. Then she opened her eyes again and evaluated her situation.

I'm in the bread room. What the hell happened?

She struggled to a sitting position. She could hear voices and strained to make out what was being said. The voices were speaking Spanish, but she couldn't quite make out what they were saying. She was thirsty and wondered just how long she had been there.

She heard footsteps approaching and the door being unlocked. It swung open and a man was silhouetted against the light that fell from behind. A knife glinted as he stepped inside. She braced as he bent over her.

It was Carlos.

"You!"

He back-handed her across the mouth, knocking her onto her side. "Shut up. You will only speak when spoken to." He cut the bindings on her legs then dragged her to her feet. "Come, El Dragon wants to see you."

Then Beth was half dragged up the stairs until they reached the main deck, where the bright sunlight blinded her momentarily. She blinked and a figure came to stand in front of her. Her eyes adjusted.

"Juan Montego-Rodrigues," she said. "How's the arm?"

Carlos punched her in the stomach. She doubled over but did not fall. She straightened once she had got her breath back and by then a second man had joined Rodrigues. She recognised him as his brother — a man she had taken a ship from and marooned on the Yucatan peninsula a year earlier. She had fought a duel with Juan and sliced his bicep badly when he had questioned her right to sell the hull.

"Let her talk," Juan said.

Beth glared at Carlos, who stood a step away with a pistol — one of *her* pistols — in his hand.

She addressed Juan. "You are the Dragon?"

"If you like. He was a fiction to get you here."

"Into a trap baited by this piece of shit." She spat at Carlos, who went to hit her again, but Juan stopped him with a gesture.

"We found out from him you are working for the American government. So, we made sure one of their agents in Havana got the information that El Dragon would be targeting their ships. Then we waited — and sure enough, you were given the task of tracking him down."

"And you led me by the nose to here."

Juan laughed at her.

"Where are my men?"

"Ashore, under guard," Juan said.

Now Carlos was gloating. "They gave up without a fight once I had you by the throat."

Beth ignored him. "Is my dog there as well?"

"He was, but he ran off after he was put ashore."

"What happens now?" Beth said, feigning an air of defeat.

"My brother Diego gets your ship, your men can walk to Panama, and you will come back to Havana with me."

Beth looked up at the pennant flying from the main mast. It was pointing directly down the bay; the wind was a complete muzzler.

"You aren't going anywhere until that wind changes."

"True, but we have time." He turned to Carlos. "Take her below, have some fun with her."

Captivity

Beth knew what was coming and was prepared to fight, but Carlos had expected that and stunned her again before tying her in such a way that she couldn't resist, then left her naked and bleeding in the bread room.

Beth did not cry. She was not sorry for herself, only for not being able to kill him — which she swore she would do, when she had half a chance. An hour later a pair of sailors came and dragged her up on deck. Her hands were released and re-tied so she could be suspended from a rope slung over the yard, her toes just touching the surface below.

Juan walked around her carrying a schooling crop. "I want to know who you really are and who you work for."

"Go to hell," she said, and spat.

"You have very fair skin. I think you will burn in the sun and that will be very uncomfortable."

He prodded her with the crop, and she spun. Men leered at her naked body.

"My men will enjoy you, maybe more than one at a time. They can be very inventive."

"Fuck off."

He swung the crop across her buttocks, it stung like hell.

"Naughty girl. Now answer. Who do you work for? I know it's the Americans — but who *exactly*?"

She didn't answer.

Hours later, Beth's skin had turned red, her arms ached from being pulled from the shoulder sockets, and she was suffering from dehydration. She struggled to hang on and started to hallucinate. Every now and then a crewman would wander by and grope her, but that had become irrelevant. Then she heard Juan say, "Bring her down and give her water; we don't want her to die just yet."

Carlos replied, "No, we don't. I want to enjoy her a few more times yet."

Then Beth was aware of Carlos standing beside her; she recognised his stink. She cracked her eyes open and he stepped back as she stared at him. That was a mistake. She used the last of her strength to swing up her legs and catch his head between her thighs. The sailors on the rope had already started to lower her, which helped, and she twisted her body sharply.

Her weight and the twist did the trick. His neck broke with a satisfying snap. Both Carlos and Beth ended up in a heap on the floor, Carlos's head pointing in entirely the wrong direction.

Beth passed out.

She came to, aware that someone was pressing a cold wet rag against her lips. She looked up into the eyes of a young girl. Beth's skin was burning, and the material of her clothes chafed.

Clothes?

She looked down and saw she had been dressed in a rough cotton blouse and a pair of sailor's trousers. Her hands were still tied behind her back. She sat up. "Damn, that's sore."

The young girl looked at her with large brown eyes.

"More water, please," Beth said.

The girl looked at her blankly. Beth tried again in Spanish and nodded at the water jug. The girl offered her a cup, putting it to her lips and tipping it so she could drink. Then Beth suddenly remembered Carlos and the look on his face as her thighs clamped onto his head. She giggled; the girl looked at her curiously.

"It's nothing, I was just remembering something funny."

The girl continued to look at her.

Beth was sore all over and her skin was dry and flaking from the sunburn. She looked around. If she wasn't mistaken, this was Stephen's cabin. It was better than the bread room, but she couldn't understand the change of location. The door didn't fit very well, and she could see light coming in from outside. A shadow told her there was a guard.

The girl went to a shelf and took down a pot. She dipped her fingers in it and smoothed some green gel onto Beth's face. It was cool and soothing. The smell told her it was aloe vera.

She heard footsteps approaching and the door opened. "Come with me," a man said.

Beth struggled to her feet and ducked through the door. Two guards stood out of reach of her legs, which they both admired and feared as weapons; they were carrying pistols, which they pointed directly at her. The man who had come to collect her stood six feet away from her as well and said, "Come with me and keep your distance."

I've rattled somebody's cage!

He led her to her customary cabin and gestured for her to go into the sleeping area. Her hands were untied.

"Get dressed. Clothes are laid out for you."

A dress was indeed laid out on the bed. Her trunk was missing, so were all of her weapons. She stripped and pulled the dress over her head, then listened. The guards were still out there, she could hear them muttering. She ran her fingers along the side rail of the cot and found what she was looking for. She had just stood upright when the curtain was pulled back.

"Put your hands out," the guard said.

She obeyed. Shackles were clamped around her wrists and locked.

"These were made especially for you."

He checked her over and tied the drawstrings at the back of the dress. "Now go into the dining room."

Juan and Diego stood as she entered. Diego bowed and gestured for her to take a chair. "Lady Bethany, please join us."

"I didn't tell you that was my name."

"No, we got the information from your captain's steward. He offered us the information in return for us keeping him on."

The door opened and she had to control her surprise — for there stood Garai, carrying a tray of wine glasses and a decanter.

"Ha, I bet he was hoping to be with his boyfriend Carlos," Beth said.

"He *was* rather upset when we showed him the body."

The spirits were right about someone close to me betraying me.

Garai kept his eyes lowered as he served the wine and stayed far enough away from her that she couldn't lash out. When Beth asked for some water, he nodded.

* * *

Beth sipped her water to buy time to think. Garai had obviously come aboard to try and rescue her and had given up her real name to do so. But what else had he given up?

"So, you know who I am. What do you intend to do with me now?"

"We did contemplate killing you and dropping your body over the side for the sharks, but then Pedro here told us you were the daughter of a famous British admiral and count. So should we call you Lady Bethany or Lady Turner?"

So, you told them I am James Turner's daughter. Clever.

"Lady Bethany is fine. So you know my father is wealthy, then."

"Exactly — and I am sure he will pay a handsome ransom for your return, prodigal child that you are."

Beth glanced at Garai, who stood behind the two Colombians, and he gave the faintest of shrugs. He must have spun a good yarn but it was one she had yet to understand fully.

She thought back through the various cover stories they had concocted and remembered one they had come up with as a training exercise. This one ensured that any message sent by a captor would be sent directly to Turner, shielding her real identity and links to her father. Turner wasn't a Count, so any letter to him with that title would ring alarm bells from the start.

The food was served, and she ate sparingly. She didn't touch the wine.

"Who is the girl?" Beth asked at last.

"That is Netta, she is deaf and dumb," Diego said. "She is my daughter."

"She is pretty," Beth said.

"Yes, but she will never marry," Diego replied, his voice full of bitterness.

* * *

Back in her cabin, Beth sat and watched Netta, who was drawing on a sheet of paper. She sat beside her and looked at what she was drawing. It was a house; the detail was well observed and the drawing precise. She pointed at the house and then at Netta, a questioning look on her face. The girl nodded; it gave her an idea.

She wrote the word "house" in Spanish under the drawing and pointed to indicate they were linked. Netta looked at it solemnly, then suddenly smiled delightedly. She pointed at herself. Beth wrote Netta and pronounced it with an exaggerated mouth movement. Netta imitated her. Then Netta pointed at Beth and she repeated the exercise.

The rest of the morning was spent naming objects and coming up with signs for actions. Netta turned out to be a prodigy, with a mind and memory as quick as a rat trap. Over the next few days, Beth taught her enough for them to start a simple conversation.

The brothers kept Garai away from her, making Netta fetch her food and empty her bucket. Then, one day, they were allowed on deck. That gave Netta the chance to learn the names of a whole new range of things. Now, her father noticed.

"What are you doing?"

"Teaching her what things are called. You never bothered."

Diego became angry and stepped forward to slap her, but Netta stepped in front of him and shook her head.

"Your daughter is bright, intelligent, and has an amazing memory. She can communicate and is also a very good artist. But I suppose you never noticed."

That stung, and Diego turned away. Beth turned Netta around so she could see her and mouthed, "Thank you for stopping him."

Netta hugged her around the neck.

* * *

They arrived at Havana, but because she spent much of the time locked in the windowless cabin she had no idea exactly how long they were at sea. However, judging by the meals and sleeps, she estimated a little over a week. She was taken to the house that looked like the one Netta had drawn. Beth guessed it must be a house belonging to Diego and Juan's family and she asked Netta, who confirmed that it was. Beth had made her understand that she was a prisoner. That was not easy, and it had challenged Beth's inventiveness to come up with a row of pictograms that got the meaning over. In the end, a caged bird gave her what she needed.

Netta frowned and pointed to the cage and then at herself.

"Yes, I think you are too."

At the Havana house, the door of their room was always locked except for at set times when Netta was allowed out to get their food and empty the chamber pots. The window was barred with an ornate wrought-iron grill and Beth examined the fixings thoroughly, before concluding that she couldn't damage them badly enough to escape.

Days passed, then weeks. The friendship between the girls grew and Netta became the link between Beth and Garai. This began when Beth spotted Garai in the garden and pointed him out to Netta. It was a calculated risk, but she needed to talk to him. And so they started passing messages via Netta.

Given a second person to talk to, Netta developed even faster and a friendship with Garai blossomed. Beth knew the two had been talking and wasn't overly surprised when, one day, the girl pulled from her cleavage a sheet of paper that had been neatly folded.

"From Garai," she mouthed.

Beth took it and saw that it was in code. It took her only a moment to translate.

Messenger from T arrived. Big surprise it is Seb. Met him in town. We will move tonight at midnight.

"Sebastian? What is he doing here?" Beth said out loud.

Netta had been watching her carefully and made a query sign. Beth signed for her to wait and asked, "Is your father here?"

"That ass is on his ship," Netta replied with a sour look.

"If you could leave, would you go?"

"If I could go with you."

"You would not miss this place?"

"No. I am a prisoner here. Like you."

Midnight came, and there was a dull thud and the sound of something sliding down the wall outside their room. Beth heard the door being unlocked; moments later, Garai stood in the open doorway. Beth glanced around the opening and saw the guard on the floor.

"Come on, Seb is waiting for us."

Beth followed him, but then stopped by a door through which snoring could be heard. "One moment."

Garai gave her a look that spoke volumes. She ignored him. She gently opened the door and tiptoed inside. Juan lay in bed with a nightcap on his head, his wife beside him. Beth reached into her bodice and produced a slim blade. It was only three inches long and had a knob rather than a handle. She stepped up to the bed and placed her hand over Juan's mouth. His eyes popped open. As soon as she saw that he recognised her, she stabbed him three times in the side of the neck. Blood spurted from the severed artery. He only struggled once, then fell still. His wife snorted and continued to snore. Beth wiped her blade on the sheet and left.

Garai whispered, "Are you done?"

"Yes, get a move on."

Netta followed them and, as they got close to the main door, stepped up and held Beth's hand. "Me too!" she signed.

Beth looked at Garai, who shrugged. She looked back at Netta and nodded.

Outside, there were men patrolling the gardens. The men sauntered along, obviously feeling secure. Beth and Netta hid behind a hedge while Garai greeted them.

"You're out late," one of the men said.

"I fancied a smoke, and you know the boss doesn't let us in the house," Garai said and stepped closer to them.

The men laughed — the boss did have his quirky side.

Then, Garai moved so fast that neither man could react. A blade ripped across the first man's throat and was then plunged several times into the other's chest as a hand was held over his mouth. Garai took their guns and gave one to Beth.

Netta watched, her eyes wide. Beth returned to her and gestured, "Come."

The girl looked at the men, then turned to Beth and held out her hand. Beth led her after Garai, towards the main gates to the property. These were open and the guards lay in pools of blood that shone darkly in the moonlight. Garai gave a low whistle, which was answered from a tree that overlooked the garden. A dark figure dropped to the ground. He was carrying a rifle. Beth immediately knew who it was and rushed forward to embrace him.

"You are always getting into trouble," Sebastian said, and led them to a carriage parked a little down the road. The girls and Garai got in the back and Sebastian took the driver's seat — just as a scream shattered the silence.

"Time to leave," Garai said.

Sebastian shook the reins and the horses set off at a canter. "Who did you kill?" he shouted over his shoulder.

"Juan."

Sebastian laughed. "That's my girl."

Reunion

Sebastian drove them out of town and along the coast road to the west. A full moon lit their way. Once out of town he slowed the horses to a trot to preserve their energy. Beth climbed up beside him and held his arm, resting her head on his shoulder.

"Where are we going?" she asked, almost dreamily.

"We decided that getting a ship out of Havana, if the alarm was given, would be too risky. So, we will board by boat from a village called Guanabo."

She lifted her head. "How come you are here?"

He kissed the top of her head. "I was recalled, and the ransom note arrived just as I got to London. As I was going to be heading out here, Turner gave me a ship and sent me to free you."

Beth hugged his arm. "Not to pay the ransom, surely?"

Sebastian shrugged. "Oh no, there was never any chance of that happening."

Beth laughed. "How long have you been here?"

"It was a week before I spotted Garai at the market and it took me another week to organise things."

She sat upright and looked at him. "Two weeks?"

"Yes, and that was as fast as we could go. Who is the girl?"

"Netta, she is going to be an orphan."

"Does she know?"

"I think so. She may be deaf but is very observant."

Sebastian left the questioning at that for the time being; he would find out more later.

The ship was hove-to a mile offshore, with its longboat and crew waiting on the beach for the party. Sebastian, Garai, Beth and Netta disembarked. Sebastian, whom the crew knew as Lancelot, slapped the horses on the rump and sent them back down the road to Havana.

A midshipman barked the orders and the ship's crew smoothly rowed out to the sloop of war *Lizard*. This small, twenty-four-gun, unrated ship was a former French corvette that had been captured during the war and was now assigned to the Secret Service.

Beth eschewed the use of a bosun's chair and climbed up the side. Garai helped Netta up onto the deck. Beth looked at the guns in the dawn light. *Carronades, good.*

Sebastian introduced the captain. "Chaton, may I present Wilfred Billingham, master and commander of this fine vessel."

"Milady." Billingham bowed graciously. "Where do you want us to go next? The admiral was quite explicit that we should follow your lead."

"Colombia — just south of Cartagena. I want my dog back. Then we will go to Panama to find my crew."

Netta stayed with Beth, not as a maid of all works as Sebastian expected, but more as an apprentice. He learnt that her mother had died giving birth to her, and her deafness was a result of that traumatic birth. Her father had wanted nothing to do with her and she only found out who he was when the aunt that had brought her up died, and Juan took her into the family's house as a servant. When she talked about him, the look on Netta's face sent cold shivers down Sebastian's spine.

He soon learnt that she was intelligent, and quite able to communicate using signs that she and Beth had come up with — which were based on the silent communications used by Secret Service agents. Consequently, Sebastian had little trouble picking them up and understanding the conversations.

Netta was also learning to read and write. Reading especially fascinated her; she was constantly asking what words meant, which stretched Beth and Sebastian immensely. The captain created a small cabin for her so she could have some privacy, while Beth shared Sebastian's.

Beth was uncharacteristically nervous that first night and Sebastian asked, "What's wrong?"

She told him about what happened on the ship. He was furious but held it in as she cried for the first time. "You killed the bastard?"

"Yes, I broke his neck."

"That was too good for him."

"Oh, I would have loved to peel his skin off his back, inch by inch. But I had to take the opportunity when it arrived."

He understood and simply held her to start with. Their lovemaking, when it happened, was gentle.

The trip down to the Colombian coast would take a couple of days and Beth took her mind off finding Fede by teaching Netta how to copy handwriting. For this, Netta didn't have to be able to read, and her artistic ability helped. Beth showed her how to not only copy the shapes but also the ways in which the writer formed various letters; where they put more pressure on the nib or turned it in a particular way.

But they arrived at the inlet where they had lost her ship all too soon, and Beth had to go ashore and search for her pup. The *Lizard* anchored outside the bay, and she was rowed in. As they drew close enough, she jumped out of the boat over the bow and walked ashore, with Garai following her. Beth looked over the sand for paw prints, but all marks had been washed away by recent rains.

The pair walked inshore and up a hill that would give them a view of the surrounding country. If Fede was here, maybe they would see him. The land was uninhabited, and Beth wondered how — if — a dog could have survived for the several weeks she had been away. Garai had his doubts as well, but kept them to himself.

As Beth walked, she called Fede's name, but there had been no response by the time they reached the top of the hill. There was no sign of him to be found, in any direction. She sighed; the search had been a long shot from the outset, and she was about to turn around and walk off when Garai threw back his head and gave an undulating call.

"Aye, aye, aye," he cried, increasing the pace of his cries with each successive call. "Aye, aye, aye, Ipeeee." He repeated the process, turning to face a different compass point each time. The sound echoed eerily.

"Is that the call Daddy told me about? The one from the Basque mountains?"

"It is one of them. It's the call for dinner."

Beth laughed.

"Well, if Fede responds to anything it will be a call to dinner."

They stood, and watched, and waited. Garai took a deep breath to repeat the calls. Again his voice echoed from the hilltop.

Still nothing.

He prepared to call a third time, then Beth laid a hand on his arm. "Wait! Look."

Down in the valley, to the north, a white shape was crossing a stream. It came up the bank and bounded towards them.

Fede's greeting, when he found them, was boisterous and wet. His belly was soaked from crossing the stream and running through the wet grass. On closer examination, they found he had fleas and ticks. On board ship this was not tolerated, and later he was thoroughly washed with an alum solution and soap, followed by a rinse with vinegar in the water. The ticks were removed manually, and he was groomed with a fine-toothed comb to remove eggs and any fleas that remained. This process was repeated weekly until he was free of the little pests.

But right now, as they were reunited, Beth observed that was no longer the size of a sheepdog — he was now around the size of a German Shepherd. He was underfed and a little skinny, but he had grown. Beth could only assume that he had survived by hunting small mammals like rabbits and mice. He wolfed down a bowl of dried meat that they had brought with them.

The next task facing Beth, Sebastian and Garai was to find their crew. Now they had Fede, they spent more time examining the beach and found a pile of stones in the form of an arrow. Under the stone at the point was a navy captain's epaulette, which told them their men had marched west. They followed the coast, hugging the shoreline as tightly as they could to try and spot them. Beth guessed — and

Sebastian agreed — that Richard would have taken his men to a place where they could find food and water. That meant a bay with a stream, or a fishing village.

As the *Lizard* rounded the peninsula, Beth saw immediately that the rocky coast was turning into a vast wetland. Beth doubted very much that the men would have tried to cross that mosquito-infested region; it was much more likely they had stayed on the shore, which was rocky but passable.

Then the mainmast lookout shouted, "Deck, there is a raft ahead with someone stood on it waving like a madman."

"Where away?" Billingham called back.

"Two points off the starboard bow."

They closed with it and in time a man, bare-chested and wearing tattered trousers, was hauled aboard. He introduced himself to Beth. "Bert Farrell, ma'am." Beth noticed that he was skinny and covered in sores.

"It looks like you have had a hard time," Billingham said. "Are the rest of the men nearby?"

"Aye, sir, they are. What's left of us, that is. The fever got some and others just gave up."

"Is Captain Brazier still alive?" Beth asked.

"He is, but he is right poorly."

"Can you guide us in?"

"I can, ma'am. The cap'n chose this spot to stop as it had deep water in close."

Bert was right, they could get the *Lizard* in close, and when they did they could see a camp by a stream that came out of the trees. About fifty ragged individuals were waving at them.

When they got ashore, they found another twenty or so lying in shelters, each at various stages of yellow jack or the black bile. Those with the black bile had only an even chance of survival, whereas the ones with yellow jack had a good chance, unless their illness developed into the black bile. The latter group included Richard; he had been ill for four days but was showing signs of recovery. He sat up when he saw Beth.

"Thank God! We had almost given up hope that you would find us," he cried.

"I came as soon as we escaped. I am sorry it took so long."

They transferred the men to the ship, keeping the sick on deck in cots. Those who died were buried immediately. Only Beth, Netta and the ship's surgeon were allowed near the men with black bile.

They sailed on to Jamaica and pulled into the Wag Water river. The *Fox*'s crewmen would convalesce at the Den. Richard was on the mend but by now two more men had the black bile, and one of those looked unlikely to make it.

The *Lizard*'s surgeon had been a surgeon's mate on the *Unicorn* under Shelby, who was a specialist in tropical diseases. Therefore, he had been trained in their treatment. Having done what he could at the camp with the few resources available, he now had access to herbs and a new medical box that Beth procured in Kingston. This allowed him to provide more effective treatment — which was just as well, because three days after arriving, Beth went down with yellow jack.

The illness made Beth wretched: she vomited, sweated with fever and chills and had excruciating aches and pains. For a while, she thought she would die. Youngs, the surgeon, and Felice the witch woman treated her with a honey-and-ginger tea. Youngs felt comfortable with that, as Shelby had recommended ginger as a treatment for fever, and he knew that honey was good for lots of things. The tea also helped to keep her hydrated. The old woman advised him to add moringa leaves. The surgeon had never come across them before and tried the treatment on himself before giving it to Beth, trusting the old woman wouldn't poison him. Meanwhile, they bathed her head with damp cloths and the windows of her bedroom were kept open to allow fresh air to circulate.

Beth's fever broke after five days, and Sebastian was allowed in to see her. She tried to smile. "I must look a fright."

He smiled and stroked her cheek. "You are as beautiful as ever."

"Flatterer."

He looked into her eyes. "They say you should be able to get up and have a bath after you have eaten something."

"I could manage some soup," she said weakly. The prospect of a bath was enticing — and she even pondered if she should get Sebastian to wash her back.

Beth recovered quite quickly after that and, when she was strong enough, visited the men that were still sick. These survivors of the black bile were on the mend, but all still had the yellow tinge to their skin. By now, they had lost nearly half of the *Fox*'s original crew.

Beth, deciding it was time to act, called for Captain Billingham and asked him to make the *Lizard* ready to sail. "We need to get my ship back," she explained.

To Catch a Smuggler

The *Lizard* sailed, with the Foxes on board, around to Montego Bay, where Beth knew there was a shipping agent and broker. She was looking for a cutter or a lugger. They pulled into the bay and, after firing a salute, anchored across from Fort Montego.

Beth went ashore with Richard and Sebastian and was met by a navy lieutenant, who looked at them curiously.

"I know that none of you is Captain Billingham, since we served together in '15," he stated upon meeting them.

"Very astute," Beth said. When he looked surprised she added, "My respects to the Port Admiral. I am Chaton. This is Major Ashley-Cooper of the 95th Rifles and this is Commander Brazier of the *Fox*."

"Flag Lieutenant Ernest Pettigrew at your service," came the reply, and he dipped a bow. "I will take you to Major Devereux. He is in charge here."

Pettigrew explained, as they walked to the fort, that he was the senior naval officer in the bay and worked for the Port Admiral in Kingston. The fort was commanded by Major Devereux of the 61st Artillery Brigade.

The fort commanded the bay and was a relic from the last century. Its guns, while serviceable, were old and the walls not particularly high. The guns were mounted on iron carriages that ran on a metal ramp to manage the recoil, which was unusual. The ramp could be pivoted to change the angle of fire and the carriage had a screw at the back to change its elevation. The downside of this arrangement was that the barrel was quite a long way from the ground, making it hard to load efficiently.

Devereux met them in his sitting room and Beth made the introductions.

"What can I do for you?" he asked, directing the question to Sebastian, whom he considered the most senior.

"We all work for Chaton," Sebastian said. Devereux frowned at that and turned to Beth with a condescending look.

Arrogant ass.

She smiled sweetly. "I need to buy a ship and I hear that there is a ship broker in the bay. What can you tell me about him?"

"There is such a man, but I know nothing about him." The major sipped his tea.

Beth was about to inform him that he really ought to know something when, seeing Beth stiffen, Pettigrew interrupted.

"If I may, Major?"

The major waved a hand.

"The broker is Clyde McMillan. A Scot in exile who dislikes the English immensely. We suspect him of smuggling and the odd act of piracy but have no proof. He is a wily one and runs several fast ships out of Jamaica and the Netherlands Antilles."

"Does he? And whose side did he support during the war?" Sebastian asked.

"Probably the French, although we have no proof of that, either."

Major Devereux looked surprised at all this. "Why was I not told?"

"My apologies, sir, but the admiral sees this as navy business," replied Pettigrew.

"Have you tried catching him in the act?" Beth asked.

"He knows all our ships, and if his captains see us coming, they dump their smuggled goods overboard."

"Then you need to get someone on the inside."

"He would never trust anyone he didn't know," Pettigrew said.

Beth put on a frightened face and adopted a Highlands accent to say, "But he may find it in his heart to protect a wee Scots lassie on the run from the English."

"Do we have time for this?" Sebastian asked.

"Yes, Diego is out at sea for months at a time and anyway, we need to get a ship from McMillan to hunt him down. In any case, it shouldn't take more than a few weeks."

Beth stripped off her dress and went to a trunk of clothes she had gathered at the Den. She took out a skirt and blouse in the local style, which she deliberately tore in several places.

"That's a bit risqué, isn't it?" Sebastian said as one of the tears exposed part of her breast.

"You attempted to rape me."

"I did? Why? You have never objected before." He grinned.

"I stuck a knife in you and escaped."

Sebastian looked a little worried at that. "Where?"

"From the ship."

"No, where did you stab me?"

"Oh, that. In the shoulder." Beth smiled.

Sebastian closed his eyes, he knew what was coming.

Beth pulled out a knife and pushed it about an inch into his shoulder .

"There — now there is proof."

That afternoon, a figure was seen rowing away from the *Lizard* in the gig, heading for the shore. A hullabaloo went up on the ship and several shots were fired. People laughed when they saw that the other ship's boats were adrift, and sailors were diving over the side to try and recover them.

Beth reached the shore and ran down into the town. A contingent of sailors came ashore and started searching for her. After a while, a squad of soldiers joined them from the fort and they started a sweep of the town.

Beth hid in a shipyard but was spotted by the workers, who grabbed her and took her to the boss when she swore at them in Gaelic.

She was dragged roughly in front of McMillan and held firmly by his men.

"What is your name, girl?"

"What's it to you, ya great oaf?"

"If it's you the English are hunting for, you will be nice and tell me your name!"

"Isla Murray."

"Of Clan Murray?"

"Aye, me father claims as much."

McMillan grinned and rubbed his hands together. "Our ancestors fought the English at Culloden. You are safe here." He turned to his men. "Take her to the caves."

"Boss?" one of the men said, troubled.

"If she is lying, we will deal with her later. For now, hide her in the caves."

They took Beth out of the room and down into the cellar. One of the men carried a lantern and went to a stone pillar that had an iron bracket mounted on it. He grabbed the bracket, turned it ninety degrees and pulled it downwards. A section of floor rose up, revealing a flight of steps.

They descended, and the floor dropped back into place above their heads. The man took Beth by the arm and led her forwards, along a man-made tunnel which in time joined another tunnel. This was more natural, with a sand floor. They followed the second tunnel for several hundred yards until it exited into a cavern. Beth could hear the sea.

"Sit down," he said, and indicated a crate.

He lit several more lanterns and now Beth could see that the cavern was stacked with crates and sacks.

"What's your name?" she asked, when he returned with a blanket.

He didn't answer, but grabbed her arm and pulled her over to a wall. There, he threw down the blanket and told her to sit on the floor. There were chains attached to the wall with manacles and he clamped one of these around her ankle.

"Can I have some water and a bucket to pee in?"

He huffed and fetched her a jug of fresh water, a beaker and a bucket.

"You empty it."

Beth found it hard to judge time in the cave. The lamps burned steadily, and she dozed. She didn't waste energy trying to get out of the manacle, although she was sure she could. They hadn't searched her and, in any case, her lockpicks were somewhere they wouldn't find them.

Footsteps woke her, as McMillan walked into the light with one of his men. He pulled up a crate and sat down opposite her.

"Why are the English hunting you?"

"I stole from the captain of the ship."

"Not in this town. I would have heard of it."

"In Kingston. I dipped his pocket and was seen by one of his men."

"What was he going to do with you?"

"Take me to Martinique and sell me as a slave." As she spoke, Beth made sure her lip was quivering.

"That's better than hanging you. Unchain her."

While his man worked on the manacle, McMillan chatted. "His men made a mess of my yard searching for you."

"What will you do with me?" Now she made herself sound frightened.

"Nothing bad. Can you read?"

She lifted her head proudly. "No, but I can count to ten!"

McMillan laughed and beckoned her to follow him.

"This will be your room," said the housekeeper, Mrs McFarlan, as she let Beth into a bedroom in the garret. It was small, and had a single bed and washstand. A small skylight let in the sun. There was a wardrobe which Mrs McFarlan opened to reveal some dresses, saying, "You will work as a maid of all works. One of these should fit you well enough. Get washed and dressed and report to me in the scullery."

The dresses were utilitarian servants' clothes and she found one that fitted reasonably well. As she changed, Beth recovered her tools and hid them in her hair, which she plaited as soon as she had washed herself. There were no shoes that fitted, so she went barefoot down to the scullery.

Mrs McFarlan noticed the lack of shoes straight away as she inspected Beth. "At least you know how to clean yourself. You are tall, and that dress is too short, but it will do for now. You have big feet for a girl."

Big feet? They are the right size for me!

"Yes, ma'am," Beth said, keeping her eyes down.

"Wash the dishes and put them away. Once you are done, I will have another job for you."

The sink was full, and she set to washing the crockery and scrubbing the pans. She did a good job and got the approval of the cook, who she discovered was a former slave named Mary. Beth's next job was to sweep the hallway. The constant flow of men coming and going from the boatyard brought sand and dust in, and she endured several slaps on her behind and a pinch or two before she was finished.

They kept her busy all day and she was grateful for her bed that night, but set her internal alarm to wake at three in the morning so she could explore the house. She woke on time and left her room — feeling her way in the dark, she went downstairs to the ground floor to find the room where McMillan met his men. Its door was locked, but that only took a second or two to remedy, and Beth slipped inside.

She lit a candle that she had brought from her room and searched the Scotsman's desk. Bills for materials, orders and other paperwork associated with a shipwright was all she found, so she extended her search to a cabinet. Again, she found drawings of ships' hulls and a couple of charts, but nothing incriminating. Soon her internal clock told her it was time to leave; she purloined a sheet of paper and a pencil, then blew out her candle before slipping out and relocking the door.

She was woken before daybreak to help prepare the men's breakfast. Bread was baked from dough that had been proving overnight in a cool place. Butter had to be churned, coffee brewed and small beer fetched from the cellar. The cook fried ham, kidneys, sausages and eggs and boiled porridge.

The table was set for ten people, and at seven o'clock the men gathered. The hot food was served on platters on the sideboard and the men helped themselves. Bread and butter were on the table. Some drank coffee, others drank small beer. It struck Beth that this was very much like a clan breakfast would be in Scotland, with McMillan as the chief.

As the maid, she was completely invisible as the men fuelled up for a day's work, so she was able to listen in to their conversations. All of the men were Scots or Irish and their accents were thick, so it took her a few minutes to tune in.

"We will lay the keel for Standish's clipper today," one of the men said.

"Good, he is paying well and wants it before the year ends," McMillan replied, speaking around a mouthful of ham. "How is Jimmy getting on?"

"He's healing. He was lucky, the silly bugger got the rope wrapped around his leg when they dumped the goods over the side. If Billy hadn't cut it so quickly, he would have either lost the leg or taken a trip to the bottom."

That's interesting. Why would they dump goods over the side?

"Did we lose them?"

"We can dredge for them. We know where they were dropped and it's only thirty or so feet deep there."

"Good. Do that when that fucking navy patrol boat is in dock."

Aah, that explains it, thought Beth.

* * *

Beth cleared the table after the men had departed for their various jobs around the yard. McMillan went to his office. Eventually, Beth got a break and went to her room. There she quickly encoded a message and wrote it on a corner of the paper she had taken from the office. Tearing off the message, she folded it as small and tightly as she could and hid it up her sleeve.

She was sweeping the hallway, again, when a visitor arrived at the door. Beth answered the knock and found a tall man, dressed in the typical clothing of a colonial planter. His goatee beard and handlebar moustache were silver grey, as was his long hair. But she wasn't fooled: it was Sebastian.

"I would like to see Mr McMillan," he drawled in a decidedly New Orleans accent.

"Who should I say is visiting?"

"Pierre Lombard, I want to speak to him about a vessel I wish to have built." He held out a card and Beth took the opportunity to pass him the message as she took it.

McMillan had her show Pierre into his office, and after a few minutes called her in.

"Get us some coffee, Isla."

As she left, she heard them discussing a leisure yacht that Lombard wanted to commission. It sounded luxurious and she decided that one day she and Sebastian would have one just like that.

The Snare

Sebastian waited until he reached his rooms before reading Beth's message. He sat in the window and unfolded the paper. He checked the date: 21 November 1824. Therefore, the key would be twenty-one minus eleven, plus twenty-four equals thirty-four. Subtract the number of letters in the alphabet and what remains is plus eight. The key was a shift of eight letters to the right like this.

thequickbrownfoxjumpedoverthelazydog

elazydogthequickbrownfoxjumpedoverth

It was a simple cypher, but one that only he and Beth knew the key to. He decoded the message.

McMillan has secret caves storing smuggled goods. Near the sea, access from cellar tunnel two hundred and ten steps long. Navy cutter searched one of their ships. Cargo dumped overboard in thirty feet of water. Will be retrieved when navy ship is in dock.

Sebastian sat back and contemplated the message for some time, then he got out a map he had drawn of the town around McMillan's yard and house.

Two hundred yards north or south of the house on the coast. North is a dock, so what is south?

He stood up and shed his disguise. He opened the window and slipped through, having checked that no one was around to see him. He had requested a ground-floor room in preparation for just such an occasion. He walked to the fort and found Pettigrew.

"Do you have a ship out on patrol?"

"Yes, we do. The *Wren*, a cutter."

"When is she due back?"

"Why are you asking?"

Sebastian handed him the deciphered note.

"Ahh, I see. She is rather good, isn't she? The *Wren* is due back in three days."

"And the caves?"

"Do you fancy a sail?"

Pettigrew changed into civilian clothes and the two headed down to the beach, where Pettigrew kept a small sailing boat. They launched it and were soon cruising along, as if out to enjoy the sea.

They passed McMillan's yard three hundred yards offshore. Sebastian lounged against the starboard side of the boat with a small telescope to his eye. He scanned the coastline, which became very rocky as they went south of the yard.

"That is coral rock and there are caves. Most are shallow, but some may be much deeper."

They sailed a mile south, then wore around and tacked back north. Back at the fort, they discussed strategy.

"We could just raid the house and cellar," Pettigrew said.

"We could only charge him with handling illicit goods if we did that. We need to catch him in the act of unloading them. Then we can charge him with smuggling."

"And hang the beggar!"

"Quite."

"What do you suggest?"

Sebastian pointed to a chart of the bay that was laid out on the table. "They will almost certainly land the goods by boat at night. We need a team onshore, near the house. We need a boat with another team hidden around this headland and we need a lookout above the cave hidden in the rocks."

"What about the ship they use to pick up the goods?"

"The *Lizard* will take care of that — as soon as we nab them in the act."

It did not take long for them to put this plan into effect. The Foxes had become used to manning the *Lizard* with their surviving Marines providing muscle. Clubs and blackjacks, along with pistols and knives, were their weapons of choice. Garai, having excellent night vision, was the lookout. The *Lizard* slipped out of harbour in the dark once the *Wren* had returned, and went out to the area that they had searched for the smugglers' ship which had dumped its cargo. The cutter's captain came along for the ride and to help them navigate into the right area.

Garai slipped down to the area above the cave openings and by listening to the sound of the waves, got himself above one that seemed deeper than the rest. He knew that Richard was commanding the longboat and should be in position soon after dark. Keen to see some action, Major Devereux led a platoon of soldiers to quietly surround the house and yard.

***

Beth waited in her room with the door cracked open so she could hear what was going on downstairs. She heard voices from below and crept out and down to the first-floor landing.

She heard McMillan's voice. "The boys should arrive around three. We need to get the stuff ashore fast, so we will all go down and make a chain. Till then, get some rest and I'll rouse you at two."

Beth went back to her room; she would have to wait as well.

Garai made himself comfortable. He had brought a night glass with him and there was enough starlight for him to see by. The only problem was that Garai wasn't used to using a night glass, and when he tried to use it he became hopelessly confused. It literally turned the world upside-down and back to front.

Ears and eyes, like in the mountains, he thought, and remembered his time in the Basque country. There he had learnt the tricks of hunting by night; listening for unusual sounds or for a lack of sound, using his peripheral vision because it was more sensitive to motion in the dark, noting any changes in the behaviour of animals or birds.

Garai sat, his vision not focused on anything in particular, and breathed steadily. He became attuned to his surroundings, absorbing the normal night sounds so they became part of his consciousness. Time passed without him really being aware of it.

Then ... something tickled his senses, a sound, then a glimmer of phosphorescence on the water. He shifted his eyes to bring the glimmer into his peripheral vision and saw that there were two lines of dots, with a faint line between, coming towards him. He heard the sound again. It was the creak of an oar. Sound travelled over water.

He waited, keeping track of the glow. The boat came closer until he could make it out about fifty yards off. He moved to the edge of the cliff and looked down. The mouth of the cave was dimly lit, but showed enough light to guide the boat in.

He moved back carefully, so as not to dislodge any rocks, and watched.

At two in the morning, the men were roused by McMillan and went down to the cellar. Beth left her room and went to McMillan's office, where she had discovered, on one of her nightly excursions, a weapons cabinet. She took and loaded a flintlock pistol, then lit a candle and moved it in a circle in front of the window.

Then, Beth stepped out of the office and found herself face to face with Mrs McFarlan, who was dressed and carrying a candle of her own.

"What—"

No sooner had Mrs McFarlan started to speak than Beth's hand shot out and hit her in the throat. Mrs McFarlan staggered back, choking as the blow cut off her air. Beth followed up, stepping behind the woman and wrapping her right arm around her head at eye height, her hand on the left temple, her left arm behind the head with her hand clamped just behind the right ear. Then she twisted the woman's head sharply. There was a crack, and the housekeeper went limp. Beth dragged her into the office and closed the door. A check of her pulse confirmed that Mrs McFarlan was dead, and the unnatural angle of her head offered additional proof. Beth stuffed the body under McMillan's desk, then went to the front door and unbolted it.

The hatch in the cellar was open and she felt her way down the stairs. Being barefoot, she made no noise as she followed the wall with her left hand and carried the gun in her right. A glimmer of light showed at the end of the tunnel, and she stopped before it illuminated her. She listened. McMillan's men were chatting as they waited for the boat.

Richard waited; his men were ready. The pistols were not cocked or primed — he didn't want any accidental discharge to warn the smugglers they were coming. A blue rocket arced up into the sky. It was the signal they had waited for and Richard ordered in a harsh whisper, "Make way, steady, no noise."

The oarsmen had packed the rowlocks with rags to kill any sound and pulled without splashing. As they rounded the headland they could see a light on the clifftop; Richard steered the longboat parallel with the shore until the light bobbed up and down twice, then turned in. He was steering on faith, as there was no other light to guide him.

He could hear the sound of waves against rocks but kept the light dead ahead. It dipped again. "Ship your oars, prime your weapons," he hissed.

The momentum of the boat carried them into the cave, and they soon discovered that it curved first left, then right. As they approached the second curve, light shone from ahead and they could see that there was a path carved into the left-hand wall.

"Marines, onto the path. Quietly now," Richard whispered.

The Marines, well used to stealthy night operations as part of the Special Operations Flotilla, quickly debarked and moved ahead single file. Richard followed, pistol in hand, but would leave their command in the hands of Sergeant Bright.

Back on land, the soldiers moved in on the house and yard as soon as the rocket went up, sweeping up the watchman and any workers as they went. Sebastian walked beside Major Devereux, aware that he had to be a restraining influence and making him wait for the signal before moving in. The major was eager and none too patient.

The ring closed in on the house, and Sebastian — with the major and six soldiers at his back — tried the latch on the front door. The door swung open and he stepped inside. The house was quiet as he led the men forwards.

"Search the rooms; if you find anybody, no shooting — but make sure they cannot shout a warning."

Four men broke off to search the rooms, with rifles slung over their shoulders and clubs in their hands. Meanwhile, Sebastian led the major and the remaining two men further on. His foot touched something, and he stopped to check it out — it was a candle holder, with a candle still in it. He felt the wick. Cold. Sebastian used a striker to light it and decided that Beth must have left it there.

He found the door to the cellar. The candlelight gently illuminated the open hatch.

"Wait here," he said and handed the candle to Devereux. Then Sebastian slipped down the stairs into the tunnel and disappeared.

Devereux shook his head and sat on a crate, placing the candle to the side. "Damn spies," he lamented, frustrated at being left behind.

Beth heard the men's voices change.

The boat must have arrived.

She edged forwards. The sound of crates being placed on the floor drifted towards her. She stooped as she walked, moving up to the end of the tunnel, and peeked around the end. McMillan's men had formed a chain and were passing crates up from a boat that had been pulled up onto the sloping shore. McMillan stood in the line, catching and passing crates with the rest of them.

Suddenly, uniformed Marines surged out of the cave entrance into the cavern. Beth stepped into the cavern, ready to stop any smugglers who tried to run back into the tunnel. Soon, the cavern echoed to shouts and grunts as the Marines and smugglers engaged. McMillan broke away and headed towards Beth. She levelled her pistol at him and pulled the trigger. It misfired; the flint was broken.

McMillan saw her try to shoot him and the realisation of her perfidy hit him like a hammer. He charged towards her, anger in his eyes and bent on revenge. Beth spun the gun around and caught it by the barrel; if it wouldn't shoot, she would use it as a club. McMillan loomed in front of her, fists swinging. She dodged him and pirouetted on her left leg, letting her right swing around and up, the power of her body behind it. Her heel connected with the side of his jaw.

McMillan staggered with the force of the blow — and as he staggered, Beth continued the spin and used her momentum to hit him on the side of the head with the pistol butt. McMillan dropped like a half-full sack of potatoes.

A slow clap from behind her drew her attention back to the mouth of the tunnel. Sebastian was leaning against the wall, grinning as he applauded. She bowed.

Major Devereux thought he heard the sound of fighting coming up and out of the tunnel's mouth. He stood up and moved to the top of the steps. He listened. Yes, it was definitely fighting.

He was about to order his remaining two men forwards when the cellar door opened, and the four soldiers who had been searching the house came down the stairs to the tunnel mouth. Two of them carried lanterns.

"House is secure, sir," their sergeant reported.

With better light, Devereux could see that there were lanterns mounted on the walls. "Get them lit," he told the men, indicating the lanterns. Devereux didn't really like the dark.

The room was aglow with lantern light by the time he turned his attention back to the tunnel. The fighting had stopped now; all he could hear was the sound of footsteps. They were gradually getting louder.

"Form up, rifles at the ready."

Then Beth and Sebastian walked up the steps and into the room, followed by the smugglers, who dragged the still-unconscious McMillan by his arms. They were followed in turn by uniformed Marines.

"Hello, Major," Beth said cheerfully. "These men are all yours."

The next morning, Beth stood drinking a cup of coffee and looking out of Devereux's office window, overlooking the bay. She hadn't slept and was tired, but the coffee would keep her going long enough for them to finish the work they had started during the previous night.

Beth noticed the *Lizard* coming into the bay with a fast cutter under her guns. She grinned. That would be her new ship until she got the *Fox* back. Then Devereux was saying something, and Beth brought her attention back to the room. "I'm sorry, I was distracted." She smiled.

"I was saying that all of McMillan's men are in custody, and he has regained his senses. He has a nasty swelling on his jaw and an egg on the side of his head."

"The goods?" Beth asked.

"Being investigated by the revenue chaps — but there isn't any doubt, it's all contraband."

Beth nodded towards the window, where she could now see the two ships anchoring. "And the *Lizard* has got their ship."

"Were any of your men hurt?" Devereux said, almost as an afterthought.

"Only a few bruises. They are skilled at that kind of fighting."

"Excellent, excellent. So, your work here is finished?"

"Major!" Beth said, feigning shock. "It's almost as if you want rid of me!"

As it was, they stayed for the trial. Beth's testimony was needed to seal the conviction, and she needed the *Cub* — as she had christened the cutter — to be released by the revenue service. McMillan was found guilty and sentenced to hang. His lieutenants would hang alongside him, and the rest of his men were sentenced to hard labour at the general penitentiary in Kingston, where they would spend years careening ships' hulls and pulling oakum.

The Hunt

Beth sent a comprehensive report to Admiral Turner via the captain of the newest vessel in the Stockley merchant fleet, the *Caroline*. Named after her mother, she replaced the original *Caroline* and was bigger and faster, being longer for the same beam, which made her more hydrodynamically efficient. She could make the crossing from Liverpool to New York in fourteen days, and needed just eighteen days to go from Liverpool to Jamaica.

Now, Beth wanted her ship back. This was not due to pride or any sense of attachment she felt for it — at least, that is what she told herself — but because it belonged to the British government and was armed with carronades.

"Where are we going?" Sebastian asked as they left Montego Bay. They were on the newly acquired *Cub*, a fast topmast cutter that was only a year old, sailing alongside the *Lizard*. Both ships had had their bottoms cleaned and the *Lizard* had been re-coppered at the new, government-owned shipyard that had once been the property of a convicted smuggler. The *Cub* had also been re-gunned, with eight twenty-four-pound carronades which had been brought from the navy yard in Port Royal.

"First we'll go to Veracruz, to see if Diego is currently based there and to catch up with Troupial," Beth replied, referring to Manuela by her code name.

"Is Diego still a threat to shipping?"

"Probably. Troupial will be able to confirm that."

They stood on the foredeck of the *Cub* and the breeze over the deck blew Beth's auburn mane out, so that the sunlight made it look almost afire. Sebastian smiled as he looked at her; meanwhile, Beth herself was absorbed in watching the *Lizard* plough through the swell. She had tried to convince herself that she was over what Carlos had done to her, but she knew Sebastian could feel the slight hesitation when they made love that told him it would stay with her for a long time.

Beth watched the *Lizard*, admiring the way the French-built hull heeled over under sail and cut through the water. Both ships were fast, but the *Cub* would have a knot or two on the *Lizard*, which had been built to an older design. That additional speed would be important when they found the *Fox*.

Beth was unaware that Sebastian was looking at her until she turned to say something. She forgot what that was as she looked into his eyes.

Fortunately, the *Cub*'s smuggler's hold had been converted into a cabin for the couple. It was not overly large and was deep in the hull, but it was dry and — interestingly — soundproof.

They arrived in Veracruz five days later. There was no sign of the *Fox* in the harbour, so Beth took Sebastian to meet Troupial/Manuela. From the outside, the house had not changed, and she knocked before opening the door. Inside it was dark, and the couple was immediately struck by the loud buzzing of flies and an overwhelming smell of corruption. Beth, fearing the worst, advanced with gun in hand, heading towards the biggest concentration of the insects.

"Ugh," she said, as a maggot-ridden corpse came into view.

Sebastian looked at it and frowned. "Why leave a dead dog here?"

Beth went to a roof beam and searched a gap that was invisible from the floor with her fingers.

"To keep people out. Aah, here we are!"

They left the house and went to the plaza by the Pastora church, to sit by a fountain and get the stench out of their noses. Beth unfolded the message she had recovered from the dead drop.

"Manuela has had to move. Diego somehow found out where I lived when I was ashore and sent men around to eliminate any friends."

"Where is she now?"

The church clock chimed midday. Beth looked around her. "There."

Manuela, a scarf covering her head, was entering the church. Beth stood up and covered her own head with a scarf.

"Wait here."

She walked into the church and took the pew behind Manuela.

"What happened?"

"They came to the house; the dog warned me, and I escaped across the roofs."

"They killed the dog."

"I know, I left it there to keep kids out of the house. You found the message?"

"Yes. Where are you based now?"

"In the top floor of a house by the Parque de las Madres. You enter through the blue door."

"Is Diego still operating from here?"

Manuela chuckled. "You are looking for your ship."

"The bastard stole it and I want his head."

"He is not based here, but has visited twice. The second time, he sent his men. I made the mistake of waving at the ship from the shore, thinking it was you, and they followed me."

"Any idea where he is based now?"

"Maybe Isla Mujeres — he was heard saying something about hunting British ships."

That made sense. Isla Mujeres was on the tip of the Yucatan peninsula overlooking the passage from the Caribbean into the Gulf. Ships from Honduras and Jamaica used it.

"He will use a British flag to get close to them and board," Manuela said.

But there was no reply. Beth had already left.

"We need to take a look at Isla Mujeres," Beth told Richard and Wilfred Billingham, the captain of the *Lizard*. She had called both men to her as soon as she got back aboard the *Cub*.

"I don't want to frighten him off if he is there, so we will go in with the *Cub*. I want the *Lizard* to be out of sight but close enough to intercept or follow him if he runs." She turned to Richard. "How are the men?"

"I am pleased to say they are all fit, or at least on the mend. We still have a couple of invalids who are recovering from the black bile, but the rest are fine."

"Good, then we have enough. When can we sail?"

"We will be ready on the tide. The fresh stores are aboard, and we just need water and wood," Richard said.

"Same for the *Lizard*," said Wilfred, who was still getting used to Beth taking command.

She noticed the slight hesitation and asked, "Given the local conditions there, where do you think the *Lizard* will be best positioned?"

He looked at the chart, which was ever-present at their meetings. "The prevailing wind is from the east, and we want that in our favour so we should beat up to be east."

Richard commented, "From here with the Gulf current and the winds we might be better going north of Cuba and coming up on it from the Caribbean side."

Wilfred had his head down over the chart and traced a course with his finger. "I don't agree. If we follow the current around to here, just off Havana, we can sail direct to the island, and it is half the distance. I can leave the *Cub* at the tip of Cuba and beat upwind ten to twenty miles and hold there."

Richard looked at Beth from over Wilfred's shoulder and nodded. Beth smiled in appreciation of his allowing Wilfred to contribute.

"Then that is what we will do. The *Lizard* can lead until you break away."

Their circumnavigation of the Gulf of Mexico took five days and then they were on the last leg from Havana to the island. The *Lizard* broke away in a flurry of flags as they passed the tip of Cuba.

"Message reads, 'Good hunting,'" Richard said. "Reply, 'You too, good luck.'"

They were sailing about as close to the wind as the *Cub* could go, since they had to consider the current rushing through the strait. They were greatly aided by the *Cub*'s gaff rig and did not need the top and gallant square sails.

Mujeres turned out to be little more than a fishing village with a lagoon behind it. There were men working on the construction of a large house, but other than that it was a sleepy sort of place. Beth went ashore and talked to some fishermen. An offer to buy their catch was enough to get them talking. They had seen a ship that matched her description of the *Fox* — it had called in to rewater. But it was not based there, they said.

"Do you know where it is based?" asked Beth.

"No, but the captain mentioned that the water here was better than that in Bonaire."

Beth took that information back to the *Cub*.

"That makes sense," Richard said. "They know we know that they were selling their loot in Cuba so would stay away from there for a while. The Dutch have a reputation for not asking questions, and Bonaire is underdeveloped enough to be a good place to pass the goods through."

"Father had a run-in with the Bonairians some time back. It will be worth a look. Finding the *Fox* at sea will be next to impossible."

Their first task was to send a boat to find the *Lizard* with instructions to rendezvous at Bonaire. Then they set sail.

Getting to Bonaire was easier said than done. The Caribbean current and prevailing trade wind prevented them from sailing to it directly. Instead, they had to sail up and around Cuba and run down to St Lucia in a series of long tacks. Then, when they had made enough westing, they turned south to cross the Caribbean.

"Is that it?" Beth said, as the island came into view.

Richard chuckled. "The ABC islands aren't pretty like the Windward Islands. They're more like coral outcrops with a few thorny trees."

What she was seeing was in fact Klein Bonaire, the small and uninhabited island that protected the mooring in the bay. As they got closer, she could see that there was a settlement on the main island and, as they tacked to get behind the small island, she saw that there were a number of ships anchored, including the *Lizard*.

A flash of silver caught her eye. A flying fish was skimming a foot above the surface of the water. Another came up and flew along beside it, and then a large fish erupted from the water and snatched a smaller one from the air.

"Good Lord! What was that?" Beth gasped.

"A tuna, I think," Richard said.

Sebastian walked over from where he had been sitting on a canvas chair, reading a book. "I have been reading a travelogue. These are rich waters and there is a reef that runs almost all the way around the island. It was originally owned by the Spanish. They noticed that the wind blew consistently from the east, hence the name Bonaire or 'good air'. Salt, dyewood and castor oil are the only products they produce, but they handle a lot of goods."

A boat was approaching. "Who is that?" Beth said.

It turned out to be the harbour master, who directed the ship to its moorings. William came aboard as soon as they were moored and they discussed a plan of action. Soon after that, Beth went ashore.

Beth assessed the town as she was rowed over. There was a fort, which looked like a recent addition, and several houses that doubled as stores. Beth went to the fort and walked in through the open gate; the guard merely nodded to her as she passed. In the central courtyard was a building that looked like an office of sorts. She knocked on the door and stepped inside.

The office was empty apart from a desk and chair, and a slave boy snoozing in the corner near a cord that ran up to a large woven mat, slung from a pivot on the ceiling. She had seen similar setups in India, where they were called punkahs and operated by punkah wallahs who pulled the cord to make the mat flap back and forth, acting like a fan. It moved the air around but didn't cool the room at all.

"Anybody home?" she asked the boy, in Spanish.

He pointed to a door at the back of the room. Beth walked over and banged on it. There was a grunt from the other side and the sound of someone moving around. She sat on the end of the desk closest to the door and arranged her dress so that when she crossed her legs she showed a slender ankle.

The door opened and a man came out, buttoning up his uniform coat. The boy started pulling on the cord.

"How can I help you?" the officer said to Beth.

"I'm looking for whoever is in charge of the island."

He looked her over; his eyes lingered on her ankle.

"That is me, I am the commanding officer. Captain Victor van den Bosse at your service."

"Rosa Collins. I am a privateer, out of Charleston."

"American?"

"Yes, I am. My ships are out in the harbour."

"Ships? You have more than one?"

"Yes, I have a former French corvette called the *Lizard* and a cutter called the *Cub*."

Van den Bosse looked at Beth, clearly reappraising her. Then: "Again, how can I help you?"

"I'm looking for a man called Diego Montego-Rodrigues. He is a Colombian, and sailing a schooner that is very well armed."

"Why do you want to find him?"

"He stole the ship from me and tried to kill me."

"I thought he'd had that ship for a long time."

Beth giggled and waved a hand gracefully. "Well, you see, I took Diego's previous ship from him when he attacked me, and sold it. Then he trapped me with the aid of a traitor in my crew, and his brother took my ship."

"You obviously escaped. What happened to the brother and traitor?"

She pouted, her bottom lip protruding ever so slightly. "It was sad; they died."

Victor frowned. He knew she was being disingenuous, but she was so damn cute! Beth, however, had had enough of play-acting and stood up, suddenly all business. "Now, I want his head on a plate — and I want you to help me."

"Aah ... this is not a thing that concerns the Dutch government."

"No, but you are an ally — and as such, you are obliged to help."

"We are not allies with America."

"But you do have a treaty with Britain."

Now Victor was really confused. Beth decided to play a straight hand. "I am sorry, I haven't been entirely honest. I am a member of British Intelligence working on behalf of the US government."

"Show me your papers."

"That is part of the problem. Diego has all my papers on the ship."

"Then I cannot help you."

Beth sighed. She had feared this would happen. "Then tell me, who does Diego sell his goods to?"

"Ernst Nigtavecht. His is the blue warehouse."

Beth paid the merchant a visit. "Do you buy and sell?" she asked him.

Ernst Nigtavecht, a tall thin man with receding hair and a bit of a stoop, looked her over. "What are you selling?"

"Anything I take. Do you ask questions?"

"No, I don't care where the goods originate from, but what does a girl like you have to offer?"

He leered at her, at which she sidled up to him. Then she moved with the speed of a striking cobra — and Ernst found a nasty curved blade on his neck, just below his ear. She was very close now and whispered in that ear, "I kill men who try to take advantage."

Then she pirouetted away, and the knife disappeared.

"I have a letter of marque from the United States navy and two ships."

"I already have a supplier with a letter of marque."

Beth walked around the warehouse looking at the goods. "Yes — Diego. I know."

"He always has plenty of goods to sell."

"Based here, is he?"

"As much as anywhere."

"You have British and American goods here. Did he bring them?"

"He might have."

Beth was getting tired of the game. "Do you want to hang next to him?"

"*What?*"

"Do. You. Want. To. Hang. Next. To. Him?"

"I don't understand."

"You see, it's like this. He has a letter of marque to attack Spanish ships. The problem is, he is indiscriminate and attacks vessels flying British and American flags too — which makes him a pirate, not a privateer."

Ernst started to look worried. "I do not know where the goods come from."

Beth lifted a sack of coffee beans and studied it. "But these are clearly marked in English with the name of the shipper — who is in Jamaica, a British island. In fact, I think I know the plantation they came from, and the owner definitely would not have sent them on a Spanish ship."

Ernst edged towards his desk. As Beth watched from the corner of her eye, her hand slipped into the hidden pocket in her skirt and closed around the butt of the pistol holstered on her thigh. She waited until he made his move. He grabbed a gun, and she drew her pistol. They faced each other.

"That is a very old pistol," Beth said, looking at it critically. "Where did you get it? From Blackbeard?"

"It is still fully functional."

Beth fired. The bullet hit the brass end cap of his gun butt, ripping it from his hand and taking out a chunk of flesh to go with it. Suddenly Garai, Sebastian and Sergeant Bright were all inside the warehouse with guns drawn.

"Hello, boys," Beth said, frowning.

Sebastian examined the wound on Ernst's hand.

"Just passing, were you?" Beth sniped, feeling rather put out that the boys had followed her.

"We were taking a stroll along the front and heard a commotion," Bright said, and smiled.

Beth wasn't convinced, but she had other things on her mind. Given that Ernst was prepared to pull a gun on her, how deeply involved with Diego was he?

"Take him back to the *Cub*."

Sebastian took Beth to the side and spoke quietly. "He is a Dutch citizen, and this is Dutch territory."

"I know, but we will not remove him from their territorial waters, and they can have him back when we are done."

"All the same, this could blow up on you. You can't do anything to him."

"I was planning to invite him to tea and to treat his wound," Beth said, and smiled.

Now it was Sebastian's turn to be suspicious, and he decided that he wouldn't be leaving Beth alone with the injured Dutchman.

The Trap

Ernst was in a lot of pain: he had never felt pain like it. The bullet that the woman fired had hit the brass end cap on his pistol and torn up through the heel of his hand. He was convinced that he had lost almost all of his blood, and the pain was incredible. Now the bitch had brought him to a ship, and he didn't know why.

"This is our surgeon. He will look after your hand."

The man who spoke seemed to have taken over custody of him from the woman. He was a well-mannered man with an upper-class English accent, but he looked at the woman fondly whenever she was around.

The surgeon sat down opposite Ernst and held out his hand. Ernst didn't understand what that meant to start with, then realised the man wanted him to hold out his own, wounded hand.

"Hmm ... looks like the bullet flattened before hitting the flesh. Tore it rather than cut it. Milord, if you could ..." The man made a sleeping motion.

Ernst felt strong arms clamp around his neck and pressure applied to the side. It didn't hurt, but he started to see his vision closing in as the blood supply to his brain was restricted.

* * *

"All done!" the surgeon chirped, as Ernst started to regain consciousness. The Dutchman shook his head to clear it and looked down at his hand, which was neatly bandaged.

"Did you have to do much?" Beth asked as she entered the cabin.

"Had to clean up the wound and cut away some of the jagged bits before stitching it up. Your beau helped by putting him to sleep."

"How considerate," Beth said, without smiling. She bent down and looked Ernst in the eyes. "Does it hurt?" She reached for the hand and he pulled it away, a frightened look on his face. "Oh, don't be silly, I am not going to hurt you." She gently took his hand and turned it over. "Can you wiggle your fingers?" His fingers moved. "Brilliant! You should be up and running in a week or so."

"Why did you bring me here?"

"To have our surgeon fix your wound and to get you out of the way. I do not want you warning Diego that we are on to him."

"Why are you so interested in Diego?"

"Two reasons. One, he is attacking British and American ships, and two, he stole my ship."

"Your ship? He has had the *Isabella* for years."

"You can't tell one ship from another, can you?" Beth said, taking in the blank look in Ernst's eyes. "I captured the *Isabella* and sold her off. He is currently sailing around in my ship, the *Fox*. Which in its former life was the *Griffon*."

Ernst looked blank at this information. He had never liked ships — nasty things that made him sick — and only paid them the attention required to acquire their cargoes.

Beth discussed tactics with Richard and Wilfred over dinner.

"It's probably best that my ship is not visible when he comes in to anchor," Wilfred said.

He's catching on!

"Can I suggest we move north up the coast to Boca Slagbaai? It's a bay where the castor oil is loaded. We can swoop down when we know he is in port."

"How will we know?" Richard asked, looking at Beth.

"See that hill to the north, the one with the two peaks that form a saddle? If you put a lookout there you can see this bay."

Beth thought about that. "The *Cub* has been seen in these waters under her previous owner. She can stay. But the *Lizard* looks like a navy ship, so she should go. When the *Fox* is anchored, we will fly a signal to alert the *Lizard*."

"You can blockade the northern channel out of the anchorage and we will move the *Cub* to blockade the southern end," Richard said.

Someone noticed that Ernst's warehouse was closed and mentioned it to another person, who mentioned it to Captain Victor, who went to the warehouse to investigate. Then a boat came out to the *Cub* with the good captain aboard.

"Permission to board?" he asked, looking up at the unfriendly faces of the crew looking down at him.

"Wait," a surly individual barked.

A few minutes later, Beth's face appeared — all smiles — and asked him to come up.

"So nice of you to visit," she said, as if he had come for tea. "You really should have told me you were coming."

A table had been set up on the quarterdeck, complete with a tea set and cake. Ernst sat there, as calm as you like.

"Are you well, Ernst?" Victor asked in Dutch.

"Healing," the merchant replied.

"Have they misused you?"

"Not at all, they are the perfect hosts."

While this exchange carried on, Beth poured tea. She then called their informal meeting to order. "Gentlemen, if you would be so kind as to continue this conversation in English, then we can all participate."

Victor muttered an apology. Then he looked at the bandage. "How did you hurt your hand?"

Beth explained politely. "A ricochet. We were comparing guns when mine went off. The bullet hit the heel of his hand and tore a nasty jagged cut. Our surgeon has dealt with it and we are hosting him while it heals." Beth smiled and passed the officer a cup and saucer. "Milk? Sugar?"

A crewman gave a piercing whistle from the top of the mainmast. Beth didn't react and simply continued to sip her tea.

"What was that?" Victor asked.

"Oh, just a crewman signalling that the *Fox* is approaching the harbour."

"The *Fox*?"

"Yes, my ship. Ernst tells me that they usually unload as soon as they dock, then the crewmen go ashore for some entertainment while the skipper negotiates the sale."

Victor stood up. "I must return to the fort."

"Whatever for?" Beth asked innocently.

"You are going to start a war in my harbour!"

"Oh, don't be silly, of course I'm not. *That* would not get me my ship back."

"Then what *are* you going to do?"

Beth smiled and indicated that Captain Victor should sit down and finish his tea.

* * *

The *Fox* slipped into harbour around midday and dropped anchor opposite the blue warehouse. As soon as she was secure, boats were pulled around and loaded with goods to be taken ashore. Meanwhile, Beth discreetly went ashore in another boat and took up residence in Ernst's usual place.

She waited, having opened the warehouse doors enough to show that someone was there. Garai and Sebastian had insisted on coming along and positioned themselves in the gloom of the warehouse's rear.

In time, their patience was rewarded. The door was pulled fully open, and Diego called out, "Ernst, are you there?"

As his eyes adjusted to the gloom, he saw that the figure now sitting with its feet on the desk was not Ernst. It was, in fact ...

"You!"

The double clicks of pistols being cocked preceded Beth's words. "Hello, Diego. Do come in." As he advanced, Diego registered that the barrels of those pistols were pointing directly and unwaveringly at his face. His eyes focused on them, then on the face behind. He turned to run.

She shot him in the backside before he had travelled more than one step. Fede, now weighing in at eighty pounds, helped him to the ground by hanging on to his arm.

As soon as Richard saw Diego fall and noted that he was held securely by Fede, he gave the order to raise anchor and manoeuvre under sweeps.

"Pull together, lads."

The jib was raised to give them a hand. Then Richard took the wheel himself and steered them precisely to come behind the *Fox*.

"Away grapnels."

Hooks were thrown and the two ships locked together. The men poured aboard the *Fox*. With half of Diego's crew ashore or in boats, resistance was minimal and soon the sound of men being thrown overboard echoed around the bay.

Victor could do nothing but assemble his few men and place the pirates in custody. That process started well, but as the word spread that something was wrong, Diego's men started to resist.

Then the *Lizard* arrived, flying the blue ensign and very obviously a Royal Navy ship. She moored to block off the northern end of the harbour and sent two boatloads of Marines over to help.

Garai and Sebastian helped Diego to his feet and dragged him in front of Beth. What scared Diego more than anything was the fact that she was totally calm, while her big white dog looked eager to rip him to pieces.

"I have some good news and some better news," she said. "The good news is that your brother is dead." She smiled and cocked her head at him. "The better news is that you will soon be joining him."

Diego became paler and shuddered. "I insist on a trial!"

"Oh, so do I. This must be done properly. We will go to Jamaica."

"The goods that you have unloaded will be held as proof," Sebastian said.

At this point, Ernst entered, having been brought back from the *Cub*. Diego saw his bandaged hand. "She shot you as well?"

Ernst simply nodded and slumped into the chair behind his desk. He knew that the days of easy money were over.

* * *

The small squadron, as it now was, returned to Jamaica once Beth had retrieved her papers from the hidden strongbox in her cabin. Victor had read them and agreed to "backdate" his knowledge and co-operation to the time she first arrived. This favour included giving her a written permission to do what was necessary under the treaty to apprehend the pirate. In return, she had agreed to ignore Ernst's obvious collusion.

Thus, Beth returned to her cabin on the *Fox* and the seriously undermanned squadron, which had spread out its resources so all three ships could sail. Luckily the weather stayed fair and the winds consistent. She spent her time, when not snuggled up to Sebastian, writing her report for Turner.

Spanish Town

They anchored in Kingston harbour and Beth went straight to see the Governor, Colonel William Montagu, Fifth Duke of Manchester, whose residence was in Spanish Town. She took a carriage and dressed in her best outfit. Sebastian and Garai accompanied her.

The carriage horses trotted along, happily pulling the landau at a steady eight miles an hour, and Beth was enjoying the breeze and the view. Then, over the sound of the horses' hooves, she heard the unmistakable sound of fighting.

"Do you hear that?"

"Yes, it's coming from over there," Garai replied.

"Stop the carriage."

The three of them dismounted and the boys drew guns. The fight was down a side road about fifty feet away, in a courtyard. Three girls were facing off against a gang of eight boys. The boys had them backed up against the wall of a house and surrounded them in an arc.

Sebastian went to intervene, but Beth stopped him.

"I want to see what happens next; they have held them off up to now."

The girls looked relaxed in a way one wouldn't expect under the circumstances, while several of the boys looked battered. The leader of the boys was angry and shouted something in Papiamento. The boys moved and the girls reacted, in one of the most graceful displays of fighting Beth had ever seen.

"Good Lord! What kind of fighting is that?" Sebastian exclaimed.

The girls moved constantly, using a rocking step, and executed kicks with their hands on the ground. The boys were coming a poor second in the contest.

"Darling, you can stop it now," Beth told Seb.

Sebastian fired a shot into the air. The boys ran for it — they let them go. Beth walked over to where the girls stood.

"You speak English? Spanish?"

"I speak a little Spanish," said one of the girls, whom Beth thought was the oldest.

"You are not Jamaicans, are you?" Beth said, noting that the girls had a distinctly South American aspect to their features.

"No, miss, we are from Brazil."

"Why are you here?"

The girls looked at each other and whispered. Beth took in their clothes, the similarity in their features and then caught a glimpse of a brand on an exposed shoulder.

"Are you sisters? Have you escaped from a ship? One that stopped off here on the way to or from Brazil?" At this the girls looked surprised, then worried. "Don't worry, we are not slave owners or idiots like those boys who thought they could take advantage," Beth went on. She wasn't certain all of that had been understood, but the older girl nodded. "Come with me, I will help you." At this, Sebastian put his gun away and Beth stepped back towards the carriage. The girls merely stood where they were, looking scared.

Beth looked back over her shoulder and smiled. "It's alright, come on."

The fact that this woman was pretty, well dressed and smiled convinced them. As she climbed into the carriage and patted the seat on either side of her, the girls very slowly walked forwards. Garai got up beside the driver and Sebastian lounged in the seat opposite Beth. The girls climbed aboard and sat huddled around Beth.

"Walk us the rest of the way," Beth told the driver, and the carriage started to move. "My name is Bethany, he is Sebastian," she told the girls.

"I am Delfina, this is Paola and Alejandra. Who is he?" She pointed to Garai.

Garai turned and grinned at her. "I am Garai, Miss Beth's head of security."

"What was that fighting technique you were using called?" asked Beth.

Delfina replied, still hesitantly, "Capoeira — it is traditional and practised to music."

"So the slave owners don't know it is used for fighting, eh?" Garai said. The girls nodded. Now they were beginning to relax, he assessed their ages. "I'm guessing you are twenty-one, she is nineteen and she is seventeen," he said in his limited Portuguese as he pointed to each of the girls in turn.

"I suppose so, we were never told," Paola said.

"What will you do with us?" Delfina asked.

Beth looked at Garai, who pursed his lips then shrugged. Then she said, "How would you like to work for me as free women?"

* * *

The Governor's residence was a mansion of impressive dimensions that dominated the street. Set in its own gardens, it had a driveway that arced around a classical fountain that created a rotunda in front of the house. The carriage pulled up in front of the steps and Sebastian stepped down and offered Beth his arm. She used it to help her dismount.

"Come, you are part of the team now," she said, and beckoned the girls to follow.

She was halfway up the front steps when a liveried footman opened the door. Beth smiled graciously and immediately put on her best airs and graces. Sebastian stepped up and announced them to the footman. "The Honourable Bethany Stockley and Lord Sebastian Ashley-Cooper to see Duke William." He handed over a pair of visiting cards.

The servant ushered them inside and told a maid to attend them while he went to the duke. The maid, a woman originally from England, eyed the girls.

"Your servants can wait in the pantry if you like, ma'am."

"They are not servants or slaves, but members of my bodyguard." Beth's tone left no doubt she found the suggestion annoying. The maid looked surprised, and then relieved as the footman returned.

"The duke will see you now."

He led them through large double doors into a reception room. The duke and his wife, Lady Susan, were waiting for them. The duke smiled warmly at Beth as she came in, but looked slightly puzzled by her entourage, who had spread out behind her.

"Bethany, how is your mother?" Lady Susan asked as she embraced her.

"The last I heard she was fine, but I haven't seen her for a while now."

Lord William also embraced her, then said, "Sebastian, how are you? Are your parents well?"

"In fine fettle, thank you, as are my older brothers."

"So, you are free to pursue your military career, eh?"

The meeting quickly turned to more pressing matters as Beth said to the duke, "We have a guest on our ship — a guest whom we need to very publicly hang."

"Aah, one associated with your mission?"

"Indeed, and that is why I am here. You see, our guest is the one who called himself El Dragon and has been taking British and American ships."

"I see; and what do you want to do with him?"

"I had in mind a very public trial, attended by the American ambassador and every reporter we can get our hands on from Colombia, Mexico and any other South American country we have relations with, followed by an equally public hanging."

"And you would testify?"

Beth frowned. "I could, if it is not sufficient for my captains to do so. I would be in disguise, of course."

"I will instruct the chief justice to arrange a special court with a jury of the good and the great. Once they are arrayed, we can put the show on."

Beth nodded and walked to the window, which looked out over the tropical garden. Lady Susan stepped up beside her and said softly, "William Anglin Scarlett is the chief justice. He has opposed William's will twice now in the courts. You will need to properly prove your case as he cares greatly for the rule of law."

Beth turned to Lord William. "Who will be the prosecutor?"

"I think Sir Euan Fitz Thompson would be the right man," Lord William said. "Scarlett respects him. The government will allocate a defence lawyer."

Beth took it all in. "Please, have Sir Euan visit me. I will take rooms in the Red Rover," she said.

"Can't you stay here?" Lady Susan asked.

"I would love to do so, but after the trial. I need to be incognito until then," Beth said with the sweetest of smiles.

They went from the mansion to the Red Rover and Beth took rooms on the top floor. Diego was being held on the *Lizard* as a prisoner of the Royal Navy.

Sir Euan Fitz Thompson visited the inn the next day. He was a thin, wiry man of around fifty years with a razor-sharp mind and dry wit. He spoke with a strong Welsh accent. His clerk, Erik, was a young man in his twenties who diligently wrote down, or at least tried to write down, everything that was said in shorthand.

Beth laid down some ground rules. "I am only to be referred to as Chaton, this man is Lancelot and this man is …" She had to think. What *was* Garai's code name? Then she remembered. "This man is Pala."

"Pala? What does that mean?" Erik asked.

"Blade," Garai said.

"Oh, thank you."

Beth continued, "Our agent in Veracruz is Troupial."

"What—" Erik started to ask, but was interrupted.

"It's a type of bird," Sebastian said. He had found a chair and sat with his feet up on a footstool, using a knife to eat an apple slice by slice.

"Can you tell me the nature of your mission here?" Thompson asked.

Beth explained in enough detail to satisfy him without giving away any secrets. Erik sat with a leather half-pint tankard full of pencils and scribbled away furiously. As he blunted one, he simply dropped it into the tankard and took another.

They were well into the evidence against Diego when Thompson called a halt. "I am in need of refreshment and sustenance."

Beth sent a message down with Delfina for the landlord to send up food and ale. While their social betters ate, Garai took the girls down to the bar.

"Miss Bethany wants you to have new dresses," he told them. "You can choose five each, two of which must be the same for all three of you. You must also each have a set of fighting leathers. She also wants you to be clean, so you must wash every day, especially after exercise. If you are not clean enough, *I* will clean you. There is a bath waiting in your room, go and bathe and be back here in one hour. Then we will go shopping."

The girls, chattering excitedly, went to their room where they found a large metal bath full of hot water. Towels, soap and washcloths were laid out for them, along with jugs of hot water. Dresses were laid out on their beds.

Delfina went first. She stripped and stepped into the bath and slid down into the water. It felt wonderful. She had never bathed in hot water before. Paola washed her back and helped her wash her hair. She emerged clean, glowing and fragrant. Paola went next and Alejandra last, by which time the water was filthy. Her sisters poured jugs of water over her as she stood in the lukewarm bath to make sure she was clean too.

The outfits were identical, second-hand, ill-fitting servants' uniforms with shoes. They dressed and returned to the bar to find Garai. He was just finishing his lunch and indicated they should help themselves to the selection on the table. The girls immediately grabbed bread and meat.

"Stop! Were you taught no manners? You are not slaves anymore, but young ladies. Use the plate and place your food on it. Use the knife to cut it into bite-sized pieces." He continued to give them a lesson in etiquette. Then he dropped a bomb. "From now on, you will be learning English. This is a plate."

Their education had started.

The shopping trip got them five new dresses, bonnets and shoes. Four of the dresses were of European style and one typically Jamaican. Then Garai took them to a weapons dealer.

"You can have one pistol and a pair of knives each."

The girls looked worried. "Sir, we are not allowed to carry weapons," Delfina said.

Garai stepped up close and asked, "Why?"

"The brands."

He had forgotten about the brands. She was quite right — a branded person was considered a slave, whether they were or not. Regardless, Garai had them choose weapons and packed them in a wooden chest. He noted that they all chose the same pistol, but their choices of knives varied. Delfina went for a pair of matching long-bladed daggers; Paola chose a pair of punch daggers and Alejandra surprised him by choosing a Mexican scorpion blade and a lightweight tomahawk with a spike on the reverse side.

"Why do you choose that and not two knives?" Garai asked her.

"I think I can use it to drag them in close so I can stick them with the dagger," Alejandra replied.

That was certainly creative, and Garai, who had seen Marty, Beth's father, fight with a tomahawk in one hand and his fighting knife in the other, respected her choice.

With the brands in mind their next stop was a tattoo artist. The girls looked at the designs curiously.

"Alejandra, come here. Show him your brand."

The artist, a Chinese man, looked at the brand then examined it with a magnifying glass.

"Can you conceal it?" Garai asked.

"Yes, it is quite stylised." He looked around at the samples and chose a chrysanthemum bloom. It was drawn on fine waxed paper which had been delicately pierced. He positioned the paper over the brand and moved it until it was just as he wanted it. He held it firmly in place and patted around the design with an inkpad, transferring the design to her skin.

The other girls watched, fascinated, as the Chinese man started to tattoo Alejandra's skin with a tap stick. He worked carefully and methodically, first making the outline in black before switching to pink then yellow. When he finished, he coated the tattoo in some kind of grease and layered brown paper over that.

"Keep in place for at least three hours. Better overnight."

He moved on to Paola; her chrysanthemum was in blue and yellow. Finally, Delfina's was done in red and orange. Before it was wrapped, Garai studied it. The artistry was plain to see, and the curves of the petals concealed the lines of the brand nicely. In fact, for any observer who didn't know it was there, the brand was now invisible.

They returned to the inn and found Beth seated on the balcony of her room, enjoying the sun. Garai told her of the tattoos; she showed the girls her own and told the story of Scarlett and the plantation slaves. The girls were fascinated and when they uncovered their tattoos, declared they wanted the iguana as well.

Garai sent the girls to their room and sat near Beth. "Are you done with Thompson?" he asked.

"For now. He is interviewing Sebastian, then Diego, and examining the goods we confiscated."

"What about Diego's defence lawyer?"

"He will be appointed three days before the trial."

The next day, the girls' education really started. They had an hour of English, followed by an hour's shooting practice. Then they were back to the classroom, where a tutor started teaching them to read and write. They met Netta in that class and soon became friends. Netta drew their portraits and caricatures of them with their weapons.

Beth taught them close combat in the enclosed courtyard of the inn. For this, she had them dress in their fighting leathers. The girls were shy to start with, as the leathers left little to the imagination. Garai laughed at them and told them they didn't have anything that any member of the crew hadn't seen before. Garai taught them knife-fighting and shooting — they would move onto other weapons later.

Beth used the methods her father and Chin had used to teach her. She walked the girls through the moves slowly, emphasising balance and positioning. The girls learnt more English during these lessons than they ever did in the classroom.

The Trial

After three months of waiting, at last the day of the trial loomed. The court was convened in the courthouse on King Street to open the trial and a public defender appointed. He was a young lawyer, confident and fiery, called Jebediah Cameron. A product of Edinburgh Law School, he was both clever and cunning.

"Will he cause us trouble?" Beth asked Sir Euan.

"He will ensure the trial is fair and that if the defendant hangs, he deserves it."

"What happens now?"

"The court will adjourn, and the defence will have a week to prepare. The prisoner will be moved to the cells under the court."

Beth thought five days excessive, especially as she had been told that the defence would be appointed three days before the trial. She was impatient to get the trial over and done with, but there was nothing she could do about it, so she went back to training the girls.

During training, each girl showed a proclivity for an individual style of fighting.

Delfina used her matched daggers very much in the way that Chin had used his butterfly swords. Both weapons moved with incredible speed, but close observation revealed that the girl's left-hand dagger was predominantly used for defence while the right was probing for openings. She could switch hands without effort and very nearly caught Beth out a couple of times.

Paola fought with knives like a boxer. Her hands were fast and she would jab away with her right or left — she was a switch hitter — before sweeping in with her other hand. The punch daggers were extensions of her fists. While boxing, Paola was a hard hitter and that continued with the daggers. If she made contact, it was over.

Alejandra was more subtle. She fought like a dancer, using balance and speed to get her into positions where the combination of scorpion dagger and tomahawk could be brought to bear most efficiently. Her aim was to use the tomahawk to snag the opponent so she could gut them with the dagger.

During this training and waiting time, Beth got to thinking about the girls' origins. To her, they looked more Mexican than Brazilian.

"Do you remember your parents?" she asked Paola one day.

"Yes."

"Where did they come from?"

"They came to Brazil from Mexico. Dad was a horse trainer and was brought down to help train horses for the ranches."

"What went wrong?"

"He was a gambler and drinker. He got the family into debt, and we were sold into slavery."

"How old were you then?"

"I was probably around eight."

That explained a lot. Brazilian slaves tended to be more African in heritage and it was rare to see people with Portuguese heritage enslaved.

The girls were natural fighters and picked up English very quickly. They had never been taught to read or write, and soaked those lessons up as well. Paola had a natural sense of rhythm and would set their lessons to a beat. That set the other two to singing, and Delfina got herself a ukulele while Alejandra picked up some long panpipes. They had never had money of their own before, so Garai helped them when they went shopping.

On the morning of the day the court reconvened, a Stockley ship arrived in Kingston. A carriage arrived at the Governor's residence and an elegant couple entered the house followed by a half dozen retainers. Viscount and Lady Stockley had arrived.

Beth didn't notice; she was absorbed in the trial. It started with the presentation by the prosecution. For this, Beth sat at the back of the courtroom in disguise. The American government representative and the reporters from North and South America sat in front of her. The first moment she was aware of her parents was when they entered the court and sat in the front row of the gallery.

Viscount Martin sat with a relaxed and attentive demeanour as the case for the prosecution began. Lady Caroline scanned the room, her eyes passing over Beth, apparently without a flicker of recognition. Beth didn't know whether to admire her mother's self-control or praise herself for a good disguise.

The judge also noticed that he had unexpected worthies in the gallery and when there was a pause in the proceedings, he said, "Viscount Stockley, welcome to Jamaica. Are you here for personal or governmental reasons?"

"I am here on behalf of the Foreign Office. We have a vested interest in the proceedings. Our American colleagues have asked for our help in the matter of piracy in the Gulf of Mexico."

"Then the agents we refer to in this trial were working under your remit?"

He bloody knows we were, Beth fumed quietly.

"They were under the Foreign Office's remit."

"Thank you, it is well that is confirmed."

Lord Martin appeared unfazed by the exchange and reassumed his air of relaxed interest. Beth wasn't fooled for a minute, her father was a master spy, diplomat and naval officer. He could assume any air he wanted in any circumstances. She looked for the slightest tightening of fingers on his cane or a slight rigidity in his posture that would indicate annoyance. She found neither.

That night, Beth's rooms at the Red Rover were infiltrated. She had gone to bed alone — Sebastian was staying at the residence — and was just dropping off when she heard a noise. It was the merest of scuffs, but sufficient to alert her. Moreover, she wasn't the only one. Garai was also on alert. He was habitually the last to bed and to sleep. He was still up when he sensed that something was wrong. He went to Beth's room.

Delfina was also still awake and heard Garai change rooms. She knew his orientation when it came to sexual partners, so no thought of a tryst entered her mind. She roused her sisters and they all dressed for war.

Thus, by the time that Antton and Matai — two of her father's Special Operations team, the Shadows — opened her balcony doors, Beth's rooms were an armed camp.

* * *

Beth watched as Matai slipped the catch on the doors and gently worked the handle. The doors swung open, and everyone in the room raised their guns.

"Hello, Daddy," Marty heard Beth say just after the last gun was drawn to full cock.

He took a breath and stepped forwards, forcing himself to relax.

"Good evening, Bethany. Are you well?"

"I am." A lamp was turned up and the room flooded with light. Beth sat on her bed, Garai was leaning on the door and three young ladies in full fighting gear were arrayed between the window and Beth, guns cocked and held at the ready.

"Stand down, girls," Beth said, and they lowered their hammers. Beth stood to embrace her father while Antton and Matai greeted Garai.

"Will you introduce me?" Marty said, nodding towards the girls.

"Of course. This is Delfina, Paola and Alejandra."

Then the door opened and Netta walked in, holding a pistol. She was dressed in her nightdress and looked worried but determined. Beth signed to her that all was well, then introduced the girl to her father. "This is Netta, she is a master at forgery and copying."

Marty recognised that the signing was similar to the silent communication his team used and signed, "Hello, Netta. I am pleased to meet you."

She blushed and ran from the room.

"Is she alright?" Marty asked.

"She is in her nightdress," Beth said, as if he should have known better.

Marty sat on the bed and looked at Beth.

"You couldn't come in the front door?" Delfina said to him.

"I don't think Beth wants anyone to know who she is yet."

Beth agreed. "Not in connection with this. I am purely Chaton or Rosa Collins for now. Anyway, you gave us plenty of warning that you were coming — unless you have become clumsy in your old age."

"Not *that* clumsy," Marty said, and grinned. He had missed this kind of verbal jousting with his daughter.

"How are James and the twins?" Beth asked.

"James is fine and will have to get his own ship soon."

"Whether he wants it or not?"

Marty laughed. "The twins are fine; Constance is in Norfolk learning how to treat and breed horses and Edwin has just been made a lieutenant in the Life Guards." His tone became more sober as he turned to current matters. "I checked with Thompson; he confirmed that they have more than enough evidence to hang the brute. I also talked to Sebastian." He looked at his daughter, his eyes full of concern, then turned to the rest of them. "Everybody out."

Netta and the girls looked to Beth, who nodded. Once they were alone, Marty held out his arms; she fell into them and started to sob. He let her cry for several minutes until the sobs started to slow down.

"You killed him?"

She nodded against his neck.

"Shame, I would have made his suffering last a while."

Beth gave a mixture of a laugh and a hiccup. "That's what Seb said."

"I always knew I liked that boy."

"Does Mummy know?"

"I haven't told her. When you do, make sure there isn't a ready supply of breakables anywhere nearby."

"When can I go home?"

"After the trial. I have arranged extensive leave for you and your team. And in any case, we have a wedding to arrange."

"Will they let me keep the *Fox* and the *Cub*?"

"I can't say. I think it depends on your next assignment. Your girls can go to the Academy while you are on honeymoon. And now I need to get back to the residence."

The next day in court went much as the first had, except that Marty had managed to divert Caroline by suggesting she visited the plantations. Sir Euan presented more evidence, Justice Scarlett listened and the defence made notes. The subject of the rape and torture of Chaton came up.

Scarlett listened to the prosecution then asked, "Is this Chaton available to give evidence?"

"She is, but only from behind closed doors, milord," Euan replied.

"This is a public court ..." Scarlett said, at which Marty stood and waved his cane.

"If I may approach the bench?"

"Oh, I wondered if *you* would intervene," grumbled Scarlett as he gestured for Marty to approach.

"This is where the requirements of the Secret Service and the court clash, and some compromise is required," Marty said.

"And what is that?"

Marty ignored his failure to use an honorific. "The evidence and examination must be held in private, but the proceedings may be entered into the public record with the correct redactions."

"Such as?"

"Names, titles, that sort of thing."

"They all have code and cover names," Euan said, trying to be helpful.

"In short, anything that can identify them must be redacted," Marty concluded.

"How, then, should I refer to the young lady agent?"

"Rosa Collins, or, preferably, Chaton."

"Bring her to my chambers in ten minutes."

Beth was called for and met her father in a deserted corridor. They walked to the rear entrance of the judge's chambers. Nothing was said. Beth was dressed as a servant girl, her hair covered by a bonnet. Clever make-up had changed the shape of her face.

Marty knocked on the door and entered without waiting for an answer. They were met on the other side by a clerk and escorted to the judge, who looked curiously at the young woman. As soon as the clerk had left the room, and only the judge, the two lawyers and a recorder remained, Marty introduced her.

"Gentlemen, this is Chaton, our agent in South America."

Beth took off her bonnet and stood proudly, pulling herself up to her full height. Judge Scarlett's eyes widened and darted between Marty and Beth. Thompson was also surprised, as he knew this woman as Rosa Collins.

"*Your daughter?*" Scarlett said what they were all thinking.

Marty ignored him and turned to Beth. He would make sure *that* remark did *not* go on the record.

"*Chaton*," he said with emphasis, "please tell the judge what happened."

Scarlett held up a hand. "You need to be sworn in first." He held out a Bible and had her repeat the oath. "Proceed."

Beth gave her testimony; her delivery was flat and factual.

"This act was sanctioned by the Montego-Rodrigues brothers?" Scarlett asked.

"By Juan, but Diego encouraged him."

"You killed Juan?"

"Yes, when I escaped from Havana with the aid of Lancelot and Pala. I killed Carlos as soon as I could after the … act."

"You have been very active."

"I like to keep busy."

"Tell me, in your own words, what you found on Bonaire."

Beth told the story. At the end, Scarlett frowned. "Why did you not arrest the fellow Nigtavecht?"

"He is a Dutch citizen, and we have a treaty with them, but that was not the only reason. The island's military commander demanded a compromise for operating on their land."

"And that compromise included immunity for his man?" Scarlett asked.

"Indeed," confirmed Beth.

Jebediah Cameron stepped up and spoke. "As my client did not directly sanction the act, I ask that it be struck from the charges."

Scarlett looked to Sir Euan Fitz Thompson, who shook his head and said, "We do not agree. The fact is, the man was jointly in command along with his brother. He neither tried to stop the act nor expressed any kind of objection. In fact, according to the testimony of Pala, who infiltrated the organisation to aid in the rescue of Chaton, he heard them laughing about it and how careless Carlos was to get his neck broken by a girl."

Scarlett considered this for a moment. "I agree with Sir Euan. The charge stands."

The presentation of evidence and cross-examinations lasted a week and on the last day, Scarlett summed up. It didn't look good for

Diego. The jury retired at two in the afternoon and returned with their verdict one hour later.

"You have reached a verdict on all charges?" Scarlett asked the foreman.

"We have, milord."

"And what is your verdict?"

"Guilty on all charges, milord."

"That is the verdict of all of the jury?"

"It is, milord."

The court was adjourned. The sentence would be pronounced on the following Monday.

"What are the options he has to consider?" Beth fumed. She wanted the whole thing to be over and done with, so that she could return to England and get married.

"Well, he has choices under the law." Marty looked to the sky. They were sitting in the residence garden watching Chin, Antton and Garai take the girls through their paces with various weapons. Chin taught Delfina to fight with her matched daggers in the manner he used with his butterfly swords. Garai taught Paola to box, and how to incorporate that skill into her knife-fighting with her punch daggers. Antton concentrated on knife-fighting with Alejandra.

"If the penalty is death, the judge could have him hanged, shot or gibbeted. Or, if he decides against the death penalty, he can choose between a number of sentences from imprisonment to slavery."

At this point Sebastian arrived and saved Marty from his daughter's worsening mood. *There are some benefits to having an imminent son-in-law*, the older man thought, then stood and walked over to where Antton was teaching Alejandra. Marty had quite some experience in fighting with the tomahawk and saw in her someone worth passing it on to.

Monday wound its way to them, and they were all back in court for the sentencing. Diego was dragged from the cells and made to stand in front of the judge. Scarlett donned a black cap.

"Diego Montego-Rodrigues. You have been found guilty by a jury of your peers on counts of piracy, torture, rape, murder and the handling of stolen goods. I will not go over the lesser charges, as for piracy, torture, rape and murder you are sentenced to death by hanging. Your corpse is to be placed in a gibbet that will hang from the ramparts of Fort Charles for three months to warn others to avoid this fate. The sentence is to be carried out tomorrow at midday."

The hanging was on a scaffold erected in front of Holy Trinity Cathedral. The hangman, a bosun from the Jamaica Squadron, ensured that Diego was hanged navy style. Consequently, the crowd was treated to a thirty-two-minute dance at the end of the rope before he succumbed. His body was left hanging for a further three hours before being cut down, encased in the gibbet and hung from a beam that extended from the ramparts of Fort Charles.

Love and Marriage

Fox, *Cub* and *Lizard* formed up behind the *Caroline* and all four ships glided out of Kingston harbour. Beth waved to Diego's corpse, which now dangled in a gibbet from the highest tower of Fort Charles. She hoped she would never see it again. Her mother stepped up beside her and asked, "Are you alright? You have been a little distant."

Beth sighed; she had to tell her at some time and there was definitely nothing breakable within reach.

"I was raped."

There was a stillness and Beth shivered as the air seemed to chill. Then her mother asked, "By whom?"

Beth nodded at the corpse. "Someone that worked for *him*."

"Is the man in question dead?"

"Yes, I broke his neck."

Caroline stopped a passing sailor. "Please go down to my cabin and bring me my rifle and a box of cartridges." Then, to Beth, she said, "I suppose your father and Sebastian know?"

"Yes."

The sailor returned and passed Caroline the rifle. It was a forty-calibre, breech-loading, pinfire hunting rifle with a rifled barrel made to use the Pauli pinfire cartridge. She loaded it and brought it up to her shoulder. She fired, and the gibbet spun as the bullet hit it. She loaded again and fired. The corpse lost a few fingers.

Marty came on deck to see who was shooting, saw that it was Caroline and heard the most unladylike language drifting across the deck. The crew had all retreated to a safe distance. He ducked back into the hatchway, intercepting Sebastian as he did so.

"Caroline?"

"Yes."

"She's with Beth?"

Marty nodded. "I don't know about you, but I have a burning desire for a glass of brandy and a coffee."

Adam, Marty's valet, was also aware of the activities on deck and had anticipated Marty's wants. He had coffee, a very good Armagnac and some Florentines waiting.

"Can you make sure Lady Caroline doesn't run out of ammunition, please?" Marty asked him, as if it was the most normal thing in the world.

"Certainly, milord."

"Oh, and ask Wolfgang to exit the harbour slowly. Very slowly."

Adam grinned.

Caroline eventually calmed down, but not until she had expended two boxes of cartridges. She waved away Adam when he arrived with a third, at which point he took the gun below to clean it.

"Feeling better?" Beth asked.

Caroline hugged her. "Oh darling, you should never have had to experience that. I should never have let you join the Service."

"You must not blame the Service," her daughter replied.

Fede, who had also stayed clear while Caroline vented her anger, approached with Hector, Marty's big Mastiff–Dutch Shepherd cross. The dogs pushed against the women, offering comfort. Fede was only two-thirds the size of Hector but catching up fast. Fortunately, Adam had got in a good store of dried meat for the canines.

Beth knelt and ruffled their heads. "In any case, I have the girls and Hector for protection now," she said.

A clashing of metal on metal from forward told them that weapons practice had started.

Caroline smiled fondly at her daughter. "Do you want to fence?"

"I thought you'd never ask."

The two women dressed appropriately, Beth in her leathers and Caroline in loose trousers and a padded bodice. Each woman tied her auburn hair in a ponytail.

The girls, who were practising with their tutors, stopped to watch.

The ladies saluted and took their guard. Antton stepped up as master of ceremonies. They started cautiously; neither had fenced for a long time and both were wary of new tricks.

Marty and Sebastian come on deck after the cessation of gunfire and stood nearby, watching. Captain Wolfgang Ackermann joined them. "Fancy a bet?"

"I'll put a guinea on Beth," Sebastian said.

The big German post captain held out his hand and they shook.

"I'm staying neutral," Marty said.

"Wise man," Shelby, the ship's physician, said as he joined them.

The competition was subtle, with each woman making probing attacks and cunning defences as they evaluated each other. They tested each other's footwork and suppleness of wrists.

"What are they doing?" Paola asked Chin.

"Testing each other. They haven't fenced for a long time, so they are checking the limitations."

Paola half understood what he meant, as her English was still limited. Suddenly, Beth launched a full-blooded attack. Sparks flew as Caroline parried, bound and disengaged. Then she stepped back and drew a main gauche from behind her back. Beth grinned and drew hers.

Matai chuckled. "Now it's going to get interesting."

It did. Blades flashed as the contestants whirled and stamped, performing a dance that was both mesmerising and terrifying. Stamina was tested, as was balance and suppleness. Beth avoided a high attack from Caroline by arching backwards, her main gauche raised to direct the slash upwards. She spun with the momentum, her sword extended, and forced Caroline to step back. Without hesitation, Beth followed up with a thrust with her dagger that knocked Caroline's sword aside and slashed low at her thigh. There was a *smack* as the flat of her sword hit home.

Sebastian caught the coin that Wolfgang flipped to him as Caroline laughed, delighted by her daughter's proficiency.

The girls approached. "Miss Beth," Delfina said, acting as spokesperson, "can we learn to use swords?"

Beth looked to her mother. "Will you help?"

"Of course, as will your father and your betrothed," replied Caroline.

It was going to be a short crossing.

They landed in Liverpool twenty days later and decamped to Marty and Caroline's Cheshire estate. The girls were wide-eyed with wonder as the big house came into view. Beth felt the warmth of a homecoming as they were met by the twins, who had come home for the reunion, and Ryan and Louise Thompson, who were the managers of the estate and of Caroline's business empire. Ryan was a former captain in the Special Operations Flotilla, the Intelligence Service's mobile unit, and Louise, who was French, was a former agent in the Intelligence Service.

The wedding of Beth and Sebastian would take place in London, as that was convenient for the majority of the guests. Caroline's family would travel down from Sheffield and her brother would take leave from the navy to be there. However, until they departed for London, much could be done in Cheshire as there was an extensive staff, including secretaries.

Lists of invitees were drawn up for both bride and groom's families. This included the bride's godfather, the king. She wrote a special note for him addressed to *Uncle Georgie*. He replied that St James's Church in Piccadilly would be made available if she wanted it.

"I have always planned to get married in St George's." Beth frowned.

"You still can, they are about the same size," Caroline said.

"But, Uncle Georgie ..." said Beth.

"Has only made an offer. It's not a royal command. In any case, St George's has bigger galleries," her mother replied.

"Is it true that he is so fat he can hardly move?"

"I am afraid so. He was large at the coronation, and now he is half as big again. Your father saw him recently and said he must weigh close to twenty stones. He has gout and dropsy."

"He will not attend, then," Beth said sadly. Although her godfather was loathed by most of the population, she had fond memories of him.

"We will see, but I do not expect so."

They put Georgie's condition out of their minds and concentrated on organising the wedding.

"Bridesmaids?" Caroline asked.

"Constance, of course, cousins Flora and Sylvia, and Lady Sarah Montague."

"Only four?"

"God, yes — any more would be unmanageable. Louise will be my maid of honour."

Marty would give her away, of course.

Caroline was full of ideas. "We will move down to London before the wedding, but in the meantime I will write to the vicar and set the date. Your father wants to hold the wedding breakfast at Claridge's."

"It will be late spring, going into summer, so it should be lovely. It's also not far from the church," said Beth with a smile.

Her mother nodded. "And another thing. Your father is trying to get the SOF recalled in time for the wedding. He says the ships are all due a refit, and if they are back then, all of their officers can join us."

A month later, the invitations had been carefully inscribed and sent, and St George's Church and Claridge's were booked. As Marty told Sebastian, "There's no going back now."

The Cheshire household decamped to the London house. Almost everyone invited to the wedding had accepted. The only refusals were on behalf of those too sick to travel or already dead. The good and the great, relatives and friends from far and wide, all travelled to London. The hotels were happy, the dressmakers and gentlemen's outfitters were very happy. Marty and Caroline were renowned for their elegance and sense of style and the ladies attending had no intention of being outdone.

The SOF was recalled and replaced by a "proper" naval squadron which was attached to the Mediterranean command. Marty, though on shore leave, got a hint from Admiral Turner that he should be ready to leave at short notice. He replied that "*short* had better not mean *before* the wedding".

The banns had been read in two parishes: Wimborne and London St George's. Announcements were made in the press, and the scandal sheets swooned at the prospect of the wedding and over how glamourous the happy couple was. Sketches of them were created by the sheets' artists which were abstract to say the least.

"At least they got my hair colour *almost* right," Beth giggled as she perused the latest batch of highly inventive drawings. "This one looks like Aunt Dora!"

Beth's wedding dress was an ivory silk satin slip covered in a transparent silk net, which was lavishly embroidered with silver flowers. She had a veil of Brussels lace — the same lace was also used to trim the sleeves of her dress — and wore her mother's diamond tiara. A six-foot train of the same material as the slip was fastened to her shoulders with diamond brooches. The whole ensemble had been made by Mrs Triaud, the creator of Princess Charlotte's wedding dress. Marty paid for it without complaint, even though it cost close to a year's income from one of his estates.

Beth and Sebastian married in the morning of a fine summer's day. Sebastian looked splendid in full dress uniform with his fellow officers in attendance. Wellington attended and placed himself on the groom's side of the church. This balanced things somewhat, as Admiral Turner, Beth's boss, and George Canning, the foreign secretary and head of British Intelligence, both sat on the bride's side.

Sebastian stood waiting at the altar when a murmur, followed by the sound of people standing, spread forwards from the rear of the church. He turned to see King George waddling up the aisle, supported by two footmen. Another two footmen pushed a large, padded chair mounted on a wheeled wooden platform, which they placed at the end of the front pew.

King George growled, "Sit down, please, this is for my goddaughter," and dropped, sweating, into the chair.

Then the organ blasted into life, playing "The Prince of Denmark's March". The bride was on her way. Sebastian glanced over his shoulder and almost swooned. Beth was angelic, beautiful, spectacular — she glowed with the light from the open church doors behind her, which seemed almost to cast an aura around her. Marty proudly walked beside her in full admiral's uniform. Beth's girls sat with the Shadows, Marty's Special Operations team, and gasped at the sight of her, with a few tears of happiness thrown in for good measure.

Everyone stood up, even the king, and as Beth passed, whispers followed her. Some guests expressed awe at her dress, others whispered encouragements. But Beth only had eyes for Sebastian, and when she reached him she laid her arm on his and gazed into his eyes. She knew King George was there, as they had delayed her entrance to allow him to get to his seat. She dipped a little curtsy, and he gave her a broad wink in return.

Bishop Robert Hodgson began the service. "Dearly beloved, Your Majesty, we are gathered here today …"

George scowled at the addition of "Your Majesty" and flapped his hand at the bishop to get on with it. This flustered the bishop, who promptly started again. "Dearly beloved, we are gathered here today in the sight of God to join together this man and this woman in holy matrimony …"

He droned on until he got to the vows. Sebastian made his: "I, Sebastian Archibald Augustus Ashley-Cooper, take thee, Bethany Anne Stockley, to be my wedded wife, to have and to hold from this day forward, for better, for worse, for richer, for poorer, in sickness and in health, to love and to cherish, till death do us part, according to God's holy ordinance; and thereto I plight thee my troth."

Beth replied, "I, Bethany Anne Stockley, take thee, Sebastian Archibald Augustus Ashley-Cooper, to be my wedded husband, to have and to hold from this day forward, for better, for worse, for richer, for poorer, in sickness and in health, to love, cherish, and to obey, till death us do part, according to God's holy ordinance; and thereto I give thee my troth."

Then, he placed his ring on her finger saying, "With this ring I thee wed, with my body I thee worship, and with all my worldly goods I thee endow: In the name of the Father, and of the Son, and of the Holy Ghost. Amen."

A quick hymn and a few more words from the bishop and it was done. Caroline was crying, Marty was proud, and Sebastian and Beth exchanged a scandalously long kiss. The king roared with laughter and clapped his hands delightedly.

Getting King George to Claridge's was a substantial logistical challenge that was superbly executed by the members of the royal household. The five-minute walk from the church would have been a marathon for George: he was short at five feet two, had a waist of some fifty inches and was grossly overweight. He didn't attempt to walk out of the church, but had his wheeled chair pushed outside, where four grooms then helped him into a coach with an oversized door. The process was probably reversed at the other end, but Beth didn't see that.

The celebration started with the happy couple greeting their guests; this was followed by lunch — a grand buffet. Beth's brother James, tanned from his time in the Mediterranean, hugged her and shook Sebastian's hand.

"I have some news," he told them.

"Is it exciting?" Beth asked a twinkle in her eye,

"For me, yes. The admiralty is giving me a ship — but that means I will have to leave Special Operations."

Sebastian patted him on the back. "You are going back into the real navy?"

"Looks like it!"

Beth hugged him again. "Does Daddy know?"

"I think he might have been behind it."

Beth smiled as she remembered what her father had said in her hotel room that night in Jamaica but kept it to herself. Instead, she asked, "Do you know what ship you will get?"

"The *Talbot* — a sixth-rate, twenty-eight-gun frigate. She is being refitted at Portsmouth."

Then Beth blindsided him with a question that had been burning in her mind for some time. "When are you and Melissa having a baby?"

James handled the abrupt change of subject with aplomb and joked, "In two months, didn't Mother tell you?"

The king asked Beth and Sebastian to present themselves in a private room off the main ballroom at Claridge's. He was obviously tired from his efforts so far and Beth curtsied deeply when she entered the room. Sebastian bowed.

"Tsk, you two do not need to do that when we are alone."

"Alone" was relative when it came to the king. He was always attended by his physician, at least two footmen and the lord chamberlain.

"I have a wedding gift for you." He held out his hand and the Lord Chamberlain passed him a rolled-up scroll tied with a purple ribbon with the royal seal attached. The Lord Chamberlain had a sour look on his face.

Sebastian took it and unrolled it.

"Good grief!" he gasped.

George chuckled.

"What is it?" Beth said and peered over Sebastian's shoulder.

"A house and lands in Surrey!"

Beth read the deed. It was for a property and ten acres of land in the village of Ripley. "Uncle Georgie, you are too generous!"

"Nonsense, you deserve it. In any case, I need to make sure my favourite god-daughter is well taken care of before I pass."

Beth hugged him, which was no mean feat, given his girth. "Don't be silly, you will live for a long time!"

"Pah, tell that to him," he said, indicating Sir Richard Croft, his physician. "Keeps telling me to moderate my indulgences or I will die an early death."

"Well, you could cut down on the food and drink a little …"

George mock frowned at her and waggled a finger. "You, my dear, are the only person who can get away with telling me that. Now, off you go and enjoy the rest of your day. I shall go back to St James's and rest."

Having been dismissed, the newly-weds went back to the ballroom and found their parents talking together.

"Well? What did George want?" Marty said.

Sebastian's father, the Earl of Shaftesbury, generally known as Cropley, raised his eyebrows at the casual reference to the king.

Beth passed Marty the scroll. "His wedding present."

"Poof!" Marty exclaimed and passed it to Cropley.

"Ye gads!"

The deed was passed back to Sebastian, who tucked it away for safekeeping. They would all have to wait to see exactly what the house was like.

While both families were wealthy, a property of their own made the couple independent. That was important, because neither was the heir apparent; Sebastian, as the youngest son, could only expect a small portion of his parents' estate and Beth was a woman, so although she was the oldest child, James would be the main inheritor.

But the guests put all thoughts of wealth aside as they danced away the afternoon until the main banquet and ball began in the evening. The ball was a high-society function, with all of the great and the good who hadn't attended the wedding having been invited.

Beth and Sebastian changed from their wedding outfits. Resplendent in an emerald-green satin ball gown, her hair woven through with strands of jewels, and wearing a diamond-and-emerald necklace and matching bracelet that were a gift from Sebastian, Beth looked stunning and even outshone her mother.

Caroline, for once, didn't mind being upstaged. She wore a pale blue satin dress by the same maker as Beth's ball gown, highlighted with diamonds and sapphires. Marty shed his admiral's uniform for a much more comfortable suit.

The army and navy types kept their uniforms on, and soon there was stiff competition for dances. Caroline and Beth had tried to ensure that there would be enough eligible girls to go around, but there was inevitably a shortage.

James danced only with Melissa, except once when he danced with Beth. The rest of the single ladies and even a few of the married ones enjoyed the attentions of the handsome officers, and not a few trysts were arranged for later on.

Ripley

The next morning, the couple looked out of the window of their room in the Stockley family home, and saw it was a fine day.

Sebastian stretched and looked at his watch — it was a half after eight.

"How do you feel about a little ride out into the country?"

"That sounds like a wonderful idea! Can we get to Ripley?"

"It's a four-hour ride or five hours in a coach."

"Let's get the coach, my backside isn't used to being in the saddle for that long," said Beth. "Is there somewhere we can stay overnight in Ripley?"

Sebastian grinned at the thought. "Being saddle sore would be somewhat limiting."

Beth threw a pillow at him and he tossed it back with a laugh.

"I remember an inn in the village called the Talbot, we could stay there — or at the house if it's furnished."

Decision made, and having asked for one of the family coaches to be prepared, they breakfasted. Marty, who was also a late sleeper when not on ship, joined them at the dining table.

"Off to see your new house?"

Beth looked excited. "We are, yes. We will come back tomorrow."

"I guessed that was the case when I saw your bags being prepared. Anyway, that gives me and your mother a chance to give you *our* wedding present. Come, she is waiting for us."

The couple followed Marty out into the hall and, to their surprise, he headed for the front door. He opened it to reveal Caroline waiting outside. They all stepped out and the newly-weds stopped suddenly, their mouths open. Awaiting them, instead of one of the family carriages, was a brand-new landau with a matching pair of Cleveland Bays. A uniformed driver was on the seat with Garai sitting next to him. Two of the girls sat on a rumble seat at the back and the other two were on the seat behind the driver. Sebastian's personal coat of arms was emblazoned on the doors.

After an exchange of hugs and kisses, they climbed aboard. The seats were of plush leather with loose velvet cushions. Before they left, Marty pointed out a couple of innovative additions to the vehicle. He lifted the front seat behind the driver and revealed a weapons storage compartment that had already been fitted out with a pair of the latest revolving pistols, a blunderbuss, a pair of rifles and several boxes of ammunition. Clothes could be stored under the back seat, in case one needed to make a quick change. The roof was of a design that made it fast to put up and secure, and the wheels were sprung with leaf springs. All in all, it was the best vehicle of its type that money could buy.

The road to Ripley took them over London Bridge and then through Clapham, Wandsworth, Richmond, Malden, Tolworth, Chessington, Claygate and Cobham. They stopped at Chessington to water the horses and grab a light lunch at a coaching inn. Beth and Sebastian were eating at an outside table when there was a shout and a man came flying out through the inn door backwards and landed on his backside. Beth grinned as he was followed by an angry hellcat swearing in Portuguese.

Once Garai had sorted things out, it transpired that the man, a waggoneer, had fondled Paola's behind — which had earnt him a kick to the chest that had sent him out of the door. Paola was joined in her pursuit by her sisters, who berated the poor fellow soundly. Garai helped him to his feet. The man complained of assault — they were only serving girls, after all. Garai then took the man aside and spoke to him quietly. They returned with the man visibly paler. He tugged a forelock to Paola and apologised.

Having finished lunch and rested the horses, the group resumed their journey. The girls, who had been giggling and chatting, asked, "What would you have done, Miss Beth?"

Sebastian answered before Beth could. "I would have called the man out for a duel."

"Would you have killed him?" Paola asked.

"I am sure the rascal would have apologised profusely before it came to that," Sebastian said, and smiled.

Beth took the opportunity to give a lesson. "When I am working, I sometimes have to pose as a serving girl. Then your backside is a regular target for men. If you are lucky, it's just a pat, but sometimes they pinch hard enough to bruise. Then, an elbow to the sternum or a heel on the instep is enough to dissuade them. The trick is to be seductive enough to attract the target, but at the same time to stay in control."

That triggered another bout of chattering as the girls discussed her points. Eventually, things settled down and soon they pulled up in front of the Talbot in Ripley. The coachman asked for directions to their house, which was called Ripley Court.

"Down the High Street and left into Rose Lane, the house is the big one just before the corner. Are you visiting?" the barman said.

The coachman explained that his passengers were the new owners and shortly afterwards the landlord came over and welcomed them.

"We heard that the house had been sold. All the staff are still there, but you need to pay them as they haven't had no money since the old owners left."

Sebastian sighed; it seemed that all Georgie's presents came with a sting in the tail.

The house was a large Regency manor house, set in an elegant garden with a coach house, stables and fields. When they pulled up in front, an elderly man came to the entrance to greet them. Garai jumped from the coach and talked to him; the man looked surprised then ran inside, only to reappear within minutes with the complete household staff, whom he lined up in front of the door.

Once they were assembled, Beth and Sebastian left the coach and Sebastian introduced them.

"I am Major Sebastian Ashley-Cooper, and this is my lady wife, Bethany. We have been given this house by His Majesty King George and intend to make it our home. Now, if you would be so kind as to introduce us?" The last was addressed to the man who stood at the head of the line.

"I am Bates, the house manager, sir." The old man bowed.

"I am pleased to meet you, Bates. Have you been here long?" Sebastian asked.

"Ten years, sir."

"Excellent, please introduce the rest of the team."

They progressed down the line. There was a butler — the elderly man who had first opened the door — a gardener, housekeeper and cook. Then came the lady's maid, footman, kitchen maid, housemaid, chief groom and stable hands. A late arrival, just as they reached the end of the line, was the handyman. He had been working on an outbuilding and had to wash up before presenting himself.

Beth followed Sebastian down the line. The younger maids looked at her with open admiration. She charmed them all, then introduced Garai and the girls — explaining that Netta was deaf and that they would all be expected to learn how to sign to her.

Inside, the house was clean but a little dated. On the ground floor it had a couple of nice-sized reception rooms, a library, a study big enough for two and a dining room. On the first floor were the bedrooms, nursery and dressing rooms. Beth immediately decided that they needed to have at least one bathroom installed. Their bedroom had a large four-poster bed, which was comfortable enough, and they decided to spend the night there.

In the morning, after breakfast, Beth interviewed the housekeeper and cook. She made her expectations clear and satisfied herself that the two women were capable of meeting them. Sebastian interviewed the manager, butler and gardener. He gave the manager money for the household account to pay the staff what they were owed, and to provision the house as required. There were outstanding debts to local suppliers, which Sebastian also covered, as he wanted to get off on the right foot with the local community. All in all, though, the house was in pretty good order.

The elderly butler, Simon, was sixty-two years old. He was unmarried and stated that he was training the footman to take over when he left the position. *And you probably want to die in service,* Sebastian thought.

The gardener complained of a shortage of horse muck, as the stables had been empty for some time. He needed more manure for the rose and vegetable gardens. Sebastian asked what was done with the fields and learnt that the former owner had bred horses and that when he died the farm manager had left.

Sebastian made a note to employ a farm manager and get some cattle and sheep. As an infantryman he was not interested in horse breeding.

"Darling," Beth said as they went to bed at the house for a second night.

"Yes, my love?" Sebastian knew what was coming.

"We should stay here a while and get everything sorted out."

"What about our honeymoon?"

"That can wait."

He understood. Beth had a nest, and now she wanted to make it her own. Sebastian sent a message to the Stockleys' house in London, asking for their things to be sent down. Caroline had anticipated that very request and had made everything ready. Almost as soon as the message arrived, she despatched a wagon filled with trunks.

Within a week the house was ringing to the sound of hammers as new bathrooms were built on the second floor and drains plumbed in for the baths and water closets. The old ovens in the kitchen were to be replaced with new ones from London. A sealed water tank was ordered for the roof space, to supply the water closets and bathrooms. It would be filled, via a pump, from the well every morning, and the water for baths would be heated by a boiler built into the back of the fireplace in the bathroom.

It was all very modern, and the butler looked upon the changes with some distaste. These newcomers were disrupting his life and household. Then there were the *other people* that seemed not to be part of the household. The big man and the girls were an enigma to him, especially as he had found them practising fighting in the courtyard. Even more strange was the fact that the lady of the house joined in, and they were all dressed in scandalous leather outfits!

The newly-weds put the word out that they were looking for a farm manager, and several men turned up at the door to apply. Sebastian and the house manager interviewed them. A young, enthusiastic third son of a local farmer was chosen and installed in a cottage on the land. Ten acres wasn't much by country house standards, but it was enough to breed some cattle and sheep to start with. A second pair of Clevelands was soon purchased from the Guildford livestock market.

A month passed; the repainting and modernisation was now complete, and the house fit for visitors. There was a lingering odour of fresh paint, but large bowls of potpourri helped to mask it. Beth invited her parents to stay.

Marty and Caroline arrived in a coach and four. The Ripley Court butler, dismayed by the arrival of yet more people, ran in ever-decreasing circles until Beth stepped in. The three Shadows that arrived with the Stockleys were housed in the rooms above the stables — this relegated the stableboys, who usually slept there, to temporary accommodation in a stall. Adam, being Marty's valet, was accommodated within the house.

"Simon, you will have to get used to this," the housekeeper chided him.

Simon gave a huge sigh. "I don't know if I can, Sylvia. The young people are changing things too quickly, and they are very strange in their ways."

"I know. Millie tells me they have weapons in the bedroom — and what *are* they doing down in the cellar?"

The story was true; having nowhere secure to store their weapons, the couple and their entourage were keeping them in their rooms. The cellar was being modified to include a barred-off area for weapons, hidden behind new wine racks; the local blacksmith was installing the bars and a carpenter was building the racks. They were both sworn to secrecy and given dire warnings of the likely consequences if they talked about what they were doing.

Marty joined the training sessions in the courtyard. He sparred with Antton in a knife fight while Beth and her mother oversaw the girls' fencing lesson. Caroline, at Beth's request, had brought four new smallswords which the girls initially wore like a new fashion accessory. Now, they were bent on turning them into usable weapons.

Netta turned out to be the fastest learner, followed by Alejandra, who had exceptionally strong and supple wrists. These two paired off under Caroline's watchful eye, and soon had the sparks flying — at times almost literally. Paola and Delfina were not far behind, and Beth gave them her full attention.

They were all aware of the faces pressed to the windows overlooking the courtyard, watching them intently. Things came to a head when the rector of the local church visited in the middle of a training session.

"Good God!" he exclaimed, as the butler showed him through to the courtyard.

Beth spotted him and registered the look on his face. She strode over to meet him. "You must be Reverend Upton."

"I am. What is going on here?"

Beth said, "Come with me, I will explain," and took him by the arm. Leading him to the study, she sat him down in one of the two club chairs. Beth sat opposite and called for tea, then crossed her leather-clad legs.

"You need to know something, but before I tell you I must ask you to swear on the Bible that you will not repeat what I say today to anyone at all."

The befuddled priest agreed and made his oath. Beth thanked him. "Now, you probably know that my husband is a major in the Rifles and my father is an admiral."

The rector nodded, not knowing where this was going.

"Well, we all are members of the British Intelligence Service run by Mr Canning, the foreign secretary. Those people training in the courtyard are in our teams, they work with us."

By now, Upton's eyes were wide. Beth continued. "I am going to ask that you help us to keep that part of our lives a secret from the villagers. All our staff members are sworn to secrecy; now, I want you to spread the word casually that we are just a couple of wealthy aristocrats who are rather paranoid about their security."

She looked the rector squarely in his eyes, which were now gleaming with excitement. This was the most exciting thing he had experienced in all his years' service in Ripley.

"You can do that?" Beth asked.

"Oh yes," said the rector, nodding vigorously. "I can."

"Excellent!" said Beth. "Ah ... here is the tea."

James dropped in on his way to Portsmouth, where he was going to inspect his ship during her refit.

"This is a nice place! I can stop off here on my way from Portsmouth to London. It'll save on rooming fees," he said.

Beth returned his teasing. "That will be nice, we will only charge you for the clean sheets!"

They hugged and laughed. James looked out across the gardens. "It's peaceful here. Quiet, not noisy and smelly like London."

It was true. All that could be heard was the sound of birds singing and the lowing of a cow in the pastures.

"We have chickens for eggs, a cow for milk, vegetables from our own garden and the farm manager says that we will have pigs, lambs and cattle ready for slaughter in six months," Beth told him.

"What about Jamaica?"

"That will depend on the powers that be, but I will be going back when I can."

James smiled — he already knew where his first cruise would take him. "Well, I am scheduled to go to the Mediterranean Squadron."

"That's nice. Does Daddy know?"

"He does, but I don't think he had anything to do with it." Then James looked around the room and asked, "Are you still going on a grand tour for your honeymoon?"

"Yes, we are. Now the house is organised we will be leaving at the end of the month. We wanted to take the *Fox*, but the good admiral said he needed it elsewhere, so Mummy and Daddy are lending us the *Pride of Purbeck*."

The *Pride* was their mother and father's private schooner or yacht. It was armed, but also fitted out for comfort. This honeymoon was bound to be an interesting trip.

Rome

The *Pride of Purbeck* awaited them in Poole Harbour, so their departure presented them with the chance to call in on their relatives in Dorset. That being done, they set sail for Rome. The voyage was relaxed, with the *Pride* making a comfortable ten knots.

The happy couple and their entourage had the ship to themselves and enjoyed the sea air. Dolphins visited and played in the bow wave, and birds performed aerial dances around the masts. The older Stockleys had asked Roland, the Shadows' chef, to accompany them, and the food was spectacularly good.

Upon reaching Rome they took rooms in a house overlooking the Colosseum and Forum. Beth and Sebastian were just another couple viewing the sights, buying souvenirs and eating in the very best of Rome's restaurants.

Beth and Sebastian were enjoying lunch in a café when a man entered from the street, having seen them through the window. His eyes darted around the room as he walked, checking out the occupants of the other tables.

Uh-oh! Beth thought, and nudged Sebastian, nodding at the man as he approached their table, hat in hand.

"Do I have the pleasure of addressing Major and Mrs Ashley-Cooper?"

Sebastian gave him a flat, unfriendly stare. "You do. Who are you?"

"The flowers in Rome are wonderful at this time of year."

Sebastian sighed; it was a recognition phrase. "But the blossom in spring is better."

The man sat down. "Wilson of the Foreign Office."

"We are on our honeymoon," Sebastian said, crossly.

"I know, and I apologise for interrupting, but we have a problem which the ambassadorial attaché in Rome, Mr Thomas Aubin, needs help with. As you are here, Mr Canning suggested that you were ideally placed …"

Sebastian was about to tell him to go to hell when Beth touched her husband's arm and said, "We can at least hear Mr Wilson out and see what the problem is."

"I will finish my lunch first!" Sebastian barked.

"Of course, darling," Beth said, and smiled.

After lunch they walked to the residence of Thomas Aubin, who greeted them in the drawing room and made them comfortable. Once tea had been served, he got straight to the point.

"There is a growing movement for a unified Italy, and we believe that this will eventually reach such a pitch, there will be a popular uprising."

"A revolution along the lines of the French?" Sebastian asked.

"Not as bloody — the Italians aren't as vindictive as the French — but it will change the way the rest of the world has to deal with them."

Beth sipped her tea and took a Florentine. "You mean that we will no longer be able to divide and conquer and have to deal with a central government?" she suggested archly.

"Exactly."

"So, what do you want us to do?"

"You will be visiting Tuscany," Aubin said: it was a statement, not a question.

Beth tilted her head at Aubin. "We were going to visit Florence after Rome anyway. What do you have in mind?"

"Mr Canning suggests that you should first investigate Giuseppe Mazzini, here in Rome. He is the architect of nationalism in Italy. Then you should meet Grand Duke Leopold the Second of Tuscany and offer to help him locate and infiltrate the secret societies that have started to operate there. He asked me to prepare a folder on Mazzini and everything we know about the secret societies."

Aubin stood up and went to a side table, from which he collected a folder that he handed over to Sebastian.

"Mazzini is a political agitator, journalist and activist," Sebastian said as he read a page from the folder. They were on the balcony of their rooms, the Colosseum in the background. Sebastian sat in a wicker chair, his feet on the balustrade. He finished the page and handed it to Beth, who was sprawled on a lounger; a large floppy hat protected her from the sun.

"So I see. He must be upsetting many governments of states affiliated to or run by the Austrians."

"Yes, and Britain has trade treaties with all of them."

"It says here that he was admitted to the University of Genoa at fourteen and graduated with a law degree last year." She checked the paper again. "He is only twenty-two."

Sebastian looked out at the Colosseum without really seeing it. "And he is already tagged as a threat to the status quo." He turned back to the folder. "He's certainly precocious — here is an essay he has written on Dante's patriotic love."

The paper was a crude translation of the original but gave some inkling of Mazzini's thinking. Sebastian summarised this: "He doesn't appear to be a socialist, rather a nationalist who has a fascination with Ancient Rome and has started to promote a unified Italy as some type of Third Rome."

"That implies he wants to get rid of Austrian rule and influence," Beth said, thoughtfully.

"He goes further than that. He wants the Italian people to divest themselves of 'princely despotism and aristocratic privilege'."

Beth sat up. "We should meet him," she said decisively.

Finding Mazzini was easier than Beth and Sebastian had thought it would be. He was practising as a poor man's lawyer in the impoverished districts of Rome. They dressed down accordingly and followed the directions they had been given. Both of them had studied Latin and that helped when asking for directions. However, the Romanesco dialect was at a stage of transition and while it had Neapolitan roots, it was growing closer to Tuscan and that made some words difficult to decipher.

They found Mazzini's house, and waited until the steady stream of visitors stopped, at lunchtime. At this point the young lawyer went to a nearby café. Beth and Sebastian followed and took a table next to his. They chatted in English, which got Mazzini's attention, as tourists were rare in that part of town.

"Excusa me, you are *Inglese*?"

"Yes, we are," Beth said with a dazzling smile. "You speak English?"

"A little. Why you here?"

"You mean in this part of town? Oh, we like to see all sides of a city when we travel. This place gives us a sense of the real Rome."

It took Mazzini a second or two to digest that. "The real Rome is the people."

Beth spoke slowly. "Oh, we agree. Italy is so much more than just the ruins of the old Roman Empire."

"My name is Giuseppe; I am happy to meet you."

"I am Bethany, and this is Sebastian."

The men stood and shook hands. Giuseppe bowed as he took Beth's hand. "I am pleased to meet you," he said in heavily accented English.

Beth and Sebastian kept the conversation light at first and gradually worked it around to politics.

"We are surprised that the Italian people are happy with so much of their land under Austrian control," Sebastian said when Giuseppe made a remark disparaging Austrian influence.

"*Si*. It is our land. Tuscany, Sardinia, Sicily, the Papal States, Venetia; these all are one country with one language."

"It is like Great Britain," Beth said in gushing tones. "All English-speaking people, unified in one glorious … thing."

The men laughed at her running out of words.

"Would you have dinner with us? I would love to hear more about your ideas," Beth asked, blushing.

"I would be happy to. Where and when?"

"There is a café near the Colosseum called Santa Isabella that serves divine food, can you make six o'clock?"

"*Si*, I will be there."

* * *

"He seems pretty harmless," Sebastian said as they reviewed the conversation and wrote a report.

Beth was twirling a lock of hair thoughtfully. "I'm not so sure. He is a fanatic — or rather, is fanatical about his nationalism. That kind of enthusiasm can be contagious. All it takes is for him to attract a group of like-minded followers and it will spread like wildfire."

"I think I see what you mean. He infects ten, who each infect ten, and so on."

"Quite."

The girls, who had been sitting just inside the open doors to the balcony, had been listening.

"He could be the Italian Bolívar," Delfina said.

"I don't know about that, but he cited the Congress of Vienna as being the root cause of the Italian peoples' troubles," Sebastian said.

"What is this Congress of Vienna?" Delfina asked.

Sebastian explained. "The powers in Europe got together to decide the new layout of Europe after the French wars. As part of that, most of Italy was given to the Austrians."

"Was Italy there?" Paula said.

"The states had delegates. The Kingdom of Sardinia, the Papal States, the Republic of Genoa, the Grand Duchy of Tuscany and the Kingdom of Sicily — which together make up what Mazzini calls Italy — were all parties to the Treaty of Paris in 1814. The problem is, due to years of dependence on Austria to provide support and some protection from the French, most of those states had become influenced, if not directly run by them — so when they held the Congress of Vienna it was only natural that they were mostly handed over."

Delfina sat back, satisfied with what she had been told. She could see parallels, even if they couldn't.

The girls were sent to watch Mazzini's premises.

"It's lucky the girls didn't go to the Service Academy in the end," Sebastian said.

"I doubt luck had anything to do with it," Beth replied.

Sebastian's eyes widened as what she said sank in. "You think Turner and Canning *knew* we would be asked to do this?"

"I think that it's all too convenient that we just happened to be here with a full team. Add to that the time it takes to get messages back and forth to London and it makes sense."

"Turner, you devious old …" Sebastian chuckled.

Beth and Sebastian were at the café early. Giuseppe was on time, which surprised them — given that, in Rome, being on time meant anywhere up to three-quarters of an hour late.

The greetings over, Beth asked Mazzini to choose dishes for them, ideally food that was typical of Rome. He ordered *bruschetta*, which was a very nice bread rubbed lightly with garlic and drizzled with good olive oil. That was followed by *fiori de zucca* — courgette flowers stuffed with mozzarella cheese and anchovy and fried in a light batter. They were delicious. Then, he asked for *rigatoni con pajata*.

"This is a peasant dish; try it and I will tell you what is in it afterwards."

It was fantastic: thick, creamy and full of flavour. All three cleared their plates. Giuseppe chuckled when they had finished and told them, "That was the intestines of baby cows that were fed on milk."

Beth almost gagged, then thought, *You eat veal!*

Sebastian looked thoughtful. "It is delicious, not something I would eat every day but a real treat. Thank you."

All of this was washed down with a couple of bottles of local red wine made from the Malvasia grape. To end the meal they had *cannoli*, an ancient dish reputed to have been invented by nuns at the end of the first millennium.

During the meal they talked, and with the couple's Latin and Mazzini's broken English they discovered his admiration of the old Roman Republic, its democracy — as he saw it — through the senate and public elections. He especially admired the way it unified Italy. He went on to expound that Italy could be reunited under a king but with a constitutional parliament not unlike Britain's.

Beth explored Mazzini's political leanings and found that he was a liberal in the true sense of the word. He didn't particularly like the new socialism that was spreading across Europe and thought that the intelligentsia should take the lead in any government. He was witty, intelligent and a good speaker — as one would expect from a trained lawyer.

"I plan to go to Tuscany soon," he told them, and immediately looked mortified at having let that detail slip.

Beth clapped her hands. "Oh, that is wonderful! That is our next stop too — we want to see the Duomo and the tower at Pisa."

A sly look passed across Giuseppe's face; he knew the authorities were watching him and now, quite unexpectedly, he had the perfect excuse to travel.

"My friends, will you allow me to guide you?"

Tuscany

"We have to decide whether or not we reveal the team to him," Sebastian said as they lay in bed later that evening.

Beth rolled onto her side and propped her head up on her hand. "Good point. What do you think?"

"Well, we can't pass them off as our daughters."

"They could pass as servants."

"Four of them? I suppose I could have Garai pose as my manservant."

Beth ran her fingers through the hair on his chest. "You are a major in the Rifles. We told him, remember?"

"Yes, well, in that case Netta can be your niece and the girls are your personal servants."

"That is excessive. Three handmaids are more than the Queen has."

"Well, what then?"

"Delfina is my lady's maid. Paola is a maid of all works and Alejandra is …"

Sebastian had an idea. "How about we tell him that they are Garai's daughters, and we brought them along as their mother died a month before we left?"

Beth instantly warmed to that idea. "And they are taking it in turns to be my lady's maid to earn their keep!"

"That is at least believable."

The problem solved, Beth let her hand slide down her husband's chest.

The team was briefed in the morning. The girls went out and bought plain dresses that were appropriate for their new personas. Their swords were put away and knives concealed. Garai, who was well used to such deceptions, had clothes in his trunk for just such a role.

Two days later, a coach pulled up in front of their rooms. It was of the landau style but only had leather strap suspension. It did, however, have a large rack at the rear to carry their trunks. It was pulled by four medium-sized horses; four spare horses were led by a groom, who rode each of them alternately.

Giuseppe arrived with a medium-sized trunk, which was strapped on top of their luggage. He sat between Netta and Alejandra, opposite Sebastian and Beth. The other two girls sat on a rumble seat with the luggage. Garai sat with the driver.

By changing horses at lunchtime, they were able to cover more than forty miles a day. Their first stop was in San Bernardino, the second was in Ponticelli and the third in Ponticino — they arrived in Florence in the afternoon of the fourth day. Giuseppe, who said he would be teaching at the university and was staying with friends, had them drop him off just inside the city wall. Garai jumped down from the carriage as soon as they turned a corner and followed him. The others continued to the Piazza della Signoria, having rented a house nearby. They would contact the British Legation on the following day.

* * *

Garai was very good at following people. His years with Beth's father, the infamous M of the Secret Service, which had begun when the admiral was just a boy midshipman, had taught him many skills. Following without being seen was just one of them.

Garai was an old agent by most standards, but still fit and capable. He sometimes thought of returning to the Basque country where he had grown up, but deep down he knew that the old country wouldn't be as he remembered it.

Giuseppe turned down a side street that resembled an alley and was empty of pedestrians. Rather than follow and risk being seen, Garai waited at the entrance and watched to see if Giuseppe walked to the end. He did, and as soon as Giuseppe turned the corner, Garai sprinted down the street to the other end of the alley. He was just in time to see Giuseppe enter a house on the other side of the small piazza the street ended in.

He waited; a face appeared at an upstairs window and scanned the square. Another appeared beside it; they talked, then disappeared. Garai stayed just inside the end of the street and watched the house until it got dark — then he went to find Beth.

Garai reported his experiences in detail. "He is staying in a house on the Piazza delle Murate. I saw four different people come and go, and another two inside the house kept looking out of an upstairs window, as if they were on watch. They all acted furtively, constantly looking around and making it obvious that they were up to something."

Sebastian snorted. "Weekend revolutionaries. How old were they?"

"All about the same age as Giuseppe. Some looked like students."

"That makes sense, universities have always been rich recruiting grounds for revolutions," Beth chipped in.

"Ideally, we would have someone on the inside," Sebastian commented. He was cleaning a pistol and had it in pieces on a cloth in front of him. Delfina watched him carefully. He finished polishing a part then put the pistol back together.

"Strip it and reassemble it," he said and passed the gun and tools to Delfina. Then he wiped his hands while looking thoughtful. "If we can't have one of our own on the inside then we will have to recruit one of theirs."

Beth grinned wickedly; she had an idea about *that*.

They watched the house and followed the occupants for a week. In that time they found out who they were, what they did and where and with whom they went to relax.

One stood out as not quite fitting in, a student at the university. He was socially awkward, on the periphery when the rest were out drinking in the evenings, and painfully single.

Alejandra got the job of insider. It was a classic honeypot mission and Beth briefed her extensively. Alie, as they had started to call her, was nervous to start with, but with Beth's guidance she soon became more comfortable with the task.

The setup was easy. The girls went out one evening with Garai as their chaperone and found themselves in the bar that the suspects frequented. In Italy at the time it was unusual for girls to go to a café, so they attracted attention and men immediately tried to talk to them. As foreign servants they were not viewed with suspicion, especially with their father in attendance. The girls were friendly, and the language barrier lowered defences.

Alie hung back and manoeuvred herself to sit near Mazzini's colleague, who sat alone looking glum. She established eye contact and smiled at him, then looked coyly away. He looked confused and then visibly blushed when she let him catch her looking at him over her shoulder.

Alie warmed to her task, and when he plucked up enough courage to smile at her, she moved over and introduced herself.

"I am Alejandra; what is your name?"

"I-I am Stefano," he stuttered.

"You speak English?"

"I am studying languages at the university as part of my studies."

"That is interesting. What other languages?"

The young man was very conscious that nobody had taken the slightest interest in him up until then, and now a pretty girl from he didn't know where was smiling and talking to him.

As she had been directed, Alie told him about her background — the only fiction in her narrative was that Beth and Sebastian were a normal couple on honeymoon, and she told him that she and her sisters had been left motherless and brought up by their father. Stefano's eyes filled with tears when he heard the story, and she took the opportunity to touch his hand. At that moment, Garai called out that it was time for them to leave.

Stefano asked, "Can I see you again?"

"Yes, tomorrow night. Can you wait for me in the Piazza della Signoria at seven?"

All in all, it was a successful evening. Garai took the girls home and Beth heard his report. She coached Alie on her next steps. The girl was to sneak out and meet Stefano, feign interest in his life and let him talk. Which is exactly what she did.

"He smells," she complained to her sisters. "I notice it when we walk together."

"Were you holding hands?"

"Yes, and they were none too clean."

But her sacrifice and tolerance were rewarded when Stefano let slip that he was a member of an organisation called the Carbonari. Beth went to see the agent who was attached to the legation. When she saw him, she recognised him as one of her contemporaries at the Service Academy.

"Brindle, how nice to see you!" she said warmly.

"Chaton, I heard you were coming to Florence. Been here long?"

"A week or so. I have a question. Who or what are the Carbonari?"

"It means charcoal burners." Brindle smirked, then frowned. "It is also the name for a network of secret revolutionary societies that have been around since the turn of the century. We think they originated in Naples and have been influenced by revolutionary groups in other countries that experienced rebellions. Mainly France, Spain and Portugal, but also Brazil."

"Do they have a firm agenda?"

"Not that we know of. They are all very patriotic and liberal but disorganised. Have you been in contact with Mazzini?"

Beth told him all they had discovered and that they had established a link with one of the members.

"So, you have not seen Mazzini since you got here?"

"No, he went into the house that we are watching, and apparently hasn't come out. On the other hand, there have been quite a lot of visitors. He doesn't know that we know he is there."

Brindle looked thoughtful. "I will talk to the envoy and see if he wants to involve the locals."

* * *

Alie was asked to persuade Stefano to take her into the house. That wasn't going to be easy as a frank request could potentially alarm him. The objective was for her to get into the building and "accidentally" meet Giuseppe Mazzini and persuade him to re-establish his connection to Beth and Sebastian.

Stefano was, as Beth put it, particularly thick when it came to taking hints — and so it took several nudges and prods to get him moving in the right direction. In fact, he feared that Alie would be attracted to one of the house's other occupants. She identified and overcame that fear with a promise sealed with a kiss.

And so, Stefano took her into the house, and she feigned surprise when she found Giuseppe sitting in the living room talking to a group of university students. He didn't recognise her to start with and it wasn't until he heard her speak English that the penny dropped.

"Alejandra?" he said when the group broke up.

"Yes. You are Giuseppe, no?"

"Yes. Does your father know you are here?"

She tossed her head defiantly. "No, he thinks I am at our house."

Giuseppe groaned inwardly. He didn't want an angry Garai descending on the house and creating a fuss. "Does he know about you two?"

At this, her defiance collapsed, and tears came into her eyes. "No, he doesn't. Please do not tell him — he would kill Stefano!"

Now it was Stefano's turn to be alarmed.

Alie turned to him. "Pappa is a soldier; he has killed many men."

Stefano's eyes were like dinner plates and his colour went even whiter than usual. Giuseppe closed his eyes to bring his rising temper under control. How could the boy be so stupid? He tried to think of a simple solution and came up with just one possibility. "I will have to talk with Sebastian and get him to persuade your father to give you permission to visit."

The honeymooners were making the most of Florence. They visited the Duomo, with its campanile by Giotto and baptistery. The gothic architecture faced in shades of green and pink and bordered in white was a delight to the eye. Inside, they found monumental statues of St John the Evangelist and David and gazed up in wonder at the richly decorated interior of the dome.

"It is a beautiful building," Beth sighed, "and so peaceful."

Sebastian nodded in agreement.

Just then, a young chorister started to sing, his voice a pure and clear alto. The acoustics were perfect and when he was joined by an older tenor, their voices melded in an angelic duet. Beth and Sebastian stood and listened, entranced.

People were filing in and out. Some to pray or light a candle, others simply to look. Out of habit, the couple kept an eye on anybody who ventured within their alert radius of twenty feet. This was an unconscious act, performed automatically, and only rang an alarm when someone approached directly or behaved oddly.

So it was that Giuseppe was spotted, even though he came at them from the side.

"Sebastian, Bethany ... Garai said you would be here."

"Hello! We thought you were busy teaching," Sebastian said.

"I am, but ... can I speak with you privately?"

Beth smiled. "You two go and talk, I want to look at the altar."

Giuseppe led Sebastian to one side. "This is very awkward for me, but I have to ask a favour."

Sebastian feigned an interested surprise. "Oh? What is that?"

"One of my students is ... well ... um ... *walking out* with Alejandra."

"Really? Does her father know?"

The nervousness induced by this comment caused Giuseppe's accent to get thicker. "Thata isa the problema!"

Sebastian looked stern. "Garai will take a very dim view of that! If she has been sneaking out, she will be in a lot of trouble."

"She said that if he knew, he would kill the boy!"

"Who? Garai? Probably not, but he might give him a whipping. I suppose you want me to intervene?"

"Could you, please? The boy is young, and he is very fond of her."

Sebastian frowned. "She will be punished; I cannot interfere with *that*, but I will ask him to leave the boy alone."

Sebastian looked Giuseppe in the eye. "Do I have your word that they were never left alone?"

"*Si*, I swear."

"How did it go?" Beth asked when Sebastian re-joined her.

Sebastian looked up at the altar.

"Splendidly!"

That evening, Stefano was summoned to meet Garai at the house. Sebastian met him at the door and led him to the drawing room. The young man was clearly frightened, and when the big Basque stepped into the room, he almost wet himself.

Garai had a long knife sheathed on his belt and on meeting Stefano he growled, "Give me one reason why I should not kill you."

Sebastian stepped in front of him. "Now, Garai, do not be so hard on this man. After all, Alejandra was the one who snuck out of the house."

"And she won't be able to sit down for a week," Garai said.

Stefano, who knew that meant she had been beaten, protested. "Sir, we never did anything, we never even kissed!" he lied, hoping that Alie hadn't told her father they had.

"If you had, I would have killed you on the spot." At this, Garai undid his belt and slipped off the knife, which he placed on a table.

Sebastian turned to Stefano. "Tell me what was going on in the house. Quickly now, I need to placate him."

"Giuseppe held meetings, students and members from out of town came to listen to him."

"Meetings about what? What did he talk about?"

The boy couldn't take his eyes off Garai, who snapped the thick leather belt until it was taut between his fists. "He talks about politics and a unified Italy!"

"And these members, where are they from?"

Garai stepped forward, which made Stefano speak faster. "From other groups in other towns. They are Carbonari and come to Florence to hear him. He is a great inspiration to us all!"

"Go on," Sebastian prompted him.

"He talks of the old Rome, how Italy should be one nation, a nation that all Italian speakers belong to."

"How many people attend these meetings?"

"Twenty, twenty-five."

"How many from out of town are there now?"

"Probably fifteen. But what has this to do with me and Alie?"

The belt snaked out and stung Stefano's upper arm. He yelped and cowered.

"Which towns do they come from?"

"Bologna, Pisa and San Marino."

Sebastian stepped back and turned to Garai. "Watch him."

Sebastian left the room, went to the next door along the hallway and entered. Inside were Brindle, Caroline and a captain of the Tuscan Security Service.

"You heard all that?"

"*Si*, I have made notes," the captain said.

"Is it enough?" Beth asked.

"It is. We will raid the house tonight. The conspirators will be rounded up then we will raid their groups in the other towns."

The Princess

The three-month honeymoon was over. They had toured Italy and France and seen the sights. Now they were back in England and settled in their house in Ripley. Sebastian went back to his regiment and resumed command of the 1st Brigade King's Rifles. He lived in barracks from Tuesday to Thursday, coming home on Friday to spend the weekend with Beth. Turner and the Service didn't have a job for her at the moment and she was quite happy about it — she had plenty to do looking after the house.

Her father had been despatched to take over the Mediterranean Squadron, so her mother came to stay. Lady Caroline only brought two servants, Mary and Tabetha. Melissa, who was Beth's sister-in-law, came too. Mary had been Beth's nanny, and Lady Caroline's hint about babies echoed loud and clear for her daughter.

Beth's brother, James, had married before they left India, and his ship would leave for the Mediterranean within the next week. Melissa had a rosy glow about her, and Beth had a strong suspicion that a baby was on its way. She herself was not ready to be a mother, she was still young, and in no great hurry to satisfy her mother's maternal instincts.

And so Beth spent her time finishing the work they had begun before leaving for Italy. Rooms were redecorated and refurnished, hangings replaced, and the gardens landscaped. She enjoyed the gardens and could often be found pottering around with the gardener, a trowel or shears in hand.

All of this ended when a messenger arrived carrying a letter that summoned Beth to the Foreign Office at her earliest convenience.

They decamped to the Stockleys' London house, which meant that Sebastian could see her whenever he was off duty. In due course, Beth arrived at the Foreign Office and was directed to Admiral Turner's office. She was admitted immediately.

"Chaton, welcome back."

"Admiral," she said, and kissed him on the cheek.

He asked about her honeymoon and the Tuscan caper, then got down to business. "Do you know Princess Katharina Alexandra Dorothea von Lieven?"

"The wife of the Russian ambassador? I met her once, I think."

"What was your impression of her?"

"Beautiful, very intelligent, shrewd, comes from a very good family. A star in the political firmament."

"And her husband?"

"Prince Christoph von Lieven? She runs rings around him; his embassy would be much less effective without her."

"We want you to befriend her. She has been instrumental in the creation of the St Petersburg Protocol to govern the future of Greek independence. George Canning and the Russians have agreed to a joint Anglo-Russian mediation of the Greek War of Independence. Unfortunately, George's health has been somewhat erratic lately and we need someone else to stay close to the princess. She also needs protection."

The revelation that Canning was unwell surprised her, as he was Lord Liverpool's right-hand man and surely had to be in fine fettle to do that job.

"Here is our folder on her. She is staying at a resort in Brighton. Canning is there as well."

The way Turner said this made her look sharply at him, but she saw not a flicker on his face to suggest that anything inappropriate was going on.

"Get down there as soon as you can."

"What about Sebastian?"

"He will be busy elsewhere."

"Mother, get packed — we are going to take the waters," Beth told Caroline as soon as she got back to the house. Fede, who had been on guard duty while Beth was on honeymoon, bounded up and head-butted her. She knelt and ruffled the big dog's abundance of neck fur.

"Oh, are we? Where?"

"Brighton."

Caroline looked at her suspiciously. "Is this an assignment?"

"Yes, an easy one."

Caroline didn't believe that for a moment. Nobody in her family got easy assignments. *But then again, at least it will be anything but boring.*

The girls were excited to be going to the seaside. Garai rounded them up and had them choose the equipment they would take. It was a domestic assignment, so they selected lockpicks, strong, thin climbing lines, folding grapnels, jemmies and slim jims. Small, shuttered oil lamps, light mineral oil for lubricating hinges and locks, putty and a diamond glass cutter were also packed for the trip. Everybody had their weapons and a small supply of loose gunpowder. In Brazil, it was usual for women to bathe alongside the men on beaches, but that wouldn't do in England, and they giggled at the heavy woollen swimming suits they would have to wear.

Fede got a new collar and a heavy leather lead. He was now as big as Lord Martin's Mastiff–Shepherd cross, Hector, and had grown out of his old collar. He was as excited as the girls and kept bringing Beth his favourite toy, a rope tied in a Turk's-head knot, which the crew of the *Fox* had given him.

"I will pack it, you big baby!" she told him.

The coach belonged to her parents and was large enough to take all of them and their luggage at a squeeze. But Caroline wasn't going to put up with that, and insisted that a second coach carried Tabetha, Mary and the girls while Garai rode beside the driver of the main coach.

They were to take the direct route, which was around sixty miles, and would travel at a comfortable speed of about eight miles an hour, changing horses every ten miles or so on the way down. The coaching inns would hold the animals in their livery stables until they changed horses on the return trip.

Beth knew that Canning and Princess Katharina were staying at the Old Ship Hotel, a fashionable destination where the Regent had held a ball in 1819. She had sent a message ahead and booked rooms for all of them. In fact, when they arrived with their entourage, they found they had been allocated an entire wing on the second floor.

The doorman almost fainted when Fede climbed down from the carriage and stretched before peeing on one of the planters beside the door. Garai jumped down and put him on his lead as he headed towards the man to sniff his crotch. The big dog sat and watched while the ladies disembarked, eyeing the doorman suspiciously as he held out an arm to help them.

A bevy of porters carried the luggage to their suites, leaving Caroline and Beth to make a grand entrance. Canning sat in a comfortable leather chair reading a newspaper. His security, comprising nondescript policemen, blended into the background. He looked up when the ladies entered and stood up to greet them.

"Lady Caroline, Bethany — what a pleasant surprise!"

Caroline kissed him on both cheeks. "George! How are you?"

"Well enough, me dear. Let me see your daughter!"

Beth stepped up and kissed him as well. He hugged her. "Are you here as Bethany or Chaton?" he asked in a whisper.

"Chaton — T sent me," she whispered back.

"Are you staying long?" Canning asked.

Caroline answered, "A month or so. We will probably return to London for the season."

By that she meant the social season, which ran between November and July. During that time, the well-to-do attended up to two balls a week, in order to network and secure their social status and find husbands for their daughters.

Canning turned to Beth. "And where is that husband of yours?"

Beth knew that Canning knew exactly where Sebastian was, but if he wanted to play this game, she was willing.

"Oh, off playing soldiers with his boys somewhere."

Just then a gaggle of women came down the stairs, led by a beautiful woman with dark hair arranged in ringlets and held atop her head in a circlet of gold. Her hairstyle showed off her elegantly long neck and fine-featured face with large brown eyes. Beth recognised the wives of several politicians and a couple of titled ladies in the gaggle.

When the beautiful lady saw Canning, she made a beeline for him and treated him to a beaming smile.

"George, *mein Liebling*!"

Canning bowed to her and brushed his lips over her proffered hand.

"Princess Dorothea, good evening. May I present Lady Caroline Stockley, Viscountess of Purbeck, and her daughter, the Honourable Bethany Ashley-Cooper."

Dorothea bathed them in her smile and spoke with a strong German accent. "I am so pleased to meet you, will you join us for a promenade?"

Beth stepped forward and immediately noticed that she was a good four inches taller than Dorothea. "Not this evening, I'm afraid, we have just arrived from London and need to rest and eat. Might we meet in the morning? For breakfast, perhaps?"

"Oh, absolutely. I would be delighted. At nine?"

"That sounds perfect. Please, do enjoy your promenade."

Beth and her mother went to the hotel restaurant for breakfast at a little before nine, to find Dorothea waiting for them. Surprisingly, she was without any of the women from the night before. They all took seats and once the greetings were over Dorothea said, "The ladies were all aflutter about you, Lady Caroline."

A waiter poured them coffee and Beth ordered poached eggs while Caroline asked for croissants.

"Please, just call me Caroline. Were they really?" Caroline said.

"Thank you, in that case you must call me Dorothea. They told me your husband is an admiral and fought a duel for your hand."

"That was a long time ago, when Martin was just a midshipman. My former beau at the time objected when he saw Martin paying attention to me, when, in fact, it was I who initiated our relationship."

Beth chuckled. "Oh, do tell, Mother. I have never heard the full story."

"Oh, it was all quite simple. Rufus was drunk and ended up slapping Martin's face. Martin challenged him to a duel and killed him."

"Has your husband killed many men?" Dorothea asked.

"For me? One or two — but then he taught me to protect myself, so now he doesn't need to."

"That is what the ladies said."

"And what did they say about me?" Beth asked and smiled.

"That you won the heart of one of the most eligible bachelors in England, the youngest son of the Earl of Shaftesbury, a major in the Rifles and one of Wellington's favourites. Your godfather is the king, who gave you a house as a wedding present."

"My, they do gossip."

"I also know that you have been in Russia."

At this, Beth immediately went on the alert. "Oh yes?"

"Yes, I was at the Summer Palace when you were there. You used another name, had dyed your hair brown — I much prefer your natural colour — and were supposed to be married to someone else. You were working with Prince Victor and helped to solve the murder of the Grand Duchess."

"I must admit that I do not remember seeing you — and I would have, for you are very memorable."

"I kept myself in the background. The duel you fought was quite impressive."

"A duel? Darling, you didn't tell me!" Caroline said, as if duelling was the most ordinary thing in the world.

"It was nothing."

Dorothea smiled. "It was far from nothing, you fought with skill." She looked at each of the women in turn and waited for their breakfast to be served. "You are both extremely capable and dangerous women. I am going to enjoy your company."

Beth tracked down Canning and asked to see him privately. They met on a roof terrace. Beth had the girls seal it off.

"She knows what I am."

Canning shrugged. "Of course she does, both she and her husband would have been briefed by Prince Victor before they came here."

"Yet you still chose to use me?"

"Yes."

Beth knew that was all the answer she would get. "Can I ask why?"

"She is highly intelligent and probably quite deadly in her own way. She is, however, a diplomat and is trying, with her husband, to come to an agreement with the government on how to solve the Greek problem."

"Surely we want them to have independence?"

"We do but not under the Russian boot. The tsar is maintaining that all orthodox countries should be controlled by Russia."

"We want an independent state?"

"Exactly. Here is the note she passed to me." It was written in French and stated that the Russians had intelligence that the Ottomans had given the Egyptians the go-ahead to conquer any part of Greece they wanted to, enslave the population and replace them with Muslims.

Beth handed it back. "Interesting, is that why my father has been given command of the fleet out there?"

"It is, and you are here to make sure nothing happens to the princess, as well as to be her confidante."

"You think the Egyptians will try something?"

"Neither they nor the Ottomans will want us and Russia to mediate."

Beth knew just what that meant.

Beth decided that the best way to protect the princess was to be with her as much as possible, and to have her under watch when it wasn't. She detailed the girls and sent a note to Dorothea, asking to see her.

Beth was dressing and had got as far as her corsets when there was a knock on the door.

"Princess Dorothea, ma'am," Delfina said.

"Have her come in."

Dorothea stepped into the sitting room and Beth emerged from her bedroom dressed in a silk robe. "Thank you for coming, we need to have a chat," she said.

Dorothea slid elegantly into a chair and looked at her expectantly. Beth continued, "I have seen the note you gave to George. It puts your life at risk, and he has asked me to provide protection for you."

Dorothea's eyes widened slightly, and she looked a little surprised. "Why you?"

"Because I am qualified to be in your inner circle socially, and I have the ear of the king and the government."

"And you are a member of the Secret Service."

"No one knows that — it's a complete secret," Beth joked. Then she crossed her legs and her robe fell open, revealing her garter-holstered pistol.

Dorothea cocked her head to the side as she looked at it. "That is not very ladylike."

Beth grinned. "You don't carry one? Tsk, we will have to change that. Delfina, can you fetch one of my Lill of Louth pistols, please?"

Delfina soon returned with the pistol and a box of cartridges. Beth loaded it and handed it to Dorothea. "Keep this in your muff. Point it at whomever you want to shoot and pull the trigger. The closer you get, the better."

"Well, that makes a change from jewels and flowers."

Beth laughed. "Let me get dressed and we will go for a carriage ride."

Garai drove them, along with the sisters, to a deserted hill outside the town. When they got down, Garai took a pair of six-foot-long planks from the roof of the carriage and set them upright, side by side in the ground. He took a piece of chalk and drew a circle at head height with a body below it.

"What is that for?" Dorothea asked.

Beth grinned and got the girls lined up. "If you have a gun, you have to know how to use it. Garai, would you be so kind?"

"Target ahead. Fire!"

Where there were no guns, guns appeared, were aimed and fired in about a second. Four holes appeared in the target— two where the heart would be and two in the head.

"*Verdammt*, you could have warned me!" Dorothea squawked.

"Now you try," Beth said.

Dorothea took out her gun and pointed it at the target. She pulled the trigger. Nothing happened. Point made, Beth showed her how to cock it. She tried again. A hole appeared above the target's shoulder.

"You are aiming too high and jerking the trigger, aim slightly low and to the left of where you want to hit." She showed Dorothea how to crank the barrels to bring the second one into line.

This time, she hit the target in the chest area.

"That is good enough to stop a man."

The lesson continued and Beth showed her new friend how to reload the gun. Another six rounds and Dorothea was hitting in a nice group.

"My hand hurts," she complained.

"That's enough for now," Beth said.

As they rode back to the hotel, Dorothea asked, "Does your gun only have two bullets?"

Beth pulled hers out and showed it. "This was specially made for me by Francotte in Belgium. It is what they call a pinfire and fires five shots that are twenty-two calibre. Francotte's normal gun is twice the size and fires forty-four-calibre bullets. This has extra-long cartridges to make up for the small bullet. Yours is a three-hundred-and-eighty-six calibre."

Dorothea compared her twin-barrelled pistol to Beth's revolver. "I see, but what happens when you run out of bullets?"

"You run. The girls and I will stand and fight."

Silence fell over the coach as Dorothea took it all in.

That evening, the ladies promenaded again, but this time Beth and her team were in attendance. The girls were spread out ahead of the ladies and Garai brought up the rear. Beth walked close to Dorothea but left space for the other ladies to talk to her. The evening ended with a dance at the hotel, which gave Beth a chance to observe the other guests.

She knew many of them by name or reputation at least, so she concentrated on the ones she didn't recognise. There was a gentleman who was in Brighton alone — which was unusual, as they usually came in groups. Beth tagged him as one to watch; there was something not quite right about him. Another couple were supposed to be on honeymoon, but having just been there herself, to Beth's eye they seemed to lack the passion that she expected. Others were evaluated and dismissed.

Set a Thief

Two weeks had passed, and routines had been established. Breakfast was followed by a dip in the sea from the bathing machines. The ladies were permitted to swim in the morning and the gentlemen in the afternoon. Caroline, who had learnt to swim in the Caribbean, and Beth, who had learnt at an early age, scandalised the other ladies by swimming out to sea away from the machines. Princess Dorothea, who couldn't swim, expressed her admiration.

The sisters began teaching Netta to swim and the princess noticed.

"What is that sign language they are using to talk to her?"

"One we came up with ourselves after she joined us," Beth explained.

"It's very charitable of you."

"It's not charity," Beth said, even though she knew it was. "She is a naturally talented copier."

Dorothea looked puzzled. "Copier?"

"Forger, if you like. She has a natural ability to copy anything she sees with great precision and can memorise anything she merely glances at."

Dorothea raised her eyebrows. "I will have to remember that, if she visits my rooms. Where did you find her?"

"In Havana, her father had rejected her."

"He didn't want her back?"

"He couldn't, I killed him."

This was said so calmly, and in tones that suggested Beth was talking about something completely mundane, that it made Dorothea shudder.

The matron who oversaw the ladies' swimming session called out that their time was up. The ladies went back into their bathing machines and dressed, then returned to their hotels. Beth had just got to her own room when Caroline barged in and practically screamed, "I have been robbed!"

She led Beth to her rooms which were adjacent to Beth's, and sure enough they had been ransacked. The doors were open to the balcony and the lace curtains billowed in the breeze.

"Send Mary to inform the hotel," Beth said, taking charge. She went out onto the balcony and examined the floor, rail and wall. Garai arrived and joined her.

"See up there?" she said pointing to a faint mark on the wall above the door.

Garai stood on a chair to get a closer look. "They came down from above. That's a boot scuff."

Beth leant on the balcony rail and looked up. "There's a window up there on the top floor which could be used to drop a rope down."

Garai examined the doors, which showed the clear marks left by a jemmy. Then the manager of the hotel arrived and started apologising profusely, while telling them he had sent for the police. Beth shut him up and, grabbing his arm, took him to the balcony. "I want to see that room," she said, pointing up at the window.

"That is a storeroom."

"Then take me to it. Come on! No time to lose."

They reached the door to the room, the manager put the key in and tried to turn it. "That's strange — it's not locked."

Beth knelt and examined the lock plate. She moved her head to catch the light. "Someone picked it, there are small scratches that are new."

She turned the knob and pushed the door open. A grubby window let light in from the outside, revealing walls that were lined with shelves on either side of the room stacked with clean linen and towels. Beth and Garai carefully examined the floor.

"There's a footprint in the dust by the window." Garai pointed to it.

Beth looked closer and was struck by the fact it looked quite distinctive. "Fetch Netta. We need to record this," she said.

Netta soon arrived with her drawing board, paper and pencils. Beth asked her to replicate the footprint, so Netta sat cross-legged and started to draw. When she had finished, she showed her sketch to Beth. It was a perfect copy. Beth congratulated her and asked her to wait.

Meanwhile, Garai examined the window. "It has been opened recently; you can see the cobwebs have been broken and there is a scuff mark on the sill."

Beth was checking the rest of the room and found marks around a four-by-four post that supported one end of the shelves on the left-hand side of the room. "Somebody has tied a rope off here."

"And there is another mark on the outside sill where it rubbed the paint off," Garai added.

Netta made drawings of all these marks and was just finishing her work when a police constable and inspector arrived. The inspector announced himself briskly. "Inspector George Gentry, Brighton Constabulary. Lady Caroline said you were up here."

"This point is probably where the thief or thieves rappelled down to my mother's balcony from, and likely returned to," Beth said, showing him.

Gentry merely looked her over with a condescending look on his face. "And you, I assume, are Lady Bethany?"

"Not Lady, just the Honourable — and my surname is Ashley-Cooper. I'm Lady Caroline's daughter. But you can refer to me as 'Mrs', as my husband does not use his title."

"She said you were investigating the theft."

"I am."

The inspector puffed up his chest. "I think you should leave this to the professionals, ma'am."

At this, Beth began writing on a piece of paper she had taken from Netta. "Please contact the prime minister's office and have him verify my credentials," she said, and handed it to him. On the paper she had written: *I am Chaton and I am here to protect Princess Dorothea on behalf of the government.* Once Gentry had read it she took it back and tore it into tiny pieces, which she put into her pocket.

Gentry looked concerned and then almost offended. Beth decided to mollify him and showed him the evidence and the drawings Netta had made.

"You seem to know a lot about breaking and entering," he finally said.

"It's all part of the job," Beth assured him.

Caroline had made an inventory of the items stolen from her, and was sitting with tears in her eyes when Beth returned.

"They took my jewels — the ones that your father gave me."

194

Beth put her arms around her mother and held her. "I will get them back."

Garai was down in the hotel's reception area, asking whether any guests had checked out. None had. He then asked the manager for a list of staff members who had joined the hotel recently. There had been only two new people employed in the last three months, both women. Garai asked to see them. One was obviously pregnant, and the other was an older woman.

Beth arrived and asked to see the guest list.

Inspector Gentry sent a message to the prime minister's office by fast messenger. He was surprised when he got a reply the next day.

You can trust her. You are reminded that her mission is a state secret and divulging any information will result in prosecution for treason.

It was signed by the PM's personal secretary.

"That's clear enough," he said to himself as he screwed the paper up and tossed it into the bin. He had ordered his constables to ask promenaders if they had seen someone descending or ascending a rope on the exterior walls of the hotel.

There was a knock on his door and Beth entered.

"Good morning, Inspector," she said cheerfully.

"Mrs Ashley-Cooper. I trust you are well?"

"Fit as a flea," she said as she sat in the chair on the other side of his desk.

"These are the guests who should be questioned first." She passed him a sheet of paper with six names on. "None of these are known to me or my mother."

"Meaning they aren't titled?" His tone seemed almost, but not quite, to be accusing her of bias.

"Not at all; we know them and their families, so to speed things up we will prioritise the others — and as you can see, one calls himself 'Sir'. But as we have never met him, we cannot eliminate him."

"I see."

"I have another question," she said with a smile.

"Yes?"

"Who are the fencers of stolen goods in Brighton, and where can I find them?"

Gentry looked at her sternly and she caught a flicker in his eye. That flicker triggered a thought. *He's on the take.*

"You cannot go harassing people without due cause," he said.

"Oh, you can't — but *I* can. Who are they?" Her tone brooked no refusal.

Gentry wrote three names and addresses on a sheet of paper and handed it to her.

"Thank you," she said, and rose to leave.

"Be careful around those men. They are dangerous," he said, nodding towards the paper.

Beth smiled back over her shoulder as she left the room. "So am I."

Soon after she left, a sergeant came in. "Was that her?"

Gentry sat back in his chair. "Yes, and she checks out."

"We will have to watch her, then. Don't want her upsetting the apple cart."

"She is going to see Samuels, Goldsmith and Payne."

"I'll send them word. They will get rid of her."

I wouldn't be so sure, Gentry thought.

* * *

Beth set a double watch on the princess's room that night and took Garai and Paola on a tour of the older side of Brighton. The Lanes formed a network of alleys and narrow roads full of shops and small businesses. Among them were pawn shops, antique shops and jewellers.

Their first target was a pawn shop owned by Payne. The front door was barred and locked on the inside, as was the window. Garai pointed to a second-storey window that was open. Beth nodded and moved along the row of shops until she found a downpipe. Then she pulled on calfskin gloves and started to climb.

Up on the roof she pulled a skein of rope from her backpack and secured it to a chimney before dropping it over the side. She connected it to the harness she wore on her lower body with a short length of rope tied with a friction hitch, and lowered herself over the side.

She dropped to the level of the window, quietly entered the room and released herself from the rope by undoing the hitch. It was a bedroom, and a man and woman were asleep in the large bed. Beth watched and waited as the rope jerked, and a minute later Garai came in through the window. Paola stayed in the street on watch.

Beth moved over to the man's side of the bed and drew a stiletto from her sleeve. She laid the point under his eye and prodded. The man awoke and immediately froze.

"Good evening," said Beth softly.

"What do you want?" The man had a terrified look on his face.

His wife rolled over and Garai stepped up with a cloth and flask in his hands. He carefully sprinkled some drops from the flask onto the cloth then held it over the woman's nose and mouth. She struggled a little before falling still.

"She will sleep," Beth said calmly.

"Are you going to kill me?"

Beth chuckled, a sound that sent chills down the man's back. "Not yet. I know that you are George Payne, a pawnbroker and fence. You have paid off the local police and have what looks like a thriving business."

The man continued to look terrified. "How can I help you?"

"Aah, I see that you will be a businessman until the end. I am going to make you the offer of a lifetime. Your life, in return for the name of the man who stole jewels from my mother, and the safe return of those jewels. If he comes to you, you are to send a message to Chaton at the Old Ship Hotel."

Payne was visibly frightened. "There are others, he may not come to me."

Beth smiled; it didn't help.

"I know, and I will be visiting them as well. If one of you is approached and doesn't give him up, I will kill all of you, and your families. You see, I tend to bear a grudge."

"What if he tries to go out of town?"

Beth prodded him a little harder with the blade. "He won't be able to; the description of the jewels will be in every paper in the land and anyone travelling from Brighton by whatever means will be searched. It will be impossible for anyone to sell the jewels or the stones that make them up. Now, enough of your what-ifs, I have other fish to fry."

Garai came forward and applied his cloth once more. Payne slept.

They found the jewellery shop run by Goldsmith. He had obviously been warned of their impending visit, as there were men patrolling the narrow lane.

"It seems the inspector is looking after his friends," Garai grumbled.

Beth was not impressed. The men were big but moved slowly, like bears.

"Let's take them out as a warning. Damage them, but don't kill them."

Beth and Paola circled around to come down the lane from the other end and, as they approached, Garai started in from his end. The two lumbering men didn't see them coming in the faint light of the gas lamps, and didn't notice them at all until they were almost upon them.

Garai took the direct approach and in three fast steps was close enough to apply his blackjack with devastating force to the man's wrist, removing the club the thug was carrying. He followed this with several blows to the ribs and head. Beth was more elegant. Paola worked her way behind the man while Beth distracted him. Then, with Paola in position, Beth launched a fearsome thrust kick to his face. His nose broke with a satisfying crunch and, as he stepped back, he tripped over Paola, who had knelt behind him. Unfortunately, he had never been taught to fall properly and landed on his head.

Paola stood and looked down at his recumbent body. "Is he dead?"

Beth checked his pulse. "No, he is still breathing, but he is going to have one hell of a headache when he wakes up."

Garai, who had rendered his victim unconscious with a deft tap under the ear, joined them. "Are we going through the front door?"

Beth nodded and knelt to pick the lock, which took only a few seconds. When the door cracked open, she reached up to muffle the bell that hung above it. Inside, the shop was a treasure trove of cheap jewellery. As they passed through to the room at the back, Beth took the lamp from her belt and opened the shutter. There was a large safe and her fingers twitched; she really enjoyed opening safes, but she put that urge aside for the moment. A door led to a staircase, which took them to Goldsmith's apartment.

Garai led the way and paused to listen at the door at the top of the stairs, which had a sliver of light showing along the bottom. He signalled, telling them he could hear voices. Beth closed the lamp and passed it to Paola. She pulled a pistol from its holster on her bodice and drew back the hammer. Garai did the same, then counted down with his fingers.

The door burst open when Garai's boot hit the lock and they dived into the room, Garai going right and Beth left. Before the men — who sat at a table — could react, they found themselves looking down the barrels of pistols and froze. Paola took pre-prepared cords from her belt and tied their hands behind their backs and their ankles together. A third cord was looped around their necks through the chairback, under the seat and tied off tightly to the ankle cord. Gags were applied and, their first job done, the group moved on to the top floor, where the bedroom was.

Goldsmith was asleep, secure in the delusion that his four thugs would keep him safe. He was dreaming of jewels when a woman appeared in his dream holding an extraordinarily large knife that dripped blood. She advanced on him and thrust the knife towards his throat. He woke with a start.

Something cold and sharp was resting just below his chin.

"Hello, Mr Goldsmith," said a very feminine voice.

He swallowed and felt the blade's edge touch his Adam's apple. He very slowly moved his head so that he could see her.

"What do you want?"

"You know what? That is exactly what Mr Payne said."

Goldsmith resisted the urge to swallow again. "Payne? You have seen him?"

"Oh yes, such a nice man. Got the message almost immediately."

"Which was?"

"Someone will probably approach you with stolen jewels, which they want to fence. You will send a message to Chaton at the Old Ship Hotel if and when this happens, and I will take the jewels. You will also tell me who the man is. If I find out that he has visited you and you have not told me, then you, Payne and Samuels will all die along with all your families. Oh, and before you ask — this thief cannot go anywhere else to fence them as the town has been sealed."

"If I take the jewels I will have to pay him. What happens to my money?"

"You will get it back, and your reward for your co-operation will be that you keep your sorry life."

He tried not to speak, but the words came out of his mouth anyway. "Surely I deserve *something* for my trouble?"

"Spoken like a true dealer. Fifty pounds to the man who gives up the thief ... if you hand him to me, tied with a bow."

Their third visit was close to dawn. The antique shop run by Samuels was in the better end of the Lanes, near North Street. Samuels also had guards.

The team took to the roofs nearby. It was too close to daybreak to start a fight. The house had a skylight, set into what once had been a servant's bedroom. Beth dropped through it after springing the latch with a slim jim. Then she went down the garret stairs, testing each in turn before putting weight on it.

The stairs led onto a hallway, which had two doors opposite each other. Beth edged forwards and listened at the one on the right. Garai indicated to Paola to listen to that on the left. Beth could hear nothing and glanced at Paola, who nodded. Just to be sure, Beth cracked open the door and looked inside. Two children lay asleep on the bed — a boy of about six and a girl who was probably around nine.

Beth closed the door and moved over to its opposite number. She tried the knob. Locked. Out came the lockpicks. The key was in the lock on the other side.

She sat back on her heels and whispered instructions. Paola went into the room with the children and Garai moved to stand in front of the door. Then Beth heard a faint click, and reacted immediately by pushing Garai to the side.

The middle of the door exploded as a full charge of buckshot blasted through it, leaving a gaping hole.

Beth looked across the door to where Garai stood with his back to the wall. They heard a gun being reloaded.

The pair moved as one. Garai kicked the door out of its frame and Beth plunged through the gap, pistols at the ready. Samuels sat in a chair, frantically reloading a blunderbuss. Beth fired and the bullet smacked into the gun's stock, ripping it from his hands.

"Now *that* was just anti-social," said Beth, as Samuels shook his hand.

Garai moved out onto the landing to cover the stairs that came up from below. He held both of his full-size, eleven-millimetre-bore revolvers cocked and ready to fire.

Beth kept Samuels under her guns, a pair of full-size Francottes. Samuels looked down the large bore of one, like a rabbit staring at a stoat.

Beth decided to open the conversation. "Now, you were obviously warned I was coming. Who told you?"

Samuels said nothing.

"Oh, I see that you're going to be tedious about this. Look, I am in a hurry and haven't the time to beat the answer out of you. My colleague is in your children's room and in five seconds I will tell her to cut the throats of one of them. So, who told you? Five, four, three, two …"

"Sergeant Richardson sent word!"

Beth was not surprised.

"At the behest of Inspector Gentry, no doubt."

"We pay them protection money," Samuels said.

"Oh, I'm not interested in that. Someone stole some jewels from a resident of the Old Ship Hotel, and I want them — and the man who stole them. This is the deal. If you are offered the jewels, you inform me by sending a message to Chaton at the Old Ship. If you present him to me tied up with a bow, you will earn yourself a fifty-pound reward. If he approaches you and you do not tell me, I will kill you, the other two fences and your families."

"That is pretty clear."

A shot rang out from the hallway.

"It is time for us to go. Tell the sergeant he will have to answer for his indiscretion."

Beth woke at lunchtime and went to find her mother. Alie told her that Caroline was with the princess, so Beth went to her rooms. The women had just returned from bathing.

"Are you refreshed?" Caroline asked.

"Yes, thank you. It was a busy night."

Dorothea looked at her quizzically.

"Beth was out chatting to some of the town's underworld last night," Caroline explained.

Dorothea leant forward conspiratorially. "Lady Dorrington said there was some trouble in the Lanes last night. Was that you?"

Beth leant closer to her and whispered, "It was."

"What will you do now? This is all very exciting!"

"I will pay a visit to Inspector Gentry to see what he has found — and to have a word with him about his sergeant's loose tongue."

They sat and chatted for a while and Beth made sure both women had their guns to hand. She was happy that her mother also carried a silver-bladed knife that the king had given her. Then she excused herself and went to find the inspector.

She didn't have to go far: he was interviewing one of the hotel's residents in an office near the reception area. She watched through the glass-panelled door and waited. Gentry finished and the man he had been talking to stood up. Beth looked at the man's feet. *Something* nagged at her, then she realised that his shoes were of the same distinctive shape, long and narrow, as the imprint that Netta had copied. She smiled at him as he left then stepped inside to talk to Gentry.

"Who was that?"

"It was Mr Alexander Mitchell of South Shields, he's here to take the sea cure for his arthritis."

Beth memorised that information as she closed the door and took the seat that Mitchell had just vacated. She looked at Gentry as he finished making a note — and when he looked up and saw her face he asked, "Something wrong?"

"There was trouble in the Lanes last night."

"So I heard."

"Men got hurt because your sergeant tipped them off. Shots were fired and property was damaged."

Gentry started to look uncomfortable and became visibly more so as Beth continued.

"I have no interest in the fact you take protection money from the fences, but when that conflict of interest interferes with my investigation, you force me to take action."

Gentry stood up, banging his fists on the table. "Now look here, young lady—"

"Sit down!" Beth barked. "I will report to George Canning what I have found here. Now, whether I mention your indiscretion or not is going to depend on the outcome of the work I'm currently doing. In short, your career as a policeman is hanging in the balance."

Gentry sat down, having suddenly realised that he was way out of his depth. This girl had connections he could only dream of. She went on. "Your sergeant — what is he called? Aah yes, Richardson. Sergeant Richardson is to resign and leave the force or face consequences from me that will not be pleasant and may be life-changing."

"You can't …"

"Oh, I can — and with impunity."

Gentry nodded. He believed her.

"Thank you. Now, tell me what you have found."

Mr Alexander Mitchell was the only suspect who did not have a cast-iron alibi for the time of the robbery. Beth waited until he left the hotel later that afternoon, carrying a bag with his bathing suit and towel. Then, she went to his room, to which the manager had given her a key. Upon entering, the first thing she did was check his windows and doors for tell-tales. There were hairs placed across the windows and on doors between the frame and the moving parts.

Now why would you do that? She smiled to herself.

Beth began to search the room, taking care to make as much mess as she could. If Mitchell was the thief, she wanted to scare him into making a rash move. She didn't expect to find the jewels in the room; he was a professional and would have stashed them somewhere else by now. However, she did find a pair of shoes with soft leather soles. She took the left one, and a bag with a couple of strands of hemp stuck in the cloth at the bottom. Then she carried on searching.

In time, she found an envelope taped to the bottom of a drawer. She opened it — and froze as she read the letter inside.

Assassination

Beth put the letter back where she had found it and finished the job. She returned to her rooms and sat down — she badly needed to think. Someone knew more than they should, the hidden letter had made that clear — and that someone was being paid by someone in government.

She remembered the signature on the letter — the letter "R" in red surrounded by a swirl coming from the leading leg. But why steal her mother's jewels? It was nonsensical, all he did was attract attention to himself. She wished she could talk to her father.

Garai came in and dropped into a chair. He looked at her and asked, "Something troubling you, Princess?"

He hadn't called her that since she was five years old, and Beth was about to chide him for it when realisation hit her like a sledgehammer.

"He is trying to distract me!"

Garai frowned. "You've lost me."

"The robbery is a distraction. He wants me to be looking the other way."

"From what?"

"From Princess Dorothea."

"Oh, so I think the next question is, *who* wants you to look the other way?"

"That is the question."

"Our man whose room you wrecked today?"

"He is probably the thief, and therefore the distraction, but that does not mean that he is the person who will carry out whatever action it is that they do not want me to see."

Garai blinked and took a second or two to sort that out. "We need to find out who and what, then."

"Yes, and at the same time we need to make them think that their strategy is working," Beth replied.

Beth went to the writing desk and wrote a message to Turner. In it she asked him to try and find out who signed their letters with a red "R". She drew a copy of the signature, blotted the letter, folded it and gave it to Garai. "Send that by messenger, please."

A horse-borne messenger could do the sixty miles to London in six hours if he changed horses every ten to fifteen miles. She had addressed the message to Turner at his home.

A little later, when Beth was alone, she pulled out the list of hotel residents and went through it. This time, she did not discount those she recognised or had met.

Lady Farquhar, husband Sir Ronald, a confirmed Tory and a member of the East India Company.

The Honourable Mable Smythe, spinster and sixty years old.

And so she went on, annotating each and every one. Then she went back and crossed out those she felt she could be absolutely sure of due to their age or position. Then she had a thought and went down to reception.

"Has anybody booked in since I got this list?"

The clerk pulled out the register and looked. "Yes, three people."

Beth leant over and spun the register around so she could see it.

"A foreign gentleman and his wife," the clerk said when Beth pointed to an entry that said *Mr Omar Kamel*.

"Do you know where he came from?"

The clerk went to a pigeonhole and pulled out a card. "He is Persian and has an address in London. Number twenty, South Street."

Beth frowned. That rang a bell.

"I need a fast messenger."

"Your man booked one just now; he will be here shortly."

"Good," she said, and took a sheet of paper and a pen to write a second note for Turner.

There was no word from any of the fences, nor were the jewels found in any of the searches. This merely served to confirm Beth's growing suspicions. Mitchell had complained to the police that his room had been broken into. That didn't remove him from Beth's suspicions, rather it confirmed that he was confident in his cover.

The more she thought about it, the more she was convinced that if an attempt was going to be made on Dorothea's life, it would be soon. The letter had said the theft should occur between the seventh and fourteenth and it had happened on the seventh. It was now the tenth. She reasoned that the assassin would only count on the theft to distract her for a limited amount of time, and that time was running out.

Alie came in. She had been following Mitchell. "He had breakfast at a café then went to the bathing machines as usual after a walk along the front," she said.

Beth was suddenly inspired. "Does he use the same machine every time?"

"Yes: I asked the attendant, and he has rented one for his stay."

Beth grinned. "Get some rest. We will be out late tonight."

That night, two figures dressed in black slipped through the poorly lit streets. Moving from moon shadow to moon shadow, they made their way along the front to the men's section of the beach. A watchman was making his rounds and walked past without seeing them as they stood stock-still between two bathing machines.

"It's the fourth from this end," Alie whispered.

The door to the bathing machine had a padlock; Beth examined it by touch. "It's a GR Patent. You have practised on it. You can pick it."

All the girls had practised picking their practice locks blindfolded, so this should not be much of a challenge. Alie took out her lock-picks and selected the appropriate pair. Thirty seconds later, the lock hasp was open. They entered the machine — which was basically a beach hut on wheels — and after closing the door, opened their shuttered lantern.

Beth panned the light across the room. "Let's see now. Where would he stash them?"

The machine had a set of clothes hooks on the left wall, above a bench seat. Along the back wall were shelves and above them a high window which had curtains. Beth closed the curtains before proceeding. Below the shelves was another bench seat. The right wall was bare.

She scanned the light along the back wall again, sighed in frustration ... and then said, "That's not a bench, it's a chest!"

The bench was indeed a long chest. It had a lock, and this time Beth picked it. They carefully lifted the lid after checking for any tell-tales or traps. The chest was half full of towels, but under those towels was a satchel, and inside that were the jewels.

"Got you!" Beth snarled before putting everything back as it was and locking the chest.

"You left them there?" Caroline asked angrily when Beth told her about their adventure the night before.

"Of course I did. They must not know we are on to them, if we are to catch whoever wishes Dorothea harm."

Caroline was not mollified. "Oh, I see," she said, hands on hips.

Beth hugged her then held her at arm's length. "I have them under watch. Now, come on, we are meeting Dorothea for our daily swim."

Beth checked the group of women who went swimming. It was made up of the usual suspects; nobody stood out or was new. She stayed close to Dorothea during the swimming session and joined her for tea afterwards.

Dorothea asked about the theft. "Have you made any progress in finding your mother's jewels?"

"Not really," Beth lied, and then sighed dramatically. "I fear we may never find them."

"That is a shame. She told me they were irreplaceable."

Just then, a porter came to their table and handed Beth an envelope. "This has just arrived by messenger, ma'am."

She broke the seal, which she recognised as Turner's. The letter inside was in his neat script.

The R signature has been traced to an independent member of parliament, Matthew Rashford, a merchant with strong ties to the Ottomans. His entire business revolves around trade with Constantinople and therefore a licence from the Ottoman government.

Twenty South Street is the house used by the Egyptian Consulate.

Be bold.

T

"Well, well, well," Beth murmured.

"Something interesting?" Dorothea asked.

Beth looked at her, suddenly all business. "Yes. How do you feel about taking risks?"

That evening, Dorothea had dinner alone and retired early to her rooms on the first floor. Beth had skipped dinner, complaining of a headache to Caroline as they passed through the crowded reception.

As usual, one of the girls was on watch in the corridor outside Dorothea's room. At around midnight, the watch changed.

The moon disappeared behind a cloud and for some reason, the street lamp outside the hotel had gone out. A figure climbed the exterior wall of the hotel, invisible to the casual observer. This was made easier by the raised brick decoration that had been used on the corners of the hotel walls. Reaching a balcony, the figure made its way horizontally from balcony to balcony by leaping the gaps between them. In due course, it reached Dorothea's.

The balcony doors succumbed to a slim jim, and the figure slipped inside Dorothea's bedroom. The sleeping princess's dark hair was spread across the pillow. The figure stepped silently across the plush carpet and picked up a cushion, held it in both hands and placed it over the sleeping woman's face.

Beth stepped out from behind the curtain, where she had hidden when she heard the door catch being slipped. Now, she positioned herself in front of the open door. She drew the hammer on her pistol to full cock.

"Put your hands behind your head."

The figure moved fast and spun, throwing the cushion at her gun hand. Her finger tightened on the trigger instinctively, and the pistol fired. The bullet went wide, and the gun was knocked from her hand as the figure barged into her. This was somebody strong, a man.

Beth grabbed him and tried to apply a hold that Chin had taught her. An elbow hit her in the ribs, and she let him go. They squared off. He was slim but bigger than her and obviously experienced. Beth tried to use reason. "Give up, you won't get away."

There was no reply, only a kick that she narrowly avoided. Beth bounced on the balls of her feet, her fists raised to chest height. Her opponent tried to circle, and Beth's left foot stabbed out with a head-high kick that narrowly missed, forcing him back the other way.

He bent down and pulled a knife from his boot then held it, point forward, with his thumb along the back of the blade. At this, Beth took a knife from its sheath on her belt and held it back-handed so the blade lay along her right arm.

They sparred, testing each other.

He attacked and Beth retreated, but her leg hit a chair and put her off balance. He closed, making the most of his advantage, his knife slashing forward at her belly. But it found only air as Beth twisted unexpectedly to her left, against her momentum. Her left hand flashed out and hit the side of his head with a crack.

***

"Who is he?" Dorothea asked. She had come in from the sitting room, where she had been sleeping on a chaise longue.

"Let's see," Beth said, and pulled the balaclava from the man's head.

It was not Kamel. Neither of them recognised him. "Get Delfina in from the corridor," Beth said.

Delfina came in with Garai, who had been waiting outside with her. He examined the recumbent assassin. "You used a peg?"

Beth tossed him the four-inch lignum vitae rod she had held in her left hand. It was the densest wood in the world and the peg was surprisingly heavy.

"Nice," he said, and tossed it back.

"I know him. He is Kamel's servant." He stood and went to the bed, laughing as he pulled back the covers. A bolster formed the body, a shop mannequin head and a wig did the rest.

There was a groan as the man started to come round. Garai rolled him onto his side and secured his hands behind his back. The would-be assassin threw up.

"Happens every time," Garai said.

Beth looked down at him dispassionately. "He's all yours." She turned to Delfina. "Let's get the suspects rounded up. Fetch your sisters, tell them to bring guns."

The next morning, a sorry-looking group was gathered in a spare room. All wore handcuffs. Among them were the servant, Kamel and his wife, and Mitchell. Paola and Alie stood guard with pistols in their hands. Beth sat at a desk, writing a report. There was a knock on the door and Inspector Gentry entered with a pair of constables.

"Are these them?"

Beth didn't look up until she had finished her sentence. "They're the only ones in cuffs, so I suppose so." Gentry gave her an angry look. She ignored it. "They are to be held until they are collected by members of the Security Service. I expect them tomorrow."

"The jewels?"

"Have been returned to my mother."

"What am I to charge them with?"

"You aren't."

"But ..."

Beth's look stopped him. "I will stay here until the princess leaves and be in charge of her security. I expect the continued support of the local police," she said.

Admiral Turner stepped down from his coach in front of the Old Ship Hotel and raised his umbrella. The weather had reverted to type, and it was raining. He walked up the steps and nodded to the doorman, who took his umbrella from him, shook it and placed it in a stand. Unencumbered, Turner strolled through the reception area and into the café, where he joined Beth and Princess Dorothea.

Beth hugged him and kissed his cheeks. "What news?"

"My, you are impatient," he laughed.

Dorothea poured him a cup of tea. He took a sip and sighed in satisfaction. "Rashford has been questioned and admitted that he bowed to pressure from the Ottomans to employ Mitchell. He is retiring from Parliament and taking up bee-keeping to amuse himself, since his import licence has been revoked. We have added him to our watch list. Kamel and his wife have been deported; they were not Persians but Egyptians, as you thought, and only here to get the servant into position. He is now languishing in prison. He was the real threat, as he is an assassin for the Egyptian government."

Dorothea leant forward. She had concluded that Turner was something to do with the security services or government.

"What news of my government's proposal?"

"George Canning is putting it to Parliament and expects their full approval. We will co-operate."

Dorothea beamed. "Excellent, so we can all return to London."

Beth laughed. "Yes, let's. I think we have seen all we need to of Brighton's attractions!"

Steam

Beth and Caroline decamped back to London with Dorothea in convoy. She had a house in Hayes Mews, which was not far from the Stockleys' house in Grosvenor Square. Sebastian was still on detachment down on Salisbury Plain, so Beth was in no particular hurry to return to Ripley.

She reported to Canning and was immediately concerned for his health. He was prime minister now, but also pale and frail looking. When he coughed into a handkerchief, Beth noticed it was spotted with blood. It was the last time she ever saw him; he died from tuberculosis just two days later.

The funeral was in Westminster Abbey, where Canning was interred. Even though he was prime minister for just 119 days, his reputation as a statesman and orator drew large crowds.

A fortnight later Admiral Turner asked Beth to meet him in his office. She left most of her weapons at home, knowing she would be searched before entering the Security Service offices.

"Morning, Chaton."

Beth knew from that greeting this was going to be a business meeting. "Good morning, T," she replied, taking the offered seat.

Turner sat behind his desk. "Johnson will succeed George as PM."

Beth knew him, he wasn't half the statesman Canning was. "Viscount Goderich? Do you think he will last?"

"I think he will have a hard time, but that's not why I asked you here. *Our* new leader is Arthur Wellesley."

Beth smiled. The Duke of Wellington, or "Uncle Arthur", who she had known since well before the battle of Waterloo and who was a very good friend of her father's, should have become the next prime minister, in her opinion.

"You have shown excellent investigative skills in your missions so far, and that has put you at the top of our list for the next one." Turner gave her an amused look. "It will keep you out of trouble until your husband returns from Tidworth."

"What do you want me to do?"

"You know that the development of steam power has accelerated, and we are on the brink of having both passenger railways and steam-powered ships. Stephenson's railway between Stockton and Darlington has been running for a year or so now, and has proven the concept. His son is developing a faster and more reliable engine, but you know that because your mother is one of his investors."

Beth nodded; she knew he would get to the point eventually.

"Stephenson Junior thinks someone is stealing his designs. He has noticed that drawings have been moved from where they were left overnight. He suspects someone is copying them." Turner leant forward, a serious look on his face. "We have a very strong lead over all the other nations in this sector, and if all goes to plan we can dominate the railway industry for years to come. However, if someone *is* trying to steal the technology, and succeeds, it could seriously damage our future economy."

Beth dredged her memory for information she had garnered from her mother's conversations about the railways. "Robert Stephenson and Company are based in Newcastle, I believe. Edward Pease was the original investor."

"Yes, and Pease remains part of the company, along with George Stephenson. Go up there and find out what is going on, and if necessary, stop it."

"I will leave in the morning."

"Good. In the meantime, please give my love to your mother."

"I will."

Beth rose and Turner came around his desk and embraced her. "Be bold."

Beth chuckled at how James Turner never said, *Be careful.*

Beth returned to the house and wrote a coded message to Sebastian, telling him she was going to Newcastle. Her mother didn't ask questions and simply helped her to pack. She could tell her daughter was setting out on a mission from the array of implements and weapons they packed, and the black coveralls her team used for night work.

Fede was not going to be left behind and pointedly carried his lead into her bedroom and dropped it onto the bed. Beth laughed, hugged him and then packed his toys.

Beth hired a coach for the trip, which would take thirty hours including stops. There was a regular service but there were six of them travelling and she didn't want to share with strangers. Also, the fare for the scheduled coach was five pounds and fifteen shillings per person inside, and as it was moving into autumn, she did not want any of the girls travelling on the outside seats. Garai was a different matter, he insisted on riding next to their driver, armed with a blunderbuss and a pair of revolvers.

The vehicle was a stagecoach, built to withstand long journeys. It was pulled by four large Welsh Cobs, the horse used by most carriage companies and easily replaced like-for-like at coaching inns.

They made themselves comfortable in the coach. The luggage was on the roof, covered by a tarpaulin and held in place with a net. Outside, it was a balmy sixty degrees Fahrenheit with the threat of rain. The driver flicked his whip and the horses moved off. Garai settled down for the long drive, with a long coat and hat to hand in case the weather broke.

They would take the Great North Road, so headed north through Camden Town and on to Whetstone, where they changed horses for the first time. They overnighted in Peterborough and were on the road again at a half-hour after six the next morning.

"Cheer up, girls, only another day and a half to go," Garai chirped at their grumpy faces.

They were passing through a wooded section just south of the village of Ranby in Northamptonshire when there was an attempted hold-up. This was unusual but didn't catch Garai by surprise. He had been watchful from the moment he saw they were heading into woodland. He lifted his blunderbuss from where it lay at his feet and pulled the hammer to full cock. The driver nodded; this was a notorious stretch. Garai stamped twice on the footplate.

Inside, Beth pulled out her larger revolvers, which she carried in a bag that lay on the seat beside her. The girls, taking her cue, armed themselves.

The driver cracked his whip above the horses' heads and the coach sped up. But this was to no avail as a tree crashed down, blocking the road. Several men came out, armed with muskets.

That's when it all went wrong for them.

Garai blasted the man standing closest to him with the blunderbuss, then immediately dropped it and pulled his pistols. The doors burst open, surprising the highwaymen. Beth burst out of one side, guns blazing, while Delfina mirrored her on the other side. Paola and Alie knelt in the doors, shooting over their heads.

There was hardly any return fire as they had taken their assailants, who only carried single-shot guns, completely by surprise. The hail of fire was beyond anything the men had expected or experienced in their lives and they threw themselves to the ground whether they were hit or not.

Silence settled after Garai bellowed for them to cease fire. Gun smoke drifted away on the breeze. A man cried out in pain.

Beth was on one knee, her guns raised. She stood and walked to the nearest man to her. He lay still, face down in a pool of the blood leaking out from his chest. She nudged him with her foot. He did not move.

She moved on to the next man, who was the one making a lot of noise. He was holding his gut. Beth pulled his hand away and examined the hole. "Nice shot, Paola!" she called out.

There were three men on the other side. One was missing most of his head, thanks to Garai's blunderbuss. Delfina checked the other two. One had been hit in the arm, the other cowered in a crouched position, crying.

"Get up. Move over there with the other one."

He did not move, so Delfina kicked him. He stood up and staggered over to his friend, who was grey with shock. Garai climbed down and searched the survivors before binding wounds and tying their hands.

They left the dead where they were — somebody else could come and get them — and the gut-shot man was loaded into the coach. The other two were tied with a rope behind them and had to walk. Netta sat on the roof with her gun, watching them.

They cleared the road by unhitching the front pair of horses and dragging the tree out of the way. The horses were re-hitched and they made their way to the village. It was very soon apparent that the village was where the men came from, so they would have to take them to Worksop. The two dead men were married and had children. The gut-shot man turned out to be single and was blamed by the widows for leading their men astray. Of the other two men, one was an eldest son and due to be married, while the other, the only man unwounded, was married with a baby son.

Beth took pity on them, partly because she was in a hurry, partly because she saw their plight. She made a point of smashing their muskets against a tree in the centre of the village, then spoke to the women.

"Your men were unlucky to come up against us and they were stupid to listen to that man." She indicated the gut-shot man. "He will die. There is no doctor who can save him. His gut is torn open, you can smell it. You can give him a quick death or let him suffer. It's up to you."

The women put their heads together and one stepped forward as spokeswoman.

"Please, miss, we do not want him to suffer but none of us has the stomach to end him. Can your man do it?"

Beth understood their reluctance. "I will: I do not ask others to do something I can do myself."

She walked into the hut where the dying man lay. Everyone was expecting a shot, but after a minute she returned.

"He is dead."

Beth had slipped a stiletto between his ribs and into his heart with surgical precision. He hadn't even felt her do it.

They arrived in Newcastle and took rooms at the George Inn, where the coach terminated. It was close to the middle of the town. Two and a half days of being bumped over the imperfect roads had exhausted them all, although Garai showed no signs of fatigue as he bullied the porters to get the luggage unloaded and up to the rooms.

Beth asked for baths to be prepared and was told that there was a bathhouse at the back of the inn, complete with changing room. It was free that morning and they could have it all to themselves. Intrigued, she and the girls went down and entered the red-brick building. Inside it was warm, and they were met by two female attendants, who directed them to the changing rooms. The attendants were scantily clad, with their hair tied up. Beth wanted to inspect the bathhouse before she stripped.

"Can you show me around first?"

There was a steam room, where they would be washed by the attendants, a room with a large hot-water pool and finally a cold room where they could rinse off.

"Where did this come from?" Beth asked.

"Mr Jack visited Constantinople as a sailor, ma'am, and saw the bathhouses there. When he bought the inn he had the bathhouse built."

Beth liked the fact there were no windows in the walls, just skylights that let natural light in. It was very private. She undressed and wrapped herself in a large towel before entering the steam room. This had benches around the walls and a stove in the middle, heating rocks that the attendants poured water over to generate the steam. She sat and relaxed, letting the heat seep into her joints.

Delfina and Netta had started the process while Beth was looking around, and the attendants now had them laid face down on what Beth initially thought were tables. The attendants sponged them down with soapy water from buckets. They weren't gentle, and applied the natural sponges with vigour. Beth noted that Netta had acquired a chrysanthemum tattoo like the sisters. The process was repeated on their fronts; modesty was not catered for.

Paola and Alie went next, when the first two moved on to the hot-water pool. Then it was Beth's turn, and the older of the two women beckoned her to take her place. When Beth lay on her towel on the table, the woman looked at her body for a long moment. She traced a scar left by a sword cut.

"It looks like madam has had an interesting life," she said as she applied the sponge.

"It's had its moments," Beth said, enjoying the sensation.

"Why lass, you have muscles like a swordsman! Your girls have as well." Her accent was pure Newcastle with an almost musical inflection.

The woman had felt something and started kneading a tight spot behind Beth's right shoulder blade. Her fingers were like iron, and it hurt to start with. Satisfied she had dealt with it, the woman moved on, working her way down Beth's body.

"Turn over, lass. Are you married?"

"I am — to a major in the Rifles."

The sponge worked its way across her upper body. Thankfully this was with a gentler action than had been used on her back.

"Another scar," the woman said, tracing a line across her lower ribs. Beth did not comment. The woman looked at her hands. "Delicate on this side and the calluses of a swordsman on this side."

Beth gave her a calculating look; she was far too observant. "I fence."

The woman grunted something in reply, which Beth did not catch, then said, "My son is in the Rifles."

"He is?"

"The ninety-fifth."

"That is my husband's regiment."

"He is a chosen man and was at the king's coronation." She sluiced the soap off with clean water and Beth sat up.

"Then he is in my husband's battalion. What is his name?"

"Graham Bell. His mates call him Dinger."

"I will mention him to my husband when I next see him and have him pass on your regards."

"He can read and write; I will write to him and tell him I met the lady with the lizard tattoo."

Beth looked down at her wrist and smiled.

The bath completed, they had supper brought up to their rooms and went to bed. Sleep came easily, and Beth dreamt of Sebastian.

The next morning, Beth and the team took a walk to Forth Street, which was a scant half-mile away. The Stephenson locomotive works was larger than she had expected, and they were stopped at the gate and asked their business.

"Chaton, to see Mr Stephenson. He is expecting me."

The man called a boy over and instructed him to "guide the lady to the office". They were taken through the factory, which smelled of charcoal forges that were heating rivets, and rang to the sound of hammers striking hot steel. A partially completed engine stood in the middle of the floor surrounded by men. A grey-haired man in a black suit detached himself from the others and walked over to join them. He introduced himself in a Northumbrian accent.

"George Stephenson."

"Chaton. Nice to meet you."

"Robert is up in the office."

Beth took some time to examine the older Stephenson. He looked unexceptional, with a high forehead. Not bad looking for his age. Obviously very intelligent, an engineer. They climbed a staircase to an office that overlooked the shop floor, and entered. A large drafting table stood in the middle with desks at the far end. A younger version of George was bent over them.

"Robert, the investigator from London is here."

Robert looked up and blinked as he focused on Beth. He looked surprised. "Pleased to meet you. You are not what I expected."

Blunt and to the point, thought Beth, who smiled and said, "I am who I am. Did you expect a man?"

He looked flustered at that but recovered himself. "To be honest, yes."

George Senior chuckled behind her. "You asked for help, and this is what they sent you."

Beth sighed inwardly; she had expected this. In so many places it was a man's world and the merest hint that a woman could do something other than keep house was unthinkable. Well, she would show them. She pulled off her silk gloves. "You appealed to the head of the Intelligence Service because you think that someone is stealing your designs. What makes you believe that?"

Robert looked at his father, then turned back to the table. "When I work, I keep my drawings in a particular order, placed on the table to make working as easy as possible. Sometimes, I arrive in the morning to find them disturbed."

That echoed what T had told her. "Have there been any indications that they have been copied?"

"Like what?"

"Pencils missing or left in odd places, paper stocks disturbed, indentations."

Robert looked confused. "Indentations?"

"What was the last set of drawings you think might have been copied?" Beth said.

Robert went to a cabinet and opened a drawer. He pulled out some papers. "These."

"Can you lay them out on the table, in the arrangement they were in before they were disturbed?"

Robert cleared the table, carefully stacking his drawings before moving the pile to his desk, then laid out the drawings as he had been working on them. Beth beckoned Netta over and asked her to remember the layout. Then she told Stephenson, "Now, move them to where they were in the morning when you came in."

Robert shifted several sheets then stood back and looked at them before making a couple of adjustments. Beth signed to Netta, "If you were copying, would you move them like that?"

Netta walked around the table, looking at the papers. She stopped and signed, "I would stand here and yes, I might disturb them if I was careless."

"What's all this finger-wiggling about?" George asked, somewhat crossly.

"Netta is deaf but has the ability to copy any document after glancing at it just once. She is also a superb artist and draughtswoman. *Finger-wiggling*, as you call it, is how we communicate."

"Hmmpphh."

Beth stepped forward and turned several sheets over. She looked across the reverse side of one in the light from the window.

"Can I have a soft pencil, please?"

She placed the sheet on the table and gently ran the pencil back and forth, so it shaded the paper. When she had finished, she showed the result to Robert and George.

"Look familiar?"

"It is the design of my new cylinder!" Robert exclaimed.

"The indentation was caused when someone rested another paper on this one and copied your drawing."

Robert looked at her with a new respect. This lady was nobody's fool.

Beth looked around the office. "Now, the questions are *who* and *how*." She went to the door and examined the lock. "Is this locked overnight?"

Robert pulled out a key ring that was attached to one end of his watch chain. "Yes, and I have the only key."

Beth turned to Stephenson. "If you look at the outside, you will see there are no scratches on the plate around the keyhole. So even though this is a simple lock, I do not believe our perpetrator came in this way."

Her next stop was the window. The dust on the sill was undisturbed; it seemed unlikely the lock had been moved since the summer. That left the skylights. "Is there a way we can get to the roof?"

"There is a ladder on the back wall."

They led her out through the workshop to a back door, and then out into a yard. Here, there were open side sheds where they stored the steel stock. Attached to the wall was an iron ladder. Beth looked to Garai; this was, for the sake of decency, a job for him. He grinned then shinned up the ladder and disappeared onto the roof. A few minutes later, he reappeared and came down the ladder.

"The skylight has been opened with a slim jim."

Beth took them all back to the office. "We now know how and what was taken. What we need to find out is by whom."

"How do you intend to do that?" George asked, now with respect in his voice.

Beth thought for a moment. "Whoever it is knows what he is looking for. So somehow, he is learning what you are working on and knows when to pay a visit."

George looked up angrily. "You mean someone here is giving away secrets?"

"Probably not deliberately. Do the men visit a pub after work?"

Robert was intrigued as to where this was going. "Of course; it is hot work, and they like a pint or two at the end of the day."

"And they probably talk about their day. Anybody who had an interest could listen in."

"Ye gads! It's that simple?" Robert exclaimed.

Beth explained. "Espionage is the art of gathering information in the simplest way possible. You only have to resort to exotic means when faced with a security-conscious organisation, like a government."

George looked at her and around at the team. "Is that what you do?"

"Sometimes."

Robert looked troubled at the thought of this beautiful woman and her bevy of pretty girls being involved in such devious activity. "So, what do we do now?"

"We lay a trap. Do you have anything you are working on that is new and exciting?"

"New, yes. Exciting? I suppose another engineer would find it so. I have a new design for a boiler."

"Talk about it to your men," Beth told him.

* * *

That evening there was a new serving girl in the Stoker's Arms. A tall, pretty redhead who joked with the customers in a near-perfect Cumbrian accent. The men from the factory came in and took up their usual tables. She served them beer and they teased her, and she joked with them. Not one recognised her as the lady who had visited two days before. She stayed in their part of the bar and listened to the conversation. Sure enough, they talked about the new idea Mr S. had for a new boiler and how it should improve the power of the engine.

There was no one obviously listening, but there were many men in the pub, all dressed similarly. Nobody stood out.

That evening Beth and Garai camped in the office, sleeping on bedrolls. Both were light sleepers, and the slightest noise would wake them. Nothing happened, nobody came. They stayed the next night … and the next.

On the third night Beth lay looking up at the skylight, wondering if the spy would ever show up, when a shadow passed over the glass. She was immediately alert and nudged Garai. They quietly moved into the shadows at the edge of the office.

A strip of metal appeared at the edge of the skylight and slid sideways to spring the catch. A rope dropped from the now-open skylight and a body slipped down it.

They waited. A lamp was lit and the person, intent on his mission, pored over the drawings on the table. He went to a cabinet and took out a fresh sheet of paper and laid it on the table, on top of the other drawings.

That was enough.

Click, click.

He froze.

"Hello," Beth said from where she stood, a pistol in her hand.

"His name is James Whitby, and he hails from America," Beth told them. "He has been gathering information to send back to his employer, who has ambitions to build engines over there."

"And does not want to pay the licence fee," George growled.

"We recovered, from his lodgings, the copies he made," Beth continued. "It seems he visited five times in all."

"What will you do with him?" Robert asked.

"He will be coming back to London with us, where he will face a closed trial for espionage."

"He will hang?"

"Probably not. But I don't expect he will see the outside of a prison for quite a while." She grinned. "Or until the designs are obsolete, at least."

Interlude

A week later they were back in London, and Beth was reporting to Turner. Whitby was incarcerated in the Tower, awaiting a special trial. The American ambassador, Albert Gallatin, arrived to meet Turner at the same time. Beth, wanting to keep her identity hidden, listened to their meeting from an adjoining office.

"James Whitby is an American citizen and I demand his release," Gallatin said evenly.

"I'm afraid that is not possible, he was caught red-handed copying industrial designs in a blatant act of espionage," James Turner responded.

"By whom?"

"By one of my agents."

"What were your agents doing, chasing down commercial problems?"

"It was a problem of national importance."

The ambassador's voice remained remarkably calm. "So, it involves trade, no doubt — or at least future trade."

He's a sharp one, Beth thought.

"When will the trial take place?"

"I have no idea, that is out of my hands. You will need to talk to the home secretary," Turner replied.

The two men said their goodbyes, cordial until the end. When Gallatin had left, Beth opened the door and entered. Turner was chuckling.

"It didn't *sound* funny."

"He knew what Whitby was up to. He wants him released so they can get the information. We will frustrate him while being as nice as you like about it. Then, when the information Whitby collected is outdated, we will release him."

"Well, given the speed at which Stephenson Junior is coming up with ideas, that won't be long."

Turner sat on the edge of his desk, looking more relaxed than she had seen him in a long time. "You can have some time for yourself and that husband of yours. The girls need to go to the Academy, and Garai wants to re-join the Shadows."

"I suppose I should look for a replacement for him," Beth admitted.

"There are a few candidates who have passed through the Academy but didn't make full agent. Perhaps one of those might fit?"

"I will contact Kingfisher about them."

"Excellent." Turner stood up and embraced her. "Now, go and enjoy life for a while. Sebastian should be home in a couple of days."

Ripley was empty, or so it seemed to Beth. She was used to having the girls and Garai around all the time. Garai had left on the first available packet to the eastern Mediterranean and the girls had gone straight to the Academy. Sebastian wasn't due home for another day.

She sighed, and decided to go for a walk. It was a chilly day, so she wore a coat and scarf, and had a muff to keep her hands warm.

She had her knife in its garter sheath and one of her Lill of Louth pistols in the muff.

"Come on, boy," she called to Fede, and they took off down the drive together. Her intention was to walk through the village and on to the River Wey. The river had been made navigable in 1653 and connected Guildford and Godalming to the Thames near Weybridge. Beth liked to watch the barges come and go.

As she walked through the village, she was greeted with polite how-do-you-dos accompanied by a touch of the forelock from the men and a little curtsy from the women. Fede dissuaded most from getting too close by his large presence alone. Once out of the village, Beth was left alone on a quiet lane.

Beth followed that lane and came to the Seven Stars pub. She had never been there before but knew that it was popular and run by a woman. She continued on to the river, which had a towpath that was well kept and ideal for walking.

They had been walking for a few minutes when Fede suddenly stopped and stared out into the water. Beth watched and waited until a coot popped up. Fede woofed, surprised — he had never seen a diving bird before. A barge approached, being pulled by a large, plodding shire horse. Beth made Fede sit next to her out of the way as the horse passed. The bargeman's wife stood on the roof of the cabin, her man at the rudder; they waved and called a hello. Beth waved back.

In time, they reached Newark lock. The gates were open at that end and a teenage boy was running down the towpath towards Beth. She assumed he was heading to the gates to close them, but no, he kept coming. Then she saw he was being chased by two other boys.

Fede saw the boy coming and assumed he was a threat to his boss. As the lad approached, he took the initiative and leapt up, knocking the boy in a heap. He stood over him, growling. Then he saw the other two. Fede barked a warning, and the two boys skidded to a stop. He stayed over the first boy, who he now sensed was frightened, and watched the other two, who seemed angry and threatening.

Beth was initially surprised by Fede's lunge to knock the boy down, then pleased when he stood over him to protect him from the other boys. She now saw that these were armed with knives.

"Stay still and he won't hurt you."

The larger of the two boys made a fighting pose, thrusting his knife forwards. "He can try, and I'll stick him."

"Really? Then I will have to shoot you," Beth said, and pulled her gun from her muff. The eyes of both boys widened as they looked down the barrels. "Now, put the knives down on the ground and back up three steps."

The boys — or rather, young men, she decided as she looked them over — complied. Beth called Fede to foot, then told the cowering boy to stand up. He seemed to be seventeen or eighteen.

"Now, why were you chasing him?" she asked the other two. The boys did not answer, they merely glared at her and the other boy. Beth turned to their quarry. "What's your name?"

"Billy, ma'am."

"Well, Billy, why were they chasing you?"

"Don't know, miss."

Beth knew all three must have been up to no good if not one of them was willing to talk about it. She pondered various courses of action and was about to take them all back to the village when a bargeman came down the path. He held a crank handle for the lock sluice, and was obviously intent on getting his barge through the lock, but when he saw the group he kept walking towards them.

He took in the tableau in front of him: two young men standing belligerently and a lady with a gun in her hand beside a third lad.

"These boys giving you trouble, ma'am?"

Beth treated him to a smile. "You know them?"

"Those two standing there are known to us bargemen. They steal from boats. That one is my nephew."

"Really, have you told the constable?"

"No point, ma'am, they don't care about us river men. We have to make our own justice."

He pointed at Billy.

"You tell the lady what was going on."

Billy was looking sheepish. "They wanted me to tell them when barges were carrying stuff worth nicking. I wouldn't, and they threatened to cut me. That's when I ran."

"Why didn't you tell me that before?" asked Beth.

"'Cos I ain't no snitch."

Beth looked to the bargeman. "Do you know the Seven Stars?"

"Yes ma'am, I do."

"Meet me there."

Fede herded the boys along the path to the pub. Beth had their knives and covered them with her pistol. When they arrived, she had them sit on opposite sides of a table. Sarah Rogers, the landlady, came over. "Can you have someone fetch the constable, please?" Beth said.

Sarah despatched a boy, saying, "Tell the idle sod that the lady from the big house wants him here double quick." Then she returned to Beth. "Can I get you a drink while you wait, ma'am?"

"Call me Bethany, and yes, some tea or coffee would be lovely."

Sarah was surprised at this. Ladies were not usually that friendly.

* * *

The constable arrived. He was an older man, and judging by his girth and the redness of his face from hurrying, he didn't move around much. He took in the boys, the dog and the gun, and then stopped dead. He focused on Bethany.

Eventually, he found some words. "Lady Ashley-Cooper, isn't it?"

Beth ignored the incorrect title.

"Yes." Beth looked over her shoulder as the bargeman arrived. "Good, then everyone is here." She went on to explain how she had found the three boys. "Now, the bargeman, Mr ..."

"Reed, ma'am."

"Mr Reed tells me that they have complained to the constabulary about these two stealing from their barges and were ignored. Now these young criminals have tried to intimidate this young man into telling them when the barges are carrying valuables. When he refused, they threatened to cut him."

"You want me to arrest them?" the constable asked reluctantly.

"Yes, and I want you to take statements from Mr Reed, Billy and myself."

The constable pulled a leather-bound notebook from his pocket and dug around until he found a stub of pencil. The notebook looked unused. Reed gave a sworn account of thefts on the river that the two young men had been seen at. Billy was encouraged to tell his story. Beth told her own tale, and signed the copy.

"Do you have manacles?" Beth asked, when all the administration was complete.

The constable, who was called Moor, produced a pair. Beth took them and cuffed the two rascals together. "Please take them to the local gaol and I will send for the inspector in Guildford."

With the two taken care of, Beth bought Reed and Sidney, his nephew, a pint of ale each. Reed sipped his after raising his glass to Beth. "Thank you, missus. No one takes notice of us bargees. We are treated as bad as gypsies."

"Everyone should be treated equally under the law. I will make sure the magistrate takes this matter seriously."

Beth was as good as her word and attended the magistrates court to give evidence. She intimidated the magistrate, who was aware of her family connections, and he sentenced the young men accordingly.

Sebastian came home after the exercise at Tidworth ended two days later, and because the brigade was now back in its barracks in Winchester, he could come home regularly. Beth didn't like the fact she couldn't see him all the time, so started looking for a house nearby. She found an appropriately large furnished house for rent in St James's Lane and it became their married quarters.

She had written to Kingfisher and in time his reply found its way to Winchester. "He has three candidates in mind to replace Garai," Beth told Sebastian.

"Does he say how the girls are getting on?"

"Yes, they have all progressed well and, in his opinion, will make a strong support team. He even says we should give them a name, like Father's Shadows."

Sebastian chuckled. "I think you should let them name themselves. It will be interesting to see what they come up with."

Beth agreed and read some more of the letter.

"I will have to go to Coleshill. Kingfisher is going to gather the candidates there."

"When?"

"Next week."

Coleshill Academy had not changed since Beth graduated, and as her coach drove through the gates she felt happy. She had done so much since leaving and her return brought back happy memories.

The coach pulled up in front of the doors and Arthur, the porter, came over to help her down.

"Chaton, it's nice to see you here again."

"Thank you, Arthur. Are you well?"

He answered as he always did and always had. "Vigorous, miss. Vigorous. Kingfisher is waiting for you, I informed him that your coach was approaching."

Beth made her way up to Kingfisher's office on the third floor, knocked and entered when he called. He was standing by the window, looking out at the exercise yard at the back of the house. He turned and greeted her. "Chaton, as always, a pleasure to see you. Your candidates are down there."

Beth joined him at the window and watched the men as they exercised. They were all obviously fit. Kingfisher went to his desk and picked up three dockets. "These are their records."

Beth took the dockets to a side table and sat down to read them. The first was Gregor Sterling, code name Badger. A Scot who had been at the Academy the year before Beth. An excellent operative but lacking the spark that would make him a good agent. He had all the skills she wanted in her team leader. The second was Stanworth Appleby, code name Storm. Again, well qualified with several years of field experience, and he had been a team leader on two occasions. The third, and oldest of the three, was Michael Holder, code name

Wolverine. He had been on active duty during the war with Napoleon and a sergeant in the Marines. He had been recruited to the Service when he was released in 1816. He had ample skills and was a renowned fist-fighter, having been the Marine champion for two years.

"I'd like to meet them," Beth said, putting the last folder down.

"Of course." Kingfisher smiled and led her out of his office and down to a room on the ground floor. "In any particular order?" he asked as they walked down the stairs.

"Storm, then Badger, and Wolverine last."

The room was a small sitting room with comfortable chairs. Beth settled into one and waited. Minutes later, there was a knock on the door and Storm entered. Tall, dark and handsome, he moved with confidence and grace. Beth, who had his docket on her lap, indicated that he should sit down. He was clearly appraising her as he took the seat opposite.

"You have a decent record and led a team. What was its make-up?" Beth asked succinctly.

"Four men and a woman. The men were chosen for their fighting skills as the mission was a raid on a suspected spy's house. The girl was on the inside."

"Did you choose the team?"

"No, ma'am."

"If you could, would you have chosen differently?"

"I would have chosen at least one good housebreaker beside me. It would have been more balanced."

They talked some more about his experience, then Beth asked, "Have you met my girls?"

"The tattooed quartet? Yes. I have spoken to the older one."

"Do you remember her name?"

"Aah ... no, I don't."

Beth asked a few more questions, thanked him and dismissed him.

Badger came in next. She instinctively disliked him. There was something about his attitude that rubbed her up the wrong way. After a few questions and answers, she thanked and then dismissed him.

Wolverine knocked, then entered when invited to do so. Once in the room, he awaited her invitation to sit down. Beth observed that he was like his code name: stocky, well-muscled, with broad shoulders and bulging biceps. He looked as if he could run all day. His hair was cut short and salt and pepper in colour. His piercing blue eyes, and their unwavering regard, were the most immediately striking things about him.

"Please, do sit down."

"I know your father, Admiral Stockley," Wolverine said as he did so.

"Do you?"

"You are the spitting image of your mother. I met her when I was a private back in '17, in the Med. She had come to Gibraltar to see your father."

"You have a good memory." Beth then turned the conversation to his training and experience in the Marines. Then she asked. "Have you met my girls?"

"I made a point of it. Delfina is a nice girl, very good at remembering things. Alie is sharp as a needle and Paola is a born killer with those punch daggers of hers. I was just beginning to make conversation with Netta; the girls showed me the signs."

That did it. She made her choice.

The Company of Wolves

Normal life continued until the fateful day that a letter arrived with Turner's seal. Sebastian sat and watched Beth open it.

"I am ordered to London for a briefing."

"No hint as to what it's about?"

"Nothing. Or where it will be held."

Beth harrumphed; as much as she enjoyed active duty, she liked being with Sebastian more. Nonetheless, she took a coach to London and sent a letter for the team at the Academy to go to the London house. Her mother was surprised to see her and divined the reason immediately. Caroline passed on a potentially vital piece of information to Beth.

"I do not know if this has anything to do with it, but your ship and its companion are moored in St Katharine Docks."

"Could it be they are sending me back to the Caribbean?"

"It would be nice if they were."

The butler entered with a message on a silver tray. He offered it to Beth, who glanced at the seal before producing a knife to slit it open.

"It's from Turner."

She read it, frowned and read it again.

"He wants to meet me at his house, tomorrow morning at dawn."

It was so early when Beth set out to Turner's home that a nightingale was singing in Grosvenor Square. It was a half-hour before dawn, and cold. Wrapped in a fox fur coat with matching hat and muff, Beth used the brass knocker to announce her arrival.

"Come in, madam, the admiral is expecting you," Edney, his butler, said. "Can I take your coat and hat? The admiral is in the library."

Beth knew where that was and, having deposited her hat, coat and muff, took herself there. Turner was seated at a table with papers spread out in front of him. He looked up when she entered.

"Come in, my dear, make yourself comfortable. I apologise for the disgustingly early time, but I have to be in Cabinet all day."

"Good morning, you look chipper."

"I have to be, the Cabinet is examining the Service funding today, and I have to be on form. But that's not why I asked you here."

Beth took a seat and looked at him attentively.

He continued. "You did a great job down in Brighton, so much so that the princess has asked for your help with her mission, since it is beneficial to both countries. She needs to move between here and Russia to complete it."

"Is that why the *Fox* and *Cub* are at St Katharine Docks?"

"It is, and both are ready to sail."

Beth furrowed her brow. "Isn't St Petersburg ice-bound this time of year?"

"It is, which is why you will have to land as close as you can and then proceed overland."

"When do we leave?"

"As soon as you are ready. The princess is ready to go whenever you are."

"I will visit her today. The team gets back tomorrow, and we need a couple of days to get fitted out with cold-weather clothes."

Turner looked at his calendar. "That should be just fine. Now, off you go, I have a lot of preparation to do."

She rose and as she passed him, kissed him on the top of the head. He held her hand briefly in farewell.

"Be bold."

After breakfast she called for her carriage and went to Dorothea's house. It was a still, gloomy, cold day and the smog hung low over the rooftops. The coach clattered to a stop at the door and Beth stepped down. The windows of the house shone with light and a face appeared at a ground-floor window before disappearing. She was halfway up the steps to the front door when it opened.

"Miss Bethany?" the girl said.

"Yes."

"Madam is expecting you, please come in."

The girl took her coat, hat and muff and showed her into a grandly furnished reception room, where Dorothea stood waiting. They embraced like old friends.

"I am so glad you could come," Dorothea said.

"I am more than happy to help. The whole Greek thing is turning into a family affair."

"Your father is in command of the British Mediterranean Squadron, isn't he?"

"He is. Now, I have two ships waiting at St Katharine Docks ready to go, but I need to outfit my team when they return from training tomorrow. I think we will be ready to leave in three days."

"That is perfect for me as well. There are a couple of things I need to close off before we go. Do you know where we will land? St Petersburg will probably be iced in."

"I know. We will land as close as we can, then travel overland."

Dorothea laughed delightedly. "A sleigh ride in the snow! I haven't done that since I was a child."

The team, including Wolverine, who within the team asked to be called Mike, arrived late the next day. They were tired, but excited that they were on another mission. Beth let them rest overnight, then took them shopping.

"This is so soft!" Paola exclaimed as she was fitted for a full-length coat of wolf fur.

The other girls were all giggling as they tried on hats and muffs. Wolf fur was the material of choice. It would blend in well in Russia, where it was worn by many women. It was, of course, horrendously expensive, and Beth did not expect the department to make more than a gesture towards paying for them.

Beth also had an extra fox fur coat made for her, with all the accoutrements. The seamstress, who was approved by the Service, made several subtle and hidden modifications.

"Can you make these additions to their coats and muffs?" Beth asked when she had finished specifying them.

"Of course. Are they your team?"

Beth didn't answer. The woman, who was in her forties but still attractive, looked at Mike and practically licked her lips as he tried on a pair of heavy moleskin trousers.

"He is particularly ... interesting," she purred.

"Mike? He's a confirmed bachelor."

"I'm not interested in *marrying* him."

Beth chuckled. *Mike had better watch his step.*

When they had completed their clothes shopping — the finished articles would be delivered the next afternoon — they went to Fortnum and Mason in Piccadilly. The girls couldn't believe their eyes at the array of domestic and exotic foods on display, but Beth had just one department in mind, the preserved foods. She explained, "We will be sailing into the Baltic and then probably travelling across land that is sparsely populated. We might have to camp out if we cannot find a lodging. Good food that stays edible in such conditions will be essential."

What Beth didn't say was that, with the exception of that served in the royal palace, she found Russian found almost inedible. She ordered preserved meats, some in tins and others dried or salted. She also purchased tinned soup of various varieties — anything being better than borscht, in her opinion — and dried and tinned pulses. All of these, plus other staples, would be sent directly to the *Fox*.

Their last stop was Black's for their camping gear. Thick, down-filled sleeping bags and ground sheets were the order of the day as well as the usual things.

The night before they sailed, Dorothea stayed at the Stockley house. Dinner was sumptuous: whitebait with thinly sliced bread and tartare sauce, rib of beef that had been spit-roasted rare, with all the trimmings, and wonderful *îles flottantes* for dessert.

Their baggage and stores had already been taken to the ships, so all they had to do was coach to the dock in the morning. When they arrived, Beth walked up the gangway, where Richard Brazier, her captain, met her at the entry port.

"Bethany, welcome!" he said, and smiled.

"You look well, are you fully recovered?" Beth asked him.

"I am, and so are the men. We have recruited and trained full crews since I last saw you." What he did not say was that they had also fulfilled a mission of their own, and done it very well. Beth guessed there had been more going on but knew better than to ask.

Fede came bounding up the gangway and almost knocked Richard off his feet. "Good grief, he is huge!" Richard said, and laughed as he fended off the energetic greeting.

"I warned our guest to wait until he had come aboard and settled, so she could make a dignified entrance," Beth replied.

Princess Dorothea delightedly watched this scene unfold. She had made friends with the big canine, and he was beginning to treat her as part of his pack. She waited until Beth had him under control and then started up the gangway, with the girls in close attendance. Mike brought up the rear carrying their small vanity bags.

"No Garai?" Richard said, out the side of his mouth.

"That's Mike, he is my new team leader."

Dorothea's arrival put a stop to the chat. Richard greeted her graciously and welcomed her aboard. She was every inch the princess. She and Beth would share a cabin, the girls had their own and Mike would bunk down with the warrant officers. Being a former Marine, he was very comfortable with that.

Some of the new sailors were taken aback by the sudden appearance of all these women on their ship. A few made crude comments, but the offenders were immediately corrected by the old hands. Below-decks justice was swift, hard and resulted in more than a couple of bruises.

* * *

The *Cub* led them out of dock and preceded them downriver. Dorothea wanted to be on deck, despite the chilly weather. She said she enjoyed watching the green English countryside drift by, as it differed so much from Russia. Beth suspected that she was actually memorising the position of the shipyards and possible landing grounds as that is what Beth herself would have done in a similar position.

Dorothea watched the crew as they exited the estuary. "Some are not wearing shoes. Do they not feel the cold?"

"Probably not, they are a hardy breed. When we get further north that will change," Beth told her.

A crewman with a black eye walked past and politely touched his forelock. As Beth did not recognise him, she assumed he was one of the new men. Dorothea noticed his eye. "Have they been fighting?"

"I do not think so," Beth said, with a knowing smile. "I suspect that he made an inappropriate comment and was shown the error of his ways."

They went below as the ship heeled over with the wind a point aft of her beam. Freshly coppered, she fairly flew. Even so, they expected the entire trip to take around ten days. As they entered the North Sea it became much rougher; their speed dropped to an average of eight knots and that was only because the wind stayed consistently from west by south-west. Dorothea started to suffer from seasickness, as did Paola and Alie; Beth and Delfina were kept busy nursing them.

The further north they got, the colder it became, and ice started to be a problem. Spray froze on the rigging and sails and the deck became coated in a sheet of ice. The men took hammers aloft and smashed it off, as the extra weight so high up made the *Fox* unstable. It was a constant battle.

They turned east by north-east into the Skagerrak to round the northern tip of Denmark, then a little east of south into the Kattegat. The Denmark Strait followed and was navigated with the aid of a pilot.

They entered the Baltic, and now the waves were high and the weather best described as variable but always truly cold. Snow, freezing rain, rain and sun could all be experienced in a single day.

"I believe we will have to land at Tallinn or Pärnu. The last ship we managed to talk to told us that the Gulf of Finland had frozen up at the western end, and that St Petersburg was ice-bound."

"Tallinn would be better," Dorothea stated. She had got over her seasickness and well and truly found her sea legs.

Richard shrugged. "Unfortunately, we will not know until we get there; but we will try Tallinn first."

Tallinn turned out to be ice free when they arrived early in the morning, though it was snowing quite heavily. They docked and Dorothea sent a message to a local contact. An hour later, a couple of two-horse sleighs pulled up on the wharf. Beth, Dorothea and Mike took one and the girls loaded into the other. A train of pack horses was loaded with their baggage.

They left with little fuss and no ceremony. This way, they could get a good few of the 230 miles they had to travel under their belts. It got dark at around half past six, so they would be looking for lodgings or making camp at five.

The route through the town of Tallinn was relatively smooth and they were soon out into the countryside, which was largely farmland. They stopped to rest the horses regularly and found a place to overnight in the village of Valgejõe. It was better than camping.

The road, if it could be called that, took them to the village of Püssi —which actually had a hotel, where they killed off the bed bugs by leaving the window open and letting the room freeze. Beth was glad of a bed that was not infested, even if it took a while to warm it up, and slept well.

When they woke in the morning it was clear that it had snowed heavily overnight, and the road had an extra foot of powder upon it. This reduced the horses to a walk. The land they were passing through was becoming increasingly wooded and wild.

Dorothea dozed; she was well wrapped up in her furs and had another fur as a blanket. The steady plodding of the horses as they moved along the road was almost hypnotic. They expected to camp out tonight, due to their slow progress. The princess thought about how she would present her progress to the tsar, and how pleased he would be at the provisional agreement with the British.

The sleigh lurched and there was a crack. The driver stopped the horses and got out. They had hit a rock and it had damaged one of the struts that supported a runner.

Mike got down and looked at it. "We can brace it well enough to get us to a village where it can be fixed."

He went into the trees carrying a tomahawk and came back with a length of fir that was about two inches in diameter. He used leather thongs to bind that to the strut.

A wolf howled; it sounded close. It was answered by another. Something did not sound right. Beth was alert and Fede sat bolt upright.

"That was no wolf," Beth said, and pulled her rifle from under the furs. Mike leant into the sleigh and retrieved his. The girls, seeing that, armed themselves as well.

"Bring the pack horses up beside the sleighs," Mike said, and Dorothea shouted the order in Russian. The men leading them looked nervous. Dorothea talked to them and then translated for Beth.

"They say there are bandits in this area."

Fede jumped down and started walking towards the forest; his white coat blended in with the snow and made him hard to see. He disappeared into the trees.

There was another howl — even less wolf-like — from the treeline slightly ahead of them. "They are positioning to cut us off," Mike said. He beckoned the second sleigh to close up, and gave instructions to the girls, who were all armed with rifles. Alie and Delfina lay on the seats and Netta and Paola knelt between the seats so they could all present their rifles on the same side.

"Get your guns ready."

While in London, Dorothea had purchased a pair of double-barrelled Mantons. Percussion-fired, they were a custom pair of short-barrelled fifty-calibre pistols that were rifled. She had practised with them in her garden, much to the annoyance of her neighbours, until she could consistently hit a head-sized target at twenty-five yards.

Beth tensed as she spotted movement in the trees just ten yards away. A man stepped out with a rifle in his hands and shouted something.

"He says they want our valuables and food," Dorothea translated.

"Tell him to bugger off," Beth snarled.

The man laughed and raised his rifle. Almost immediately, six more rifles appeared from behind trees.

The man was shouting something else when Mike suddenly threw something black and round with a faint trail of smoke behind it. It landed between two trees and fizzed. The men looked at it confused.

Then it exploded and Beth fired her rifle. The man dropped to the ground and crawled back into the treeline. A volley of rifle fire erupted from the second sleigh: they had fired high, as Mike had instructed them, and the impact shook a small avalanche of snow from the branches, impeding the bandits, who fired back rather ineffectually.

Rifles were swapped for pistols and a gun fight broke out, with the advantage decidedly in the girls' favour. Beth counted the shots fired and the opposition's reload time, and when she figured most were reloading, she leapt out of the sleigh and charged through the snow. Mike and the girls followed.

She was almost to the treeline when a man stepped out, pistol levelled, aiming straight at her. She chose that moment to stumble over a hidden rock or branch.

Her shot went wide.

He grinned and took aim.

Then a white shape rose up behind him and slammed into his back, knocking him to the ground. Powerful jaws clamped down on the back of his neck. Fede shook his head and there was a loud crack.

Beth got to her feet and stepped past them both. The man she had shot was lying behind a tree, a bloody rose on his furs at his shoulder. He looked at her with hopeless eyes and she shot him between them. Then she moved around to flank the men she knew were ahead of the sleighs. Fede moved ahead of her. He stopped, and she dropped to a knee behind a tree. She looked down at her fox fur coat and wished she had gone for wolf. The red stood out horribly against the snow.

Well, you live and learn.

Fede was slinking forwards with his belly low to the snow, which was shallower under the trees. Beth heard two voices.

The shooting behind her had stopped. All was silent apart from the creak of the branches as they shifted under the weight of snow. Then Fede moved out in an arc, instinctively going to the far side of their quarry. Beth gave him time and, when she thought he would be there, moved forward. There was a shout as she was spotted, and as she ducked behind a tree, a bullet hissed by and slapped into another tree behind her.

She moved on, trusting that Fede would move with her. A man was reloading his pistol and a second peered around a tree from a little further along. He raised his pistol and she snapped off a shot that hit the tree near his head. He ducked, then screamed.

Beth reached the first man and kicked the pistol from his hands. He fell backwards and pulled a long, curved knife. She shot him twice in the chest, then stood over him and shot him in the head.

The other man was still screaming. She stepped around the tree and saw that Fede had his teeth sunk into his groin. She let him play for a few more seconds, then shot the man in the chest.

"Leave him."

Fede let him go and Beth made sure the man was dead. She wanted no one left behind them with a grudge. She found the others and confirmed that they had finished off the rest of the gang, then got everybody back to the sleighs. The driver of her sleigh was still cowering behind it.

Dorothea spoke sharply to him, and he got back onto the driver's seat. He was visibly shaking, so Mike took the reins and drove until he recovered.

They camped out that night, pitching tents beside the road and covering the sleighs with tarpaulins. The ground sheets and sleeping bags kept them warm and they ate from the preserved foods Beth had brought from London.

Mike turned out to be a real woodsman and made a large fire which lasted all night. He also scheduled a watch among the team; they would take an hour and a half each, including Beth.

Real wolves howled in the distance and Fede stayed alert. This was an enemy he instinctively understood. His ancestors had been protecting herds of sheep and goats from wolves for generations.

He dozed, ears twitching as they listened to and tracked the progress of the predators. Suddenly, his head came up and he moved, growling low in his throat. The pack had got too close.

He knew precisely where they were, his nose and ears tuned in to the slightest smell or sound, and came face to face with a big male. He did not hesitate and charged, catching the beast by surprise — he expected to have time to examine the stranger.

The wolf yelped as he was bitten on the shoulder and realised he was in a fight for his life. Fede was bigger and stronger and would have won easily but for the rest of the pack arriving and mobbing him. He was surrounded, but still confident.

There was a yell and a shot. A wolf fell dead and fire lit the woods. The rest of the pack retreated both from the noise and the flames. Then Beth was there, holding a bang stick in one hand and a burning branch in the other.

"Good boy, Fede," she said.

His mistress had praised him, and the world was good.

Beth stood watch until dawn after that. She wanted to watch Fede, as his instincts were likely to get him hurt. Her abiding memory of the incident would be how he faced the wolves so confidently and refused to back down. She made a mental note to visit the Alps and find out more about her dog's ancestry.

As soon as it was light, they set off again and made better progress —it had stopped snowing, and the previously soft snow had firmed up. On the next few nights, they found villages to overnight in, and then St Petersburg came into view. They encountered a cavalry patrol and once Dorothea had identified herself, went straight to the winter palace.

Rooms were made available, and the party made comfortable. Dorothea was taken to see the tsar and spent a day with him and his ministers. She returned in time for dinner.

"How did it go?" Beth asked.

"It is good; the protocol is holding and has been presented to the French. They are a strange people; their government is for the Egyptians and Ottomans but the people are almost completely for the Greeks. The Ottomans, Austrians and Prussians have rejected it."

"What do you think will happen?"

"The British and Russians will intervene alone."

Beth frowned as she thought through the consequences of that. "Doesn't that go against the congress system?"

"It does, but both Russia and Britain want that system ended."

Beth blew out her cheeks; there was more going on than she knew. "What happens next?"

"I think the Egyptians and Ottomans will try to take over Greece and live up to their agreement. Then we will intervene, whether we have the support of the other powers or not."

"Then my father will be in the thick of it," said Beth, thoughtfully.

Home for Christmas

The trip home was easier. The tsar provided comfortable transport and an escort of Cossacks to get them back to Tallinn and their ships. They got there just in time, as the ice was getting close to shutting the port. As it was, the *Fox* had to lead to allow the smaller *Cub* to make way without damaging her hull. Then, when they were in clear water the *Cub* led, scouting out ahead as usual.

They cleared the Denmark Strait and rounded the headland into the North Sea. *The last leg,* Beth thought, and smiled to herself — they would be home in time for Christmas. She was on the main deck, taking the air while the weather co-operated for once, and was enjoying a little time on her own. She wore a wolf fur coat and hat that Dorothea had given her.

Mike approached and stood to one side, waiting for Beth to notice him. Beth sighed and walked over. "You want to talk to me?" she said.

"Just a quick word. The girls want you to approve the name they want to give the team. They got the idea because your father's team has one."

"Yes, the Shadows. What do they want to call themselves?"

"*Los Lobos*, the Wolves."

Beth laughed delightedly. "We all look the part, don't we? Yes, that is a good name."

"Then I will tell them; they are talking about getting wolf-head tattoos."

"As long as they are somewhere they cannot be seen when they're dressed."

Mike laughed. "They want me to get one as well." He pulled up his sleeve to show a fouled anchor. "I will have to find space for it."

Beth looked at her wrist with its small iguana tattoo and smiled. Maybe she should get a wolf's head, somewhere it would only be seen by her husband …

They docked in London and Beth prepared to part company with Dorothea. The two had become firm friends but had no doubts that their friendship would not get in the way if duty demanded it.

"You will head home?" asked the princess.

"Probably to Winchester, unless there is a message from Sebastian telling me to go to Ripley. What are you doing for Christmas?"

"The Embassy will throw a ball and dinner. I will have to be there. Would you like to come?"

Beth smiled. "I would rather spend time with Sebastian, if you don't mind. We spend so little time together."

Dorothea touched her arm and smiled. "That's what I expected. Enjoy your time with your pack."

Beth looked surprised. "Pack? Oh! You heard the girls want to be called the Wolves!"

"Mike told me. It is a good name."

Their coaches rolled up at the dockside and their luggage swung out in nets to be loaded. Richard joined them.

"What are your orders, Richard?" Beth asked.

"The ships are to move down to Chatham, and we get shore leave for the season. We are to be back and ready to sail by the middle of January," he said, then grinned.

"The orders also say that we are to prepare for warmer climes."

"Do they? Some warmth would be nice." Beth sighed.

Richard held out an envelope. "This arrived with my orders."

It was from Turner.

My Dear Bethany,

I have managed to delay your next mission until the new year, so you can spend Christmas with Sebastian. His brigade will be deployed at the end of July. Report to me by the fifteenth for your orders. Sebastian has been given leave and is at Ripley waiting for you.

Juliet and I wish you all the joy of the season.

T

The south-east of England had no snow, only rain that year, and Beth's coach splashed its way to Ripley along muddy roads. The horses could only manage a trot at best and even Mike chose to ride inside. They entered the gates to the house just before dark and the glow of light from the windows was the most welcoming thing Beth had ever seen.

The front of the house had been decorated with boughs of pine and holly. The door bore a wreath of evergreens. As the coach pulled up, the door opened and there stood Sebastian. Beth leapt from the coach and threw herself into his arms, her legs wrapped in a most unladylike way around his waist.

The staff grinned as they circumnavigated the couple, who were engaged in a long and passionate kiss, to fetch the baggage. Life was never dull when madam was home. The Wolves made their way to their rooms for hot baths before supper. Sebastian carried Beth to their room, and they tore each other's clothes off. The bath could wait.

Beth almost purred as Sebastian washed her back. They were both in the large, double-ended enamelled bath in their private bathroom. The water steamed and was scented by fragrant oils and soap.

"So, you got my letter at the house?" Sebastian said.

"No, I received a note from Turner as soon as we docked. He said you would be here."

"Did he? What else did he say?"

"That your battalion would be deployed at the end of July, and I was to report for new orders by the fifteenth."

"We are being sent to Malta, along with the Welsh Guards."

"Dorothea thinks the Ottomans and Egyptians will try to subdue the Greeks next year."

"Then it could be war."

"I hope Daddy can stop that before it starts."

Sebastian kissed the back of her neck and worked his way around, under her ear. Beth closed her eyes and forgot about the future.

The household settled down and was busy preparing for Christmas. It was a week away when Caroline arrived. As Marty was away, Beth had invited her to stay with them. Having his mother-in-law in the house for Christmas didn't faze Sebastian at all.

Beth had decided that she would provide for the poor of the parish and called in on Reverend Upton, who lived in the vicarage beside the church. The housekeeper, Mrs Fellows, answered the door and showed Beth into the drawing room. She served tea and asked Beth to wait while she fetched the vicar.

"Mrs Ashley-Cooper, this is an unexpected pleasure. How can I help you?"

"I would like your help in giving the poor of the parish a Christmas dinner to be provided by my husband and me."

"Oh, that is most gracious and charitable of you. May I suggest we hold it in the parish hall? We built one last year, for parish meetings and the like."

"Could you make sure the right people are invited? The genuinely needy?"

Mrs Fellows, who had been serving tea during the exchange, put her teapot down and clapped her hands in an excess of excitement. "Gawd bless you, ma'am, the church ladies would love to help."

Upton smiled benignly. "The parish has recently made a survey of those in need and there are four families who have fallen on hard times; there are also several women living on war pensions, some with children. We provide clothes and the church ladies help with food, but a Christmas dinner would be a wonderful gesture. I think I can safely say that St Joseph's, the Catholic church, will support it as well."

Beth finished her tea and stood up. "Excellent! Mrs Fellows, mobilise your ladies and organise the hall crockery and silverware. My people will bring the food down in well-insulated crates so that it can be eaten warm. Reverend, can you prevail upon the local publicans to provide refreshments? Ordinary ale in moderation for the men and cider for the women."

Upton nodded. "I will, but I will warn them not to send too much. We do not want any drunkenness to spoil the celebration."

Beth thanked them both and left. It occurred to her that she would have to be seen to attend services while she was home, even though she was not that much of a believer.

Sunday came, and for the first time, religion split the team. The girls were Catholic by birth and wanted to attend St Joseph's. Caroline, Beth, Sebastian and Mike were Anglicans and would attend St Mary's. Beth dressed in her Sunday best and the girls put on nice dresses and covered their heads with scarves. Sebastian and Mike wore fashionable suits under heavy, warm coats and hats. Mike wore a bowler, while Sebastian wore a silk top hat.

The vicar gave a sermon on the holiness of charity and then announced the dinner for the poor. Beth heard one woman haughtily state to her husband that some didn't deserve such charity, as the men were drunkards. Beth noted who she was for future reference but didn't have to worry — Caroline had heard her as well and cut her to the quick with an "innocent" comment.

The farm and gardens supplied most of the produce for the household's Christmas feast, which would see everyone — down to the scullery maid — around the same table. This was to be held in the early evening, after the dinner for the poor, which was to be in the mid-afternoon.

A joint of pork, a rib of beef, a goose, a ham, a capon and a brace of pheasants were hanging in the cold room. Ice had been brought in to chill the desserts and wine, and to make ice cream. Red Cup potatoes had been grown for roasting, and Brussels sprouts, kale, parsnips, swedes and carrots came from the walled gardens. Plum puddings had been steamed for hours and thick cream, saved from the top of the milk from their Jersey cows, was chilled in jugs. Lemon ice and cheesecake would be served as alternatives. The meal would finish with cheeses, nuts and port.

Beef and pork bones were roasted, then boiled with herbs, onions and root vegetables to make stock. That was clarified with egg, turning it into consommé to be the core of the gravy. Wines, port and brandy were delivered from the Stockley warehouses. Fortunately, Caroline's business interests included a wine and spirit import business.

For the poor's dinner, beef and pork would be roasted and served with vegetables and gravy. Plumb duff and custard to follow. Not as sumptuous as the house dinner, but infinitely better than anything available at home and the most nutritious meal that several of them would get all year.

Christmas Day came; there was no snow, but that didn't dampen the feeling of celebration pervading the house. They exchanged presents in the drawing room, which was decorated with evergreens and paper chains.

Beth gave Sebastian a gold, full hunter chronometer that chimed the hours and quarters. It was made by Charles Frodsham, the best horologist in England. The watch came with a gold chain with a toggle for his waistcoat buttonhole and a golden locket with her picture on the other end.

Sebastian gave Beth an exquisitely wrought emerald-and-diamond necklace and bracelet set and, as a joke, a stiletto whose sheath was designed to clip onto her bodice between her breasts.

Caroline gave Beth a brooch in the form of a golden kitten with sapphires for eyes. She loved it. Sebastian was given a figurine in brass of a rifleman. The brass was from a French cannon, captured at Waterloo. The couple presented Caroline with a portrait of themselves, which they had sat for in Winchester.

The couple gave the girls silver crucifixes and chains, and Mike got a craftily designed leather cuff that held a set of four throwing knives. They were all delighted. The Wolves gave the couple a pair of silver inkwells, with wolf motifs, for their desks. Gifts were distributed to the staff as well; no one was left out.

At midday the food for the poor was packed into dishes and then into straw-lined crates. The dishes had been heated to keep the food warm until it was served. When all was loaded into a cart, they went to the hall and handed it over to the church ladies. The poor arrived, children dressed in rags and adults in their threadbare best. Beth had sourced serviceable second-hand clothes which were parcelled up and handed out as presents. Each adult was given alms, a purse containing a few coppers and shillings to help them through the winter. Of course, some would waste it on drink, but Beth was not their conscience.

That done, they returned to the house and their own celebration. The table was large and so full of food it groaned. Sebastian, as the master of the house, carved. The knife was, naturally, razor-sharp.

After the meal, they played games. This was the one time of the year when the staff and their master and mistress interacted in such a relaxed manner. By popular demand, the first game was snapdragon. This potentially dangerous game started with a bowl of brandy into which raisins were scattered. Then the brandy was lit. Players had to pick the raisins out of the brandy with their bare fingers. Speed was of the essence to avoid being burned. It was a game for the young and foolhardy, so of course Beth participated. Older and wiser heads sat and watched. Next came a game of blind man's buff, and Caroline joined in with this. The house rang to laughter and singing until midnight.

Boxing Day was a time of rest and recuperation; meals were basically the leftovers from the day before and included cold meats, chutneys, pickles and bubble and squeak. What was left over after the household had eaten would be sent to the church to give to the poor.

One of Beth's favourite snacks was the crackling from the roast pork, and the staff left bowls out for her to nibble on during the afternoon and evening. This year, she had competition. Fede discovered them and emptied a bowl before anyone spotted him.

The following days were marked by a series of deliveries to the house. One came in a closed box-back cart with no markings. The village was awash with speculation. Beth ordered a large bonfire to be built in the paddock and had a notice put up in the village inviting the villagers to attend a spectacle on New Year's Eve at midnight.

People turned up from eleven o'clock onwards until there was quite a crowd. Mulled wine and cider were served, along with apples coated in caramel toffee that had hardened to a shell. At eleven thirty the fire was lit. As the church clock struck the first bell of midnight, a rocket flew into the air and burst into a brilliant star. This was followed by a display that went on for fifteen minutes. The year 1827 had been welcomed in style.

A Family Affair

Beth arrived in London on the fourteenth of January and walked into Turner's office on the fifteenth as ordered. She wore a fashionable dress with a rather cheeky fascinator on her head. Heads turned as she made her way through the Foreign Office and she heard a low whistle more than once.

Turner did not bat an eyelid at the stunning figure that stood before him. He just smiled and indicated that she should sit down. He looked tired and strained.

"This Greek war of Independence is starting to dominate my time. With your father commanding the Squadron and Songbird running the intelligence network from Corfu with that former Shadow, I am short of a team for an important mission. Which is why you are here."

He looked at a file that lay in front of him on his desk. "Some time ago your father cleaned up Malta and took the criminals to Constantinople for trial. Now we have a different problem, that of Egyptian and Ottoman spies operating on the island."

Beth looked him in the eyes. "You want us to go there and clean them out?"

"Not at all. I want you and your team—"

"The Wolves."

"Wolves? Fine. You and your Wolves are to go over and set up house with your husband. Then you are to feed false information to the enemy agents to set the trap for your father to close."

"Then we kill them?"

Turner smiled; Beth was nothing if not conscientious.

"If you think it necessary."

Beth returned to Ripley and told Sebastian, who was delighted at the news. "I can't complain at that. How will you get there? We are going on a converted seventy-four as part of a convoy."

"We will go on the *Fox* and bring the *Cub* along as well. She will be ideal for sending messages to the fleet. When do you leave?"

"It takes months to organise the brigade and all the logistics for a posting like this. We will embark on the thirty-first and sail on the first. They tell me it will take the convoy about three weeks to get to Valletta."

Beth gave him a superior smirk. "The *Fox* can do it in two." Sebastian poked his tongue out and Beth sat on his lap. "It's not my fault your transports are old and slow."

He kissed her on the nose. "If you get there a week earlier you can find a house and have it all ready for us when I arrive."

"Oh, can I?"

Sebastian tickled her. "Yes, wife, do as your master commands!"

The conversation dissolved into a play fight that ended up with their clothes strewn across the floor and left them exhausted and content.

The *Fox* sailed on the thirty-first and anchored in Valletta harbour on the fourteenth of August. As they waited to be boated ashore,

Sebastian was still somewhere in the Mediterranean, plodding along on a decommissioned warship that had seen much better days and would not arrive for another week.

Turner had the local agent, who worked for Songbird, rent a house for Beth and Sebastian. Beth was to meet the agent ashore.

"Your boat awaits, ma'am," Richard said with a little bow.

The boat was at the entry port and Beth hoicked up her skirts to drop down into it. Mike was already aboard with the girls. The crew grinned as she climbed down, giving them a perfect view of her shapely legs. "Eyes down!" barked Midshipman Christopher Wiggins.

Beth stepped into the boat, undid the clip that held up her skirt and arranged it nicely before sitting. She knew all the men at the oars, as they were old hands, and the two stern men grinned at her. She returned the grin with a wink.

There was no one at the dock, so she started walking towards the steps that led up to the town. The Wolves spread out, with Paola and Delfina leading and Netta and Alie behind. Mike stayed on Beth's left shoulder.

There was a clattering of shoes on stone and a man came careering down the steps. He skidded to a stop when Paola and Delfina intercepted him with knives in hand.

He looked beseechingly at Beth and said, breathlessly, "The roses bloomed late this year in Somerset."

"But the daffodils were early in Kent. Let him go."

"I am Briar, I am sorry I am late. I expected you on the other side."

Beth had no idea what the fool was talking about. "You have a house for me?"

"I do, near to the barracks the Rifles will be billeted in."

"And where is that?"

He pointed to the other side of the water, where a castle stood on a point. "Over there. You see the castle? That is Fort St Angelo. The harbour extends between it and the next promontory, and at the end is where the barracks is — at the Couvre Porte. Your house is on San Duminku Street, here is the address. It has five bedrooms as requested and is furnished."

Mike walked back to the dock and gave a piercing whistle. Midshipman Wiggins looked over his shoulder; they were halfway back to the *Fox*. Mike beckoned, and with a shrug Wiggins pushed the rudder over to return to the dock.

"At your service," he said with a touch to his forelock.

Beth treated him to a dazzling smile. "Chris, it appears we have landed on the wrong shore. Would you and your wonderful men take us over there, please?"

"Of course, boss."

The house was part of a row and accessed through a front door in a practically blank wall. That, however, was deceiving because inside, the door led into a large hall with a grand staircase up to the first floor. The landing opened onto two large bedrooms and a stair to the third floor, where there were a further three bedrooms. The ground floor was divided into two reception rooms, a dining room and a kitchen at the back of the house. Behind the house was a courtyard and garden.

"It will do nicely, thank you, Briar." Beth looked at the man, who visibly relaxed. "What is the name you use on the island?"

"Frederick Stilgoe."

"I am Bethany Ashley-Cooper. My husband is Major Ashley-Cooper of the 1st Battalion, 95th Rifles. As far as this mission is concerned, Chaton does not exist."

"Understood. May I ask what your mission is?"

Beth gave him a wolfish smile. "If I told you, I would have to kill you."

He wasn't sure if she was joking or not.

Beth got them settled in. The girls and Mike took the three rooms on the third floor. Beth took the biggest on the second floor for herself and Sebastian. The house came with a cook and a housekeeper. Beth decided that would be enough staff.

The cook was a middle-aged Maltese and an average chef. Beth wished she had Roland, her father's chef, whose food was unbelievably good. He was Royalist French and had joined her father as a Shadow when he was but a midshipman during the Napoleonic War. He had turned out to be an excellent chef as well as a demon with explosives. She made a mental note to find herself a Roland as part of her team.

Sebastian arrived two days late. The *Warwick* had a filthy bottom, which slowed her down even more than expected. When Beth saw her, she expected that bottom to drop out at any minute and hired a boat to get her beloved to shore as quickly as possible.

Frederick was a fount of information on the enemy agents, and turned out to be a good investigator but not a great field agent.

"The Ottoman has a stand in the Is-Suq Tal-Belt market and sells Turkish food and sweets. The market is very popular with the soldiers and sailors. I think he picks up a lot of information by listening to conversations and by being friendly to the wives."

"Interesting," Beth said, and twiddled a lock of her hair. "What about the Egyptian?"

"Aah, now he is an interesting one. He is passing himself off as being Arabian, but he is not very good at it. I speak Arabic and his accent and dialect give him away. He is a porter in the docks and a womaniser."

Beth now had two targets — all she needed was a steer on the type of misinformation to feed them. And to get that, she needed to talk to her father.

"Darling, how do you feel about going on a sailing trip for a few days?" Beth asked Sebastian that evening. She was sprawled on a chaise longue with a book lying — unread — on her stomach.

Sebastian saw straight through her. "Let me guess, you want to visit your father."

Beth huffed and sat up. "I need to know what false information I should feed the Ottomans. He is the only one who can provide it."

Sebastian put down the copy of *Frankenstein* he had been trying to read. "Well, I have to stay here. I heard he is somewhere off the Ionian Islands at the moment. Will you take the *Fox*?"

"No, the *Cub* is faster and better suited. She can do the round trip in a week." She gave him puppy dog eyes and pouted. "Can you bear to be without me for that long?"

"I will suffer, but I will survive," Sebastian replied dramatically.

The *Cub*'s commander, Stephen Donaldson, met Beth when she boarded with her entourage after dark. His ship was, as always, ready to sail at a moment's notice.

"Where to, boss?"

"The Ionian Islands, as quickly as you can make it. We need to find the Squadron."

"Aye, aye, ma'am."

At dawn he bellowed orders and the crew jumped to raising the anchor and making sail. The *Cub* carried thirty men, almost all of them new apart from a handful of old hands from the Caribbean. Beth noticed their looks and muttered comments and decided that she needed to put them straight once and for all.

They carved a sparkling bow wave as they exited the harbour under full sail and heeled over a good fifteen degrees with the wind from the north-west. The ship levelled as they turned west, and the wind came more on their port quarter. "Twelve and a half knots," the mate running the log shouted.

Stephen rubbed his hands together. "Excellent. We will have plenty of sea room, so don't need to slow down at night."

"How long to get there?" Beth said as she came up the stairs from below, dressed in her fighting leathers.

Stephen hadn't seen her dressed like that for a while. "Um …" he said, then pulled himself together. "A day and a bit; we should be near the islands in around twenty-seven hours."

"Good, then we have some time for weapons practice."

The girls were dressed in fighting leathers like Beth, and there were several wolf whistles from above. Stephen raised his head to stop the men, but Beth placed a hand on his arm. "Leave this to me," she said firmly.

She walked down to the clear area behind the main mast, her hips in full motion. "Do you want to join in, boys?" she called up to them.

"You lot! Down here now!" Stephen shouted.

The men came down in a rush. Beth saw a couple that she knew and waved them away.

"You can watch. The rest of you will provide opponents for us girls to practise our unarmed combat skills on."

The men nudged each other and grinned. *This will be fun.*

Less than a minute later they were all lying on the deck, groaning.

"Oh my, you lot aren't much good as fighters, are you?" Beth said innocently. "Come on, up you get. Try again."

Richard sidled up to her and said in her ear, "Please try not to damage them too much, they are my best topmen."

Beth just grinned at this. The whole crew was now out to watch. Fifteen minutes later, she let them go. The men were a little battered and bruised in places but reasonably whole. *Then* the girls' weapons training started in earnest.

It was four bells of the afternoon watch when they sighted a sail. The lookout called down thirty minutes after it was first spotted.

"It's a British schooner. She's signalling. It's the recognition signal and the number two, four, three."

"That's the *Eagle*," Richard said. "Give our number and spell out *Fox*."

The *Eagle* turned towards them and the two ships quickly came within hailing range as they paralleled each other.

"Is Miss Bethany aboard?" Captain Trevor Archer called across, and when he got an affirmative response, said, "Heave to. I have a message from her father."

The ships backed their sails and came to a stop. Trevor had a boat pull him across. Beth met him with the side party. "Hello, Trevor," she said.

"It's an absolute pleasure to see you, Bethany. How's that soldier boy of yours?"

"He is in rude health and loves being on detachment with his brigade. Are you heading to Malta?"

"Absolutely — mail from the Squadron and all that. I have a special message for you from the admiral. Were you heading over to see him?"

"I was. What is the message?"

Trevor handed a sealed packet over to her. "He also said to tell you not to try and find the Squadron as they will be moving somewhere the Ottomans and Egyptians cannot see them."

"Oh, I was quite looking forward to seeing him."

Trevor took her hand and looked into her eyes. "He is playing a game of cat and mouse. He sends his love and says for you to 'be bold'."

Beth shook her head; her father and Turner were two peas in a pod.

"Well, we had better return to Malta."

Beth read the note from her father.

My Dearest Bethany,

First of all, I hope you are well. Your mother wrote and told me you have been playing with the Russians again. That must have been fun. Now you are in Malta. T told me he would send you, and I have a job for you. The Ottomans, Egyptians and Algerians are building an armada to suppress the Greeks. I command a fleet of British, Russian and, I hope, French ships to oppose them, supported by the Treaty of London.

I want you to spread a rumour that the Russians and ourselves are not getting on, and that the French are unlikely to show up. This will encourage the enemy to gather and move for a fast strike.

The Russian commander is Lodewijk Van Helden, a

Dutchman who fled the Batavian Republic and joined the Russian navy. You can tell people that he holds a grudge against the French (which is a fallacy) and is refusing to co-operate if they join. He is, in fact, a jolly nice chap and an excellent commander.

You can also say that the British fleet will return to Malta for replenishment, which is true. I will see you there.

Your loving father,

M

"Well, I know what I have to do," Beth signed to Netta, who was busy drawing her portrait in pastels.

"Keep still," the girl signed.

Beth sat with the letter held as if she were reading it. Netta frowned in concentration, a loose lock of her hair hanging over her face. Her nimble fingers drew, smudged and blended colours on her paper. Then, satisfied, she looked up with a grin.

Beth stretched a kink out of her shoulders from sitting still for too long.

"Well, let me see it!"

The picture captured her in a reflective yet determined mood. With an air of anticipation, perhaps?

"My hair is a mess," she signed.

"Looks good that way," Netta signed back.

"Can I give this to Seb?" she signed, using the shortened version of his name they used when signing.

"Of course."

Beth carefully put the portrait away, then signed, "Come on, we must be near Malta by now."

The pair went up on deck and, sure enough, they were approaching the entrance to Valletta's harbour. They had started out at dawn and were returning at twilight.

Ashore, she surprised Sebastian, who was sitting in the drawing room sipping a glass of brandy and reading. She sat on his lap and kissed him soundly.

"Sweetheart, I'm home."

"I can see that, how come?"

"We met the *Eagle* coming the other way. We almost missed them, but Trevor has a lookout with exceptional eyesight. They were carrying mail and a message to me from Daddy."

"So, you know who you are to kill, then?"

"Nobody, yet. I am to become a rumourmonger."

"You are a woman, you all like to gossip."

Beth sat up and twirled a lock of hair. "That's true, isn't it? You've just given me an idea."

The Rifles officers' wives held a regular tea party, which Beth attended. They all knew who her father was. She told them — in strictest confidence, of course — that he had written to her and complained about the Russian admiral and his reluctance to work with the French. Adding scornfully that they were unlikely to show up anyway. She used a conspiratorial tone, telling individuals or a couple of people at a time. She also told them that the fleet would be coming in for reprovisioning soon.

Now there was nothing the ladies liked better than to think they knew something that other ladies did not know, and Beth knew they would not be able to resist telling others. The rumour spread like wildfire through the British military contingent.

One day, Beth went to the market, with the Wolves spread out to provide security without being seen to do so. Beth did not think she needed this, but it kept the girls sharp. The Ottoman trader was there, and she approached his stall. He had a large selection of baklava, which she perused.

She was just selecting different flavours to make up a box when Mrs Fotherington-Bridger, the wife of a Guards brigadier who did not attend the tea party, approached her.

"Mrs Ashley-Cooper, how are you?" she gushed.

"I am in rude health, thank you. How are you? And the brigadier?"

"We are well — and how is your father, the admiral? I hear he is having a hard time with the Russian admiral."

Beth exulted inside; the rumour had grown with retelling.

"Daddy is managing," she said modestly, "despite that damn Dutchman letting his hatred of the French cloud his judgement."

Mrs Fotherington-Bridger put on an air of sympathetic understanding. "So I heard. Mind you, I cannot say I blame him. Having to leave Holland because the French invaded and ending up in Russia — who would *not* hold a grudge?"

Beth looked slightly annoyed. "Napoleon has been gone for twelve years — he should have got over it by now."

Then she smiled.

The Ottoman pretended to be filling Beth's box but soaked up every word. Confirmation of the rumour by the daughter of the admiral of the British Fleet himself! It did not get better than that.

That evening, he made his way to the fishing dock. There he met the skipper of a boat, who was sympathetic to the Ottomans. He passed him a message and asked him to take it to Amir Tahir Pasha, the commander-in-chief of the Imperial Squadron at Alexandria. The boat left immediately, following the rest of the fishing fleet out to sea.

Mike watched from the shadows. He had been following the Ottoman since he closed his stall. He now knew where the man lived and who his contact was. Beth would be happy.

The fleet came into harbour and immediately started loading the stores that the *Eagle* had pre-ordered. Admiral Martin Stockley came ashore and was greeted by his daughter. A certain dock worker was close by, ostensibly helping to load the stores.

"Bethany, my dear! It is so good to see you!" her father cried as he climbed the steps. He enveloped Beth in a hug and kissed her cheeks.

"And you, Daddy." Beth hugged him tightly, her fingers pressing his back in their silent language, warning him that they were being watched.

"Where is that husband of yours?"

"On duty, I am afraid. Have things improved?"

Martin took the hint and replied, "With the Russian admiral? Not really, he is still very antagonistic towards the French. But I have my doubts whether they will arrive anyway."

The dock worker almost jumped for joy, but maintained self-control and moved to another crate, to keep the pair within hearing distance as they strolled towards a carriage.

"How is your mother?" the admiral asked.

"Busy with her businesses — she has started trading in spices from the Middle and Near East now. Constantinople is a great source of saffron, apparently, and that is worth more per ounce than gold."

"Yes, and my orders could disrupt that. It will take money from my own pocket!" her father quipped.

All that was said was put into a report and sent to Cairo, where the Egyptian ships were waiting to join the Ottomans. Again, the Wolves followed the agent and identified the communication channel.

Beth, Sebastian, her father and her brother James, now the captain of a frigate, were gathered in her living room.

"We sail as soon we hear the Egyptians and Algerians have joined the Ottomans at Alexander and sailed," her father announced.

"My job here is done, then," Beth said.

"Not quite," James said as he passed her a glass of wine.

"Oh?"

"James is right, there are some loose ends to tie up," Martin said.

"You want the agents eliminated?" Sebastian asked.

"No. We know who they are, and if we eliminate them, we have to start again. No, I want you to keep watching them until Songbird returns with that overgrown husband of hers. I will send her back here once the Ottomans agree to the terms of the Treaty of London."

"Oh goody, I get to stay with Sebastian, then!"

"Until then, at least. I can't speak for James or Arthur," Marty said, referring to Turner and the Duke of Wellington. "Who knows what skulduggery they will want to involve you with next."

Epilogue

Songbird returned to the island with Billy, her husband and a former Shadow. She took over the agents' watch duty, using her local resources, and Beth was able to relax and enjoy being with her husband.

In England, James Turner and Arthur Wellesley, First Duke of Wellington, sat and shared a pot of coffee sweetened with a dash of brandy. They were discussing world events. Arthur summarised one of his main concerns.

"South America continues to be a problem. Dom Pedro is going to abdicate as emperor of Brazil and hand the role over to his daughter Maria. That will finally separate Brazil from Portugal. However, his brother Miguel is dead set against it. Colombia and Peru are on the verge of war, Bolívar is running out of patience. Colombia is riven with rebellions."

Turner nodded sagely; he thought South America would always be a mess.

"We need someone out there keeping an eye on things. A married couple with a team would be best."

Wellesley looked at him down his eagle's beak of a nose.

"You think? And who do you think fits the bill?"

James Turner looked sly. "Oh, someone who speaks Spanish and Portuguese and has a husband who is also a trained agent."

Arthur Wellesley knew exactly who he meant. "He will have to lose his command."

Turner looked pious. "It is the price of duty."

"I will issue an order recalling them both. They will need her ships."

"That is not a problem, I've already ordered a refit for both when they return," Turner said, and smiled.

THE END

Author's Notes

In the early nineteenth century, the British hangman's noose did not have the hangman's knot. Instead, executioners used a rope with an iron or wooden cleat set into the end, through which the rope was threaded to make a loop. The cleat was commonly placed at the back of the neck, ensuring that the condemned suffered a slow and agonising death by strangulation.

Modern maps of Bonaire show the location of the town called Kralendijk which, at the time this story is set, was merely a port with a fort. Rincon was the capital of Bonaire in the early nineteenth century, while Slagbaai port on the north coast served several plantations in the north which raised cattle and grew dye wood, maize and castor oil. The south of the island was given over almost completely to salt production, and is where most of the slaves were employed. The prevailing wind is from the east for more than ninety percent of the year, meaning the port has an offshore breeze. Wind reversals occur during the late hurricane season and the following wet season, when storms to the north affect the wind patterns.

Until 1872, Spanish Town was the capital of Jamaica and the Governor's residence was in King's Street. The earthquake of 1692 sank two-thirds of Port Royal, leaving a narrow peninsula which was mainly occupied by Royal Navy installations, including the hospital.

George Canning was prime minister for the shortest time in British history until Liz Truss beat his record by staying in power for just fifty days. Canning was lauded as a brilliant statesman and orator, and was responsible for the destruction of the system of Neo-Holy Alliances known as the "Concert of Europe", that threatened to dominate Europe.

The Lume & Joffe Books Story

Lume Books was founded by Matthew Lynn, one of the true pioneers of independent publishing. In 2023 Lume Books was acquired by Joffe Books and now its story continues as part of the Joffe Books family of companies.

Joffe Books began in 2014 when Jasper agreed to publish his mum's much-rejected romance novel and it became a bestseller.

Since then we've grown into the largest independent publisher in the UK. We're extremely proud to publish some of the very best writers in the world, including Joy Ellis, Faith Martin, Caro Ramsay, Helen Forrester, Simon Brett and Robert Goddard. Everyone at Joffe Books loves reading and we never forget that it all begins with the magic of an author telling a story.

We are proud to publish talented first-time authors, as well as established writers whose books we love introducing to a new generation of readers.

We won Trade Publisher of the Year at the Independent Publishing Awards in 2023. We have been shortlisted for Independent Publisher of the Year at the British Book Awards for the last four years, and were shortlisted for the Diversity and Inclusivity Award at the 2022 Independent Publishing Awards. In 2023 we were shortlisted for Publisher of the Year at the RNA Industry Awards.

We built this company with your help, and we love to hear from you, so please email us about absolutely anything bookish at feedback@joffebooks.com

If you want to receive free books every Friday and hear about all our new releases, join our mailing list: www.joffebooks.com/freebooks

And when you tell your friends about us, just remember: it's pronounced Joffe as in coffee or toffee!